Done with Ho[pe]

A hapless journey through Charlie's chaotic life

Chapter One – where did it start?

Who is Charlotte? An ordinary girl brought up in a middle-class family in a small village outside Hull. She had an older brother, Stewart, and two loving parents who gave her as many opportunities as they could to blossom and flourish and called her Charlie for short. Even as a small child Charlie was an incredibly positive person. She had embarked on a life of exceedingly high ups and incredibly low downs, but whatever she was faced with she would put on her brave face and carry on.

Charlie had a good childhood. Both of her parents were working, and she was lucky enough to have a place at a private girl's school. Her mum worked in Social Services and her dad was a mechanical engineer with his own small company. They were not rich, but comfortable, and in those days the private schools used a sliding scale for the amount of fees due, so it was not too costly. Her brother, Stewart, had been smart enough to win a free place to his school.

Mum was very independent and a career woman and encouraged the same in Charlie. Dad was practical and taught her to do many things around the house and was always there to help regardless of how busy or tired he was.

There was only ever one thing that Charlie's mum did to her that she would not forgive for many years. Charlie had mid-length mousy brown hair and at one visit to the hairdressers in the village her mum decided to have it chopped really short. It was more like a shave than a cut and made Charlie feel like a boy, and even made her get teased at school. Her mum assured her it was the for the best because it meant it would grow back thicker and stronger and would be beautiful, but Charlie still had her doubts.

When she was as young as a primary school pupil, Charlie had begun to show she was going to be predisposed to accidents and adventures. On one incident she was running into the school changing rooms with the other girls, even though they all knew they should not run. It was summer and she had some new sandals on that her mum had bought with a sort of brown crepe sole. They must have had no grip at all, as all of a sudden, she was hurtling along the floor headfirst towards the metal shoe cages at the bottom of the coat hangers. There was blood everywhere and she was taken off to the school office. They dabbed her up as much as possible and put her in the car to Woodmansey hospital to be checked out. Mum was to go straight from work to the hospital. The nurse at the hospital had to stitch her up so she left with four big black stitches right across the front of her forehead.

It was not long after that and she had another accident, although it was not so much of an accident. When her mum's mum, her Gran, used to come and stay, Charlie had to move out of her bedroom and move into the top bunk in her brother's bunk beds.

One night Charlie and Stewart were fighting as they often did, he was two years older than her, and he liked kicking the bottom of her top bunk and lifting her up with his feet. Charlie lent over the bed to try and batter him to stop him, and he pulled her arm, and she went tumbling down to the floor with a crash. It hurt a lot and she screamed. Her mum and dad came running up the stairs to see what was going on – they were very used to the normal squabbling between Charlie and her brother – they were not expecting to see half of Charlie's arm bent in the wrong direction. This time it was her dad's turn to take her to Woodmansey hospital so off they went. As usual he shouted at her and told her off for getting hurt. It was just his way and Charlie was used to it, somehow, she knew it did not mean he did not love her any less. Charlie was given an x-ray on her arm and the doctors decided it was a dislocation of the elbow and they were going to pull it straight. This meant Charlie having some gas and air to numb the pain. She had not had this before and had no idea what to expect but knew she had to grin and bear it. They manoeuvred her into position and pulled and twisted her arm until they were happy, and she herself was pleased that she did not feel too much pain. Unfortunately, whether it was the shock or the gas and air she would never know, but as soon as they had finished, she threw up everywhere – all over the doctor's coats and her dad's feet. That did not go down too well so she kept her head down and kept quiet. They were soon on their way back home with the added extra of a sling.

Mum was glad there was not too much damage, and she knew her brother Stewart was sniggering away behind mum. She hoped he was glad it was not too serious but knew he found the whole thing amusing.

It was not too long after this incident that Charlie was to get her next lot of stitches. Charlie and her brother Stewart were really close with their neighbours Sophie and Oliver as they were the same age. Their parents were close too, and from an early age because Charlie's mum worked long hours as a social worker Charlie and Stewart used to get the train home from school and let themselves into the house until their parents came home. As young as seven she was getting the train and walked to the station from school with her friend Jilly who lived in Bridlington. Her mum told her when she was older that for the first few journeys to the station that Charlie had made, her mum had followed her in the car to make sure she knew the route. It was only when she was older that Charlie had doubts about whether this happened as to get to the station from the school, she had to go through the middle of two parks and they had no roads in them.

The official arrangement was that Charlie, and Stewart, were supposed to go straight to the neighbour's house when they were home instead of letting themselves in to their own house. Stewart had worked out that with a long stick or brush handle he could put it through the letter box at the bottom of the front door and then twist it up with his wrist and knock the latch open on the inside. This way they could get into their own home. Even though their parents knew they were doing it there was never any worry as Sophie's mum was in next door and Charlie's mum could not have been accused of leaving young children home alone which would not have helped her position in social services.

Then there was another incident. As usual Stewart and Charlie were fighting when they were home alone. All the doors in the house had small glass panes in them. Stewart used to have little soldiers and trainsets and all the things he loved out all over the floor and Charlie could be wicked and kick them around. Stewart was holding his bedroom door to keep Charlie out and she was kicking at the narrow wood panel at the bottom of the door in her socks to get into his room. Then, all of a sudden, her foot slipped upwards and went straight through the bottom glass pane in the door. It was when she screamed and pulled it back that all the damage was done – it looked like her foot was hanging off and blood was oozing out everywhere. Stewart limped her to the bathroom and ran next door to get Sophie's mum. Unfortunately, Sophie's mum was not too good with the sight of blood but between her and Stewart they managed to wash Charlie's foot and get as much glass as possible out of it. The bathroom had a brand new fluffy white carpet and Charlie and Stewart were worried that their mum would go mad with them for ruining it.

Eventually their mum arrived home. By this time Sophie's mum had poured herself a few whiskeys and had calmed down after the shock and Charlie was sat on the settee with a towel wrapped round her foot. Stewart had gone back to his room to tidy up his soldiers, back to the way they should have been. After surveying the damage and telling them all that it really did not matter about the carpet, Charlie's mum was able to see Sophie's mum home and get Charlie into the car back to Woodmansey hospital. She was beginning to think with all these accidents her daughter was having that she would be called in and accused of child abuse but luckily no such thing happened.

This time Charlie had twenty-three stitches in her foot. The motion of pulling her foot back out of the broken glass had sliced the side of Charlie's foot like a chicken fillet and it needed to be attached back in the right place. The nurses and doctors warned Charlie and her mum that she might not have full sensation in the side of her foot once it was all healed but that it should not cause her any problems and would knit nicely.

From an early age, Charlie loved ponies and horses, even having the Thelwall wallpaper on her bedroom wall and any books about horses she could get her hands on. Having spent 2 years learning to ride with her friend and neighbour Sophie at a local farm she begged and begged her mum and dad to buy her a pony. After a number of months of pestering and discussing they finally relented – on the condition that she forego any pocket money and other extras that may arise. Luckily one of her friends at school was upgrading her pony, so Charlie jumped at the chance to have Cloud, a fluffy white Welsh Mountain – Shetland cross that was 11.2 hands. He was an old boy, but he was the perfect pony to start with. He was gentle and docile and mostly eager to please. He did have a habit of stopping at jumps to look over the other side which could catch you unaware and send you over the top of the jump.

Charlie's confidence grew enormously with Cloud. She lived near to the sandhills, and the beach so was able to take him on long hacks with her friends. Even her brother managed to bounce around on Cloud's back without falling off. Cloud turned out to be a star at handy pony classes at the local pony shows as nothing phased him, and he turned out to be excellent in the Gymkhanas.

Charlie did not have a horse box so if she was in a gymkhana competition her dad would borrow a horse box from the local chicken farm owner and take her when he could. Sometimes she would hack for miles to the shows with her dad dawdling along in the car behind her.

It was during this time with Cloud that Charlie had her next two mishaps. Surprisingly, they were nothing to do with riding. The only pain Cloud had caused was when Stewart was riding him on one of the old farmers' fields on the sandhills. The horsey crew had set up some little jumps on the field with logs, branches and bricks, and any other useable equipment they could find. Stewart was trotting up to a little jump on Cloud but in his usual manner Cloud decided to stop to look over the other side. Stewart went with a bang onto Cloud's withers, and it was obvious that Stewart was of an age now where this was extremely painful. Everyone else found it hysterical.

Charlie's next accident happened whilst her best friend and neighbour Sophie was helping her parents spread some gravel around in the front garden. The houses had square brick pillars at the end of the drive entrance and the girls used to sit on them and chat to each other. On this occasion Sophie and Charlie had taken a break from spreading whilst the boys, her brother Stewart, Sophie's brother Oliver, and all the parents continued. All she could remember is laughing hysterically and then the next minute toppling off the pillar and landing ungainly onto a broken brush. The wooden brush handle was broken so that it was like a spike.

It was summer and they all had shorts on, so the spikey end went straight into Charlie's leg at the very top inside of her thigh. More screams and her dad came running and pulled the brush out. There was a massive hole and blood oozing out. Yet again Charlie was patched up and whisked off to her usual hospital. This time the nurses checked the wound for fragments of wood, cleaned her up, and gave her another three of the big black stitches that had been put in her forehead and foot previously. She was bandaged up and sent home. At least it got her out of gravel spreading although they had all been having a wonderful time, the families together.

Her next accident happened back at school. It was in the gym where Charlie loved doing gymnastics. She was average at it – never a star but good enough to get all her BAGA badges and was so proud of herself when she finally managed to do a back flip. One area she had never been particularly good at in the gym was the ropes. She could hang on to them but was rubbish at climbing then. Her school friends said it was just a knack because she had the strength and agility to do it so they all decided they would do some practice together. The PE teacher was in the changing rooms sorting out the bibs for netball for her next class, so the girls saw no harm in getting out the ropes and setting up the benches in advance of the lesson. The plan was to swing the rope to someone standing on the bench so they could leap for the moving rope and use the motion to start them off on the climb. One by one they tried, and most were getting more success in climbing up the rope. Then it was Charlie's turn. She sprung off the bench towards the rope but somehow managed to miss it and landed with a large bang on the wooden floor – she had even managed to miss the mats and fly past to the solid wood.

Her schoolfriends came over to see what she had done whilst one or two went to get the teacher. They were expecting to be told off for messing in the gym unaccompanied, but the teacher was really nice and just set about sorting the mess out. Charlie was delivered to the school office, and they arranged for her to go back to Woodmansey with one of the teachers and her mum to meet them there. At the hospital they took an x-ray of her arm, the opposite one to the previously dislocated one. There seemed to be a problem when they were comparing the two arms and their movement as there did not appear to be any difference although one was obviously injured. In the end the doctor decided he could see a hairline fracture in the x-ray of the newly damaged one and the difficulty had been because the dislocated one had not healed completely straight. Charlie was bandaged up again and sent home with her mum. She was determined it was not going to stop her carrying on with her riding but had to accept that she would stay out of the swimming team for a while.

Very sadly, Cloud had to eventually move on. Charlie had outgrown him, and he was passed on to another loving home to give them all the fun and joy Charlie had. The search for a new, bigger pony culminated in Charlie's mum buying Magic. Magic was a 13.2 Blue Roan Welsh Mountain who was stunning to look at. The only reason Charlie's mum bought him was because when they went to see him and try him out her mum had a massive hangover and liked his legs. He was also loving and followed his previous owner around the arena like a loyal dog. Charlie was twelve by now and experienced in looking after her own pony.

On the day Magic was delivered from his previous owner Charlie was off school for the holidays and her dad had taken the day off work. Charlie's dad tied Magic to the pillar on the porch and they said their goodbyes to the horsebox and previous owner. A few minutes later, Magic broke free from his tether and started trotting down the road away from Charlie's house and appeared to be following the horsebox. Charlie was screaming as they watched, and then at the end of the road, a T junction, the horsebox turned right towards the way out of the village, but Magic stopped and looked and clearly decided turning left onto the sandhills was a better idea. Charlie was running after him, and her dad went to get his car. Charlie followed as fast as her legs would take her down the rough track in the sandhills but was quickly losing site of Magic in the distance as he went over the higher sandhills. She could hear her dad driving somewhere behind her, but by this time she had gone off the road and ventured into the scrub and walking paths. As she got to the top of a sandhill she could see Magic in the distance, making his way onto the golf course between their village and the next town. She kept on going, following him, as he ran around the golf course greens, digging them up with his hooves as he ran and turned. Eventually he came to a stop and Charlie was able to catch hold of his headcollar, and what was left of the lead. At last, Charlie could breathe and relax as her dad approached on foot. She led Magic back to where her dad had left the car and then back down the dirt track with her dad following in the car behind. They had decided to take the errant pony directly to the field he would be living in so he would be safely secured and could get to know his new surroundings.

As Charlie released him into the field she watched as he approached the other ponies and horses and she checked there were no personality clashes before heading back with her dad to their house. She would have stayed all night watching him but knew she would not be allowed by her parents and planned to be back down at the field first thing the next morning. Over the next few days her dad altered the end of the garage into a stable so he could be in there in the winter. He also sorted it with people he knew who were in the golf club, although he did not golf himself, that there were no damages that could be claimed from Magic's running across the greens. It was treated to an act of nature and not a deliberate act of vandalism. Every morning Charlie rode him down to the local field before school and back in the evening throughout the winter. Charlie's dad used to laugh that it was like an alarm clock for the people in their street as he used to watch the lights going on in the houses as she clip-clopped past.

Magic turned out to be a star – Charlie and Magic worked together as an excellent team, and he started winning everything at the local competitions. Charlie and her friends Claire and Abigail still tended to only go to competitions they could hack to as her dad was sometimes away working, and they had no desire to pursue competition in a serious way, the fun of having a pony was riding across the sandhills laughing and free.

Charlie also had a passion for swimming and was in the swimming team at the local pool – between her pony and the swimming she had little time for anything else. All her spare time was spent riding across the sandhills with her friend Claire and her pony Shilling, and later with Abigail and her pony Donut.

She had no time for boys in her life, but under duress and peer pressure went to a youth club disco in the next town with some friends from school. Charlie was not a particularly popular girl at school and kept to herself a lot of the time. She had some friendships that were growing and, in an attempt to be in with the in crowd she went to the disco. It was not a pleasant experience. Dancing with her friends was fun, but when the slowies came on an older lad asked her to have a dance. She was well out of her comfort zone, and it was not helped by some of the girls laughing at her dancing with him and then telling her afterwards he was the local creep. That put an end to her wanting to try that experience again.

Chapter Two – Coming Out

Throughout her teenage years her mum had been instrumental in setting up a youth club in the scout hut in the village, along with other parents and eventually an official youth leader. Mum worked for Social Services and had all the contacts to help it run smoothly. Charlie helped her mum with the tuck bar and the shopping for it from the cash and carry and gradually got to know more and more of the teenagers who attended – her social circle was growing slowly, but ponies and swimming were still the most important parts of her life. Charlie's home was like a second youth club throughout her teen years as many of the locals who congregated saw Charlie's mum as their own or second mum. She would frequently arrive home from school to find other teenagers had let themselves in to put the kettle on. The key hiding place was known to all.

On one occasion when Charlie was down at the youth club with her new friends, she was messing about outside with them and started walking along the kerb in some stiletto shoes she had borrowed off her mum to impress the gang and the new shiny and tight black leggings she had bought. The film Grease was in the cinemas and all the girls wanted the Olivia Newton-John look. Charlie had even had her long mousy hair permed so she looked the part. It was not a successful stunt. Charlie had already showed herself to be a tad accident-prone in her younger years and on this particular occasion she went over on her ankle off the kerb and heard an almighty crack. Her friends helped her back inside the youth club to show her mum.

Mum decided they had better go to accident and emergency to see what the damage was so off they went in the car after her mum had arranged cover at the youth club. When they got to Woodmansey hospital Charlie was sent for an x-ray but to everyone's joy nothing was broken, it was just a bad sprain that needed to be strapped tightly. She was duly bandaged and given some crutches which were a challenge to get the hang of. By the time they reached home the youth club was all closed up for the night, so it was off to bed for a rest. Charlie did not sleep well as she kept wondering about whether she would be able to ride and look after her pony or even swim for a while. By the morning, the pain had subsided some-what and she was able to hobble around with her new crutches.

It was around the age of fourteen that boys started to play a part in her life. A lad from the village asked her out and she said yes. This only lasted 24 hours as when he tried to kiss her, she changed her mind and ran home. After this followed a period of growing confidence and the ability to flirt. When she got off the train from school in the village there were some lads on mopeds that used to hang around under the footbridge. Charlie and Claire used to play at racing their ponies against the boy's mopeds down the path alongside the railway line and got to know them all better. Some were from the village and some from the nearby small towns.

At the same point in her life Charlie was really struggling with her Latin teacher at school. Latin was compulsory up to 'O' level and Charlie hated it, probably because the teacher seemed to hate her and pick on her. This went on for months until Charlie's mum had heard enough.

She came into the school and demanded to see the Head and the Latin teacher and had words with the latter. It made things a bit better in class for Charlie, but it was too late to do much to improve her chances of passing the main exams. It was one subject that she would just have to accept she was no good at along with French. It was doubtful that she would pass her French oral exam, even though her written French was fairly acceptable.

Up until this point Charlie, and her riding friend, had experienced bullying from some of the local girls. Both Charlie and her friend went to different private schools, and they lived on opposite sides of the railway line. Both had been chased and tormented on their walks home by some of the girls in the village which they could only put down to inverted snobbery. This went on for quite a period of time and was the main reason Charlie's friends in the village were either male or into horses. She had also been a target of bullying in school, to the point where one girl, Emma, had hit her and thrown her on the floor in the PE changing rooms with others laughing. An experience she never wanted again. She had suffered verbal abuse and teasing from some of the girls in her school even as far back as primary school. One particular incident stuck in her mind from Primary school where she was one of the witches in a play. Charlie was only ever given background parts and in this one she had to say 'horror, horror, horror' along with some others. Both the teacher and her classmates constantly teased her because the way she said it sounded like 'howwer,' but it really upset Charlie, and became an ongoing thing to pick on her about.

There was a potentially life ruining period of Charlie's life in her early to mid-teens. She was also good friends with a girl called Paisley who had joined the girls' school from a local catholic school. She too had a pony and Charlie and Paisley hit it off well. At this point Charlie was wearing palette braces on her teeth and had to get the train regularly from the station near school to Bridlington to visit the dentist for a check-up and tighten up of her braces. This usually meant leaving school a bit early or going at lunch time and going back but never actually making it. Paisley had decided she was going to accompany Charlie on these regular trips and skive off school. One day Paisley convinced Charlie that it was easy to steal things from Woolies. Charlie did not yet have pierced ears but loved the magnetic ones that were new to the market. Woolies had a fabulous selection of these and other jewellery on display in the big Bridlington shop and Charlie followed Paisley's lead and popped some in her school blazer pocket whilst they were walking round.

Unfortunately for the pair they had been seen. As soon as they started to exit the shop the security guard stopped them at the door. Charlie was terrified as she was led with Paisley to the back office to the manager or whoever he was. He asked them to produce their pickings which they did, with Charlie shaking like a leaf. Charlie only had the one pair of earrings and was scared that the manager would tell the school. She was more worried about the school finding out than her parents. After a serious telling off and threat to report them to the school, police, and their parents, he told them they could leave. Charlie was so relieved and the pair of them ran as fast as they could back to the station.

Down at the village shop one day, the lad who lived above the DIY shop collared Charlie and told her that Brett wanted to ask her out and would she wait there. She waited as he went round the block and village green on his moped a few times until he eventually asked her. Charlie said yes and it was to be a relationship that would last quite some months. Brett was a bit of a lad with the girls and Charlie eventually ended it after hearing rumours he was also chasing another girl. At one point, Charlie was standing on the roof of her parent's house – it had a flat roof with a wall all around it built in a Greek villa style. They had moved to this house when she was thirteen from across the road – her mum had always loved it so as soon as the owners told her mum and dad that they were selling up Charlie's mum and dad jumped at the chance. From the roof she saw Brett going down to the sandhills along the track with another girl from the village, Gill, on the back of his CB50 moped. He pleaded innocence of course but Charlie had already heard rumours about his philandering from other people that she knew and decided enough was enough and she was not going to be humiliated. At this point she chucked him and went out with one of the other moped boys from the village, Ethan.

The boys were all a bit wild on their mopeds, and frequently went into the sandhills to muck around on them. On one particular occasion Ethan, Brett and Dan decided to stray with their mopeds onto the golf course as there were no fences on the sandhills side of the course. Naughtily they also road the bikes across the fairways and made a mess with tyre tracks and digging up the greens.

Then they rode back to Skipsea to Dans house but unknowingly to them someone must have seen the direction they had headed off in. Not long afterwards, Skipsea village was swarming with police. Presumably the golf course had informed them and somehow, they knew that the biker vandals had taken refuge in the village. Brett and Dan had parked their bikes at Dans house and gone inside, and Ethan had gone to Charlie's house with his bike. Eventually the police caught up with the three lads and they were taken off to Caunce Lane police station for questioning and processing. There were no witnesses to what they had done but as time went on their parents were asked to bring a change of footwear in for the lads as the trainers that they were wearing were to be sent off to forensics for matching the soil. Brett and Ethan's shoes were clean, and Dan had changed his biker boots for some trainers already, but unfortunately Dan's mum brought the boots in to the police station that he had changed out of. The police noticed the boots and they were sent off for testing instead of the clean trainers he was wearing. It was a match after testing, and all three lads were charged with malicious damage and had to wait for their day in court. They all pleaded guilty and were charged. Only Brett was old enough to be told he would have a criminal record for it and even managed to get his name in the local papers, Ethan and Dan were a year younger and as such the ongoing consequences were not as bad, and their names could not be reported. It was an experience that they may learn from, although it was only meant to be a bit of fun and not malicious in any way. Charlie's dad thought it was amusing that although he did not condone the boys' actions, he did think it was unfair that Charlie's pony, Magic, had actually done more damage to the greens on the day he was delivered than the boys had done in their wild actions.

It was fairly common within the group of teenagers that some would split up and go out with another member of the group. After Charlie and Brett split up, Brett went out with Natalie, another of Charlie's friends from school who lived in the village. Natalie had come from South Africa where she had been born but her British parents had relocated back to the UK whilst her older two sisters stayed in South Africa.

Charlie, after some time of seeing him, decided to 'go with' Ethan and this moved their relationship to a whole different level which did not agree naturally with Charlie. Lots of her friends were at it including Brett and Natalie, so she felt pressure from all-round to give it a go. It was not long after her 15th birthday and she spoke to her mum about it. Her mum was a wise lady and very supportive and arranged to take Charlie down to the family planning clinic in Hull so she could start on the contraceptive pill. Moments were sneaked when parents were out or when Charlie was babysitting. She had managed to get a job babysitting regularly for one of the local farmers and his wife. She knew many of the local farmers and villagers due to her pony riding and the fact that she had grown up in the village with many of their children.

There came a time when Charlie was outgrowing her dream pony Magic. They were still doing really well in competitions, and more importantly enjoying trekking across the sandhills and farmers' fields. There were plenty of places to ride around the village Charlie lived in. There were the sandhills and beaches from Tunstall to Hornsea, the pinewoods, the stubble fields, and various other woods and tracks.

Before her 16th birthday, Charlie's cousin was engaged to a lady who was selling her 15.2 horse called Molly. She was a young mare at 5 years old, but this did not phase Charlie as Magic had been 4 years old when they had purchased him. Charlie and her parents drove to Newark to see Molly and they hit it off straight away. She was a skittish mare and according to her cousin's fiancée, worked back to front. When you pulled on the reins she would want to go forward, and when you squeezed or kicked her sides with your legs she would want to stop. Charlie reckoned they could work with this together and come to some sort of mutually agreeable arrangement. Molly responded well to Charlie when she trotted her around the paddock so the decision was made that they would buy her and find a new loving home for Magic.

It did not take long to find someone who wanted Magic. A 12-year-old boy, whose family ran a bicycle business, was desperate for him. He rode him beautifully when he came down to the field to try him out and Magic seemed quite keen on him. The parents did their negotiations whilst Charlie chatted with Simon about his plans with Magic. He wanted to do working hunter and enter some serious competitions. Magic was a looker, as far as ponies went, and certainly would do well at the cross country and show jumping as these had been Charlie's favourite competitions with him. She was not sure about the dressage part of the competitions as she had done truly little dressage with him, apart from the occasional Pony Club competition, but knew the girl that had owned Magic before her had done some basic dressage training with him. Simon Invited Charlie and her parents to see where he was going to keep Magic and Charlie jumped at the chance.

Magic had been part of her life and family for nearly 4 years and it was very heart wrenching to know he would be leaving her although she knew she had to be practical as she could nearly wrap her legs all the way around his tummy.

In due course the horses were swapped, Magic was delivered to his new home and Molly arrived. This time her parents had arranged for Molly to be delivered to the farm where the horses' field was, especially after Magic escaping all those years earlier when he was delivered. It took a few weeks for Molly and Charlie to be working as one team, but they eventually got there. Charlie worked hard at gaining the mare's confidence and love and eventually Molly would come trotting over to her from the other side of the field when she was called. By the winter Charlie's dad had built a wooden stable in the waste land part of the garden as Molly was too big for the end of the garage. Her dad had lots of help building the stable from Charlie's brother and the kids from the youth club that all adored her mother and would do anything to help her. Riding Molly was a dissimilar experience to riding the ponies she was used to. It was a more sedate affair, none of the mad galloping around, but still enough for Charlie to really love her time out riding with her friends.

That summer was Charlie's time for her 'O' levels. Her brother was 2 years ahead of her so was sitting his 'A' levels so it was real study time in the house, except her brother did not seem to be doing much of it from what she could see. Charlie's dad was away quite a lot at the time as he was doing some subsea tests on a subsea diving bell that he had built in his engineering company workshop. The tests were being done in deep water in Scotland, so it involved him staying away for days at a time.

On the day of her last 'O' level, Charlie finished at lunch time and went straight to the field from the train to get Molly to ride. As she trotted into the village it was still early. Some of the lads that finished work early were in the habit of meeting Charlie and Claire under the footbridge at the station after school, and when Charlie got there only Mark was there. He was one of the gangs that had started coming to Skipsea due to their links with Ethan and as everyone else did, had welcomed Charlie's mum's friendly attitude with open arms and were more of the gang often in her house when she got home. Mark had never ridden so Charlie said he could have a walk round the block on Molly with Charlie holding on to her bridle to be extra safe. He was just going to be walking so it all was a safe plan.

It turned out that letting Mark ride Molly was a really bad idea. As they walked down the road something spooked Molly, Charlie would never know what it was, but Molly suddenly ran forward and Charlie's loose grip on her reins did not hold, and Molly trotted off down the road. Mark was pulling on the reins to try and stop her and wobbling all over the place, but in true Molly fashion, the more he pulled, the more she ran. Charlie never saw exactly what happened, but it appeared afterwards that Mark had pointed her at a parked car to make her stop and unfortunately, she tried to jump it. By the time Charlie had caught up with them around the corner, Mark was on the road next to Molly and a crushed car. Somehow in the mayhem that followed someone raced to Charlie's house and her brother arrived from home on his Honda Express.

There seemed to be commotion everywhere and before she realised other people had arrived – and altogether there was her mum, Brett, a vet, a wagon, people trying to get home or just coming for a look.

She vaguely remembered the vet or someone telling her there was nothing they could do for Molly as she had broken at least one of her legs and had to be put down. The wagon was from the knackers' yard and was for taking Molly away. Charlie was screaming, crying and hysterical. Her mum and brother dragged her into her mum's car and took her out of the way whilst the vet did his business with Molly. Mark was taken off to be hospital to be checked out and as Charlie was escorted into her house by her mum, she could still vividly see Molly lying on the road in pain.

She could not remember how she managed to get through the next few days. Instead of celebrating with her friends, the end of the exams, she just felt miserable and sorry for herself. Every time she walked round to her friend Abigail's house in the village, she had to walk past the place where it had happened and there was still blood ingrained into the faded tarmac. It brought back fresh tears and sadness. She could not help wondering why all these catastrophes and disasters followed her around. A few days earlier she had been so happy, looking forward to the long summer off as was normal after exams had finished, spending time riding and having fun with all the people she knew.

In true mum and dad fashion they were secretly arranging something to cheer her up. She did not know as it was something that she had never been involved in, but Molly was insured and the insurance company not only agreed to pay her parents for the values of the horse and tack, but also for the replacement for the car she had tried to jump which was a write off.

It was not until later down the line that she heard that Mark had tried to claim off the insurance for his injuries as well and she was mortified as apart from a couple of bruises and hurt pride, he had escaped lightly.

When she did find this out, she determined to have nothing more to so with him - ever. Charlie's parents had decided that using the insurance money and a bit more they would encourage Charlie to get a new horse, so the search began. After much research and scouring horses for sale adverts and asking around with people she knew, they all went to see a horse called Sydney. He was also only young at 4 years old, and he was 16.2, so bigger than Molly. He had been reared as a racehorse and was a thoroughbred, but the stables he was from were into hurdling and he had not proved successful at this type of racing. He was great on the flat, but slowed too much for the jumps, so he was not a horse they wanted to invest time and money into. Charlie loved him at first sight. He had lots of character and took to her straight away and so the deal was done. It was the best thing her mum and dad could have done, as although she would never forget Molly, at least having Sydney took her mind off the accident to some degree.

There was one moment she remembered in her relationship with Ethan where he had bought himself a new motorbike. It was a Yamaha RD350LC, and he was old enough to progress to such a big bike from the Suzuki AP50. Unfortunately, within weeks of having it, he was leaving a friend's house in the village and had not put his side stand up properly. As he decked the bike round a gentle left-hand bend by the village, the side stand caught on the floor and flung him and the bike off towards the sandstone wall at the back of the pub. The handlebars went all the way down the wall, along with his right hand which, as it was un-gloved, suffered some considerable damage. Charlie's Dad picked him and the bike up. Some of Ethan and Charlie's friends took the bike back to her house whilst Charlie and her dad took Ethan off to hospital.

It turned out apart from the obvious skin damage from the wall, he had smashed two fingers and was very shaken up.

Over the next few months, after the bike had been repaired, it took Charlie's dad a lot of patience and perseverance to persuade Ethan to get back on the bike. Eventually he was back out on the bike and had his confidence back, but by this time Charlie was fed up with being the pillion passenger, and with her dad's but not her mum's blessing, decided at 17 she was going to have her own bike. At 17 she was allowed up to 250cc without passing her test, and in conjunction with all her biker boyfriends and her dad they decided that a CB100n was best for her. It was her dad's doing as he wanted her to have a 4-stroke and not a 2-stroke, the reason for which she never did understand. They found a suitable one second hand and her dad insisted they put crash bars front and back to protect her should she have a fall.

There also followed a bit of negotiation with Charlie's school by her mum to allow her to use the bike for getting to school and back. It was not really done for private girl's school pupils to be turning up on motorbikes in the sixth form, but her mum was a very persuasive woman and the school agreed. At 17, Charlie also started learning to drive and using the bike every day for school and going to the horse field, really helped with her road awareness.

Her group of friends at this time in her life was all the biker boys, some who had moved onto cars. Brett had a Marina which had been altered to include a 1.8L twin carb engine, and Ethan had a 1275GT mini.

Charlie learned to drive in her mum's Fiat 127 and her friends, and her brother found it very handy to get her to drive her to various pubs around the area so they could have a few drinks. The good thing for her was that she had plenty of practice and ended up only booking half a dozen driving lessons to polish her manoeuvres up before her test. The others had all only recently taken their own tests so took her for lots of practice around the local test routes, doing reversing round a corner, 3-point turns, and hill starts.

Charlie was 17 in June and passed her car test in August and her bike test in September. Her car test was very strange. She was in her school uniform as it was on a school half day and for some reason that pleased the examiner. It was a warm day, and she was taking the test in her mum's pale blue Allegro as she had swapped the Fiat. The examiner asked her to open his window, so she had to lean over him in the passenger seat to wind down the passenger window. She thought it was strange at the time, but in her later years when recanting the tale to others, it dawned on her that it was really creepy, but she passed first time anyway and should have with all the practice she had received driving the others around.

During her final year at school in the upper sixth, the girls had an 'A' level geography trip to the Lake District. They were to stay in Ambleside youth hostel as a base for their field trip work. Some of the girls had arranged for their boyfriends to come up and visit and all the boys were sneaking in up the drainpipes, emergency stairs, and wherever else possible to get to the girls' bedrooms. Unfortunately, some of them were caught and the school as a whole was banned indefinitely from the youth hostel.

This was an absolute disgrace for the private girls' school, and the girls never heard the end of it, even those like Charlie who had been innocent in the whole debacle. It was not that she was prim and proper, it just had not occurred to her to mention it to Ethan and the others, and they were all in work during the day anyway. Ethan had started working for her dad in his engineering company after he had done some electrical training with a local firm, and Brett worked full time at Allied bank in Bostee.

In the meantime, Charlie continued with her A levels and university applications. She was doing a really strange mixture of A levels at school – Mathematics, Geography, English Literature and General Studies. After much discussion with her mother and the rest of the family she chose a BA in Applied Sociology at Worcester University, due to start in the autumn. It was not her first choice to go to university. By this time, she had accepted her mum's advice that she should get her degree and then decide what she wanted to do afterwards as there was no rush. When Charlie was in the sixth form, still very few teenagers went to university. It was still seen something of an elite thing to do with only some 15% of 18-year-olds going to university. Most would go straight into jobs or do an apprenticeship.

But that was not enough challenge for Charlie – she had to do something else. Charlie used Lady magazine to apply for a job in France as an au pair for the summer and possibly a year, with a view to postponing university for another year. It was fortunate that this was agreeable to the University. Charlie had regularly scoured the adverts in Lady magazine for suitable positions.

She had truly little experience of babies and children apart from the occasional babysitting stint so wanted to be an Au Pair rather than a nanny. She managed to find an ideal position with a family outside Rouen in France that were seeking an Au Pair and someone to look after their horses. It could not have been more perfect.

Chapter Three – Spreading her wings.

In the early summer, after her A levels, Charlie packed up her case and set out on the drive to Rouen with her mum and dad. It was an eventful journey with her dad's Chrysler overheating on the motorway and big delays for the ferry. On arrival in the village of Poses the French family had cooked a welcome meal for Charlie and her parents (which she later found out was rabbit stew, much to her horror) and then she was duly deposited into their care whilst her mum and dad went off to their B&B. The French family lived on a large plot next to the banks of the Seine. The large house was the grandmothers, in which Charlie was to stay, and on the other side of the plot was the house with her son and his wife, a 4-year-old boy, and 4-month-old twin boys. These children were to be Charlie' charges for the duration of her stay.

The first few days were busy with Charlie learning the routines, meeting the locals and where to buy groceries, getting used to the old Citroen she was to drive, and being shown the horses and their requirements. Charlie got on well with the grandmother but did not click so quickly with the mum and dad.

After a few weeks Charlie got herself into a routine. In addition to childcare and horse care, she had to prepare a lot of the meals – spending hours topping and tailing green beans and preparing other vegetables were frequent chores. Charlie also had to complete all the shopping and do the cleaning.

The shopping and horses were her chance to escape for a bit of solitude and even cycling down to the village with the milk urn to get it refilled and collect the bread sticks was relaxing. It was during cleaning that Charlie formed the opinion that (some) French men did not have particularly tidy toilet habits and she was shocked at the number of porno magazines stacked up next to the father's throne. Duties would often finish in the late evening and Charlie had developed friendships with some of the locals, mainly male, in the village. The meet up place was the local café which served alcohol as was typical in France and as her new friends did not speak much English at all it was a really effective way for Charlie to improve her spoken French as well as unwind.

On one rare day off, Charlie decided to take a train trip to Rouen to have a look around the city and have some 'me time.' The trains from Paris to Rouen stopped at Poses so it was an easy trip – but it was to all go pear-shaped. After spending a delightful day looking around Rouen, Charlie jumped on the train back to Poses, but mistakenly caught the express to Paris, arriving in the late evening. Through her pidgin French she was able to ascertain that there were not any more stopping trains back that evening, no buses, and taxis far too expensive for the over 100km journey. She had to think on her feet. Charlie did not know the phone number of her au pair family so her only choice was to ring her mum and dad at home and, as usual, take their advice. After queuing for the public telephones Charlie rang home, panicking and worried. Her mum and dad calmed her down and checked that she still had her American Express card with her. They had made her apply for this card before travelling as there was no limit on it and it was a charge card and not credit card.

It was to take the money from her parent's bank account automatically but was only to be used in the case of dire emergencies – luckily, this was deemed to be one of them. Mum and Dad told her to find a local B&B or Guest House and stay there until she could get back on a stopping train in the morning. They said they would speak to the French family and explain what had happened.

Throughout this phone call there had been a number of local lads hanging around the public phone area. One of these lads, a good-looking Black guy, spoke to Charlie when she had come off the phone. His English was excellent, and he expressed his concern for the predicament she was in. It did not occur to Charlie that he had obviously been listening in to her conversation. He offered to take her to a reasonably priced and charming hotel that she could check into for the night. Charlie had always been overly trusting and believed in the best in people, so off they went on foot. He took her to a lovely little hotel that was a short walk and helped her check in and waited whilst she confirmed everything was sorted to her parents from the hotel phone. He then suggested as it was not too late, he showed her the sights of Paris by night.

Charlie threw caution to the wind and took the stranger up on his offer. For the next 4 hours in the beautiful and calm Paris evening Charlie saw sights she would never experience again. Along the banks of the Seine in the late evening/early morning there were artists and entertainers, many of which her new friend knew. There were food stalls that served delicacies that satiated her appetite, musicians that played enchanting music, and happiness and romance in the air all around. Eventually, it was time to go back to the hotel and get some shut eye, she slept well and peacefully.

The train back to Poses was due to depart at 10am and as Charlie left the hotel in the morning, her new friend was there to escort her to the station. Charlie thanked him from the bottom of her heart and made her way back to the family.

Returning to the family brought her back to reality. Not only had the family been less than supportive from the beginning, with the exception of Grandma, during her unexpected jaunt she had had some time to think. She was doing three times as many hours as au pairs were expected to do for little more than pocket money. She had become virtual full-time cook, nanny, shopper, cleaner and everything else. Since arriving Charlie had constantly had minor cuts from chopping vegetables and the cuts frequently became infected and she was concerned that things may not improve. Unexpectedly, the family announced that they were going on holiday to Nice for 2 weeks to their house in the south of France. Although she had doubts about how long she could stick out her role, Charlie decided that the opportunity to spend time somewhere else could only be good. Her own mum had suggested that she may just be suffering from homesickness, and that a change may make all the difference.

The drive was long, packed in the car with the family of five and luggage, but on arrival the villa was fantastic. Set in a beautiful garden full of multi-coloured flowers and located a short walk from the beach, Charlie settled in and unpacked everyone's clothes and the food that had been brought with them.

The first few days were good, with the family spending more time together. Things started to deteriorate when friends of the mum and dad started to arrive on the Cote d'Azur, and they started to spend more time socialising. It did not seem to matter whether they socialised at home or out – if they were at home Charlie ended up being a personal servant to the frivolities, if they went out, she was full time nanny again. Parts were good – she had one day off in the 2 weeks and was able to chill out on the beach and meet some new people, and even managed to stay out quite late having fun. Overall, Charlie thought if she had to rate the trip it would get a five out of ten.

Back in Poses, after the long drive home, Charlie was thrown back into her thoughts of how long she could stay. The job was supposed to be for a year, but she knew that she would not be able to endure that long. With the exception of Grandma, she had grown to dislike the whole family. In her view Dad was a chauvinistic pig who was used to being pampered to – she felt sorry for his work colleagues. Mum was weak, unlike the maternal figures in her own upbringing – the contrast was stark. Charlie often wondered whether the mum had any ambitions at all, or whether any previous versions of her had long since been squashed by becoming a wife and mother. They were not mean or nasty, nor were they uncaring, they were just not Charlie's kind of people or what she aspired to. The 4-year-old boy was spoilt and refused to take no for an answer, especially from his mum, and Charlie was fed up with struggling to get one of the 4-month-old twins to sleep just as the other woke up. It was certainly enough to put her off motherhood for a long time.

She had now been with the family for nearly 12 weeks and made the decision that she had to return home. As ever, this involved a lengthy reverse charge phone call from a phone booth to her parents. They were loving and reassuring as always and said they would help sort it all out. Charlie' mum rang the university and was able to move the degree offer to the current year. It was now early September, so it was amazing that this could be arranged. The next challenge was in telling the family. Part of the job arrangements were that the family paid for Charlie to travel France at the start of the job and then to return home at the end of the job. Needless to say, they argued that because Charlie was leaving early, she would have to make her own arrangements. Charlie's own parents stepped in and made and paid for the arrangements for her. The next 7 days were awkward and unwelcoming. Even Grandma had changed in her attitude towards Charlie and despite apologising nothing seem to lead to a change in their attitudes. Boarding the plane home Charlie knew she had made the right decision. She was overjoyed to be greeted at the airport by her mum and dad. They stopped for tea at a lovely pub on the way home and Charlie was able to fill her parents in on more of her adventures. Getting back to her own house and bedroom was the best feeling ever.

Charlie had little time to get herself sorted before she went to university – a week to be exact. In that time, she also had to sort a new car. The old mini she had from seventeen had been sold when she went to France, but Charlie, with the help of her friends and brother, was able to find another old gem of a mini.

The mini was loaded up to the brim with bedding, 'portable' TV, record player, clothes, and other student essentials as Charlie waved goodbye to her parents and set off on the drive to Worcester. Because of the short notice she had not been able to find a place in the halls of residence but had a place in a shared self-catering unit with nine others. Charlie felt this would suit her better anyway as the thought of being in the equivalent of a massive hotel with hordes of others did not particularly appeal.

Two and a half hours later Charlie arrived at her destination, excited but at the same time nervous of what this adventure and new chapter in her life would bring. The door to the block was unlocked – Charlie was in J block on the left-hand side. She rang the doorbell and was greeted to two fellow students. They introduced themselves to Charlie and quickly showed her up to her room, adding to come back down to the kitchen to join them once sorted. The blocks were set up as ten individual bedrooms over a few levels with shared bathrooms and a shared kitchen/diner and lounge. After a while of chatting to the other students Charlie was surprised to find out that she was the only fresher in the block and first year students nearly always went into the halls of residence, and then moved out to the self-catering accommodation in year 2. The girls in the accommodation were fabulous and it turned out to be quite an adventure to be with the year 2's as they were able to show her the all the aspects of university life.

It was not long before Charlie secured a job in the student union bar. She had worked in the local pub when she was eighteen as a holiday job so had gained valuable experience. The union bar was fun to work in and in those days required excellent mental arithmetic.

As an example, the university rugby team would come in after a match and order a pint of optics and other beers. The pint of optics involved a shot of each spirit topped up to a pint with beer. The prices were all on the drinks and pumps and there was no computerised till, so the totals had to be added up in your head as you went along. Some of the other staff in the bar were not good at this she had overhead the bar manager John saying to his colleagues.

The other advantage of working in the bar was that the porters (as they were known as in the eighties) and other staff from the University came in for drinks. This meant Charlie got to know them well and they were truly kind and let her into music gigs and other events for free. One particular night it was Simply Red, and another the Boomtown rats.

By this time Charlie had also made friends with people on her course. One particular friend was Iris who had been a nurse and had decided to do the same degree as Charlie. She had a lovely old Morris Minor, that although looked fabulous, was always needing repairing. Meanwhile Charlie had her mini to get around in. She had also made other friends through the course and the bar, and in her second year moved into a rented house with them. The other three girls were from much wealthier families than Charlie, but they got on well as a foursome. Charlie used to take them out for days to stately homes and other visitor places and they had great fun with picnics and enjoying free time. It really was an enjoyable time. There was no particular man in Charlie' life at this point.

Having left her home village and moved to University Charlie parted company with her boyfriend Ethan that she had been with for nearly 3 years.

This caused some issues with him, and she was told by her friends at home that he even made a threat to end his own life which luckily, he never followed through on. When she regularly returned to her home village to visit parents and friends, luckily, he had moved on to a neighbouring town and made new friends so there were no uncomfortable moments when she was at home.

As always in her life Charlie had male friends at university. There was a group of lads in a rented house that Charlie and her house mates became close to. One of the girls dated one of the boys for a period of time. They all used to have great fun together, attempting to cook dinners and have evenings where they had to dress up smart for a laugh. One particular evening it was the girls turn to cook, and Hannah had made a plum fool. The most vivid memory Charlie had from that night was that a couple of the lads crashed on the sofas in the girls' house as usual after excesses of alcohol, and Charlie awoke and came down to regurgitated plum fool all over the living room carpet. What a delight that was for them all to clean up.

Charlie worked hard at her studies and essay writing and was enjoying life in general. By the end of her second year, she had met a student who had finished his Politics degree called Liam. He was not working and used to frequent the bars in the student union. He asked her out after a while, and she sort of said yes. A relationship started. He was quite political and used to argue with Charlie because she had not voted in the last election which was unacceptable after all the trouble women of the past had gone to for woman to vote.

Charlie always replied the same – that the fight was for the right to vote, not that you had to.

Liam was from London and his separated mum lived in a lovely house on her own. Liam himself did not seem to show any attempt at even looking for work and this grated on Charlie a bit. He had finished his degree with a good result, and he just was drifting. He even liked to wear jumpers and cardigans with holes in, just to make a point she thought, and an old army coat from a charity shop. Eventually, the relationship fizzled out.

Charlie was nearing the end of her final year when one night she was in the entertainment bar after finishing work in the main bar. The entertainment bar hosted bands, a disco and a later bar closing time. It was here that she met Daniel. According to his friends, he had been watching her for some time plucking up the courage to ask her out. Charlie was beginning to wonder if this would be the story of her life and wondered why men were scared of asking her out.

They got chatting and it turned out that he had finished a Geology degree down in London and had started his first year as a trainee accountant with one of the big firms in Worcester. This was something they had in common as although it was not the original career plan, the accountancy firms and others did what was called the 'milk round' in the universities where they were touting for recruits. Charlie had been for some interviews with various firms and had offers from a few to start an accountancy training contract in London in the September after her degree finished.

Again, Charlie was not ready to start work and settle down. Charlie and one of her friends from the rented house at university decided they were going to take a year out. They planned and planned and decided on an around the world trip using a company called Trailfinders in London.

The trip was one price round the world as long as they kept going East or West and did not back track. The countries they planned to visit were India, Thailand, Malaysia, Singapore, Bali, Noumea, New Zealand, Australia, Tahiti and then finally America.

In the meantime, Charlie contacted the firm she had accepted the accountancy training contract with and asked if she could defer starting for another year. To her surprise they agreed. Hannah and Charlie had also managed to get work visas for Australia with the plan of topping up funds for the rest of the trip whilst they were there.

Chapter four – exploring the world.

As a sort of practice session, Hannah, and Charlie both decided to spend the summer in Greece. That turned out to be an experience in itself – working in kitchens, and cleaning apartments that had mostly been slept in by English tourists who had had too many drinks the night before and had left their rooms to go to the beach or pool in unsavoury states. They managed the planned 6 weeks of the summer holidays doing this, sleeping in a campsite with a lot of other 'travellers' from many different countries. Some of the people staying there did not have tents or proper sleeping bags and were eaten alive by the mosquitos. The bend on the road outside the campsite was also an accident black spot for mopeds and motorbikes. The two girls saw lots of horrific injuries from the bikes sliding on the roads, but the holiday makers did not seem to want to let it ruin their holidays and tended to get back up and grin and bear the pain they must have had.

It was soon time to return to the UK to make the main around the world trip. Daniel came down to Hull to see Charlie and it really was quite a sad parting. He was adamant they should stay in touch throughout, so Charlie agreed to try her best.

Down to Heathrow the girls went. All the flights were scheduled flights as that was the way the agent that they had used for the booking worked. The first flight was straight to Delhi, arriving in the incredibly early hours of the morning, just after midnight. They had no accommodation booked – the plan was to find travellers digs rather than tourist hotels to save money.

When they exited the airport with their rucksacks, they were approached by a number of friendly Indian faces offering to help. They had to choose so one rickshaw driver was picked who said he could take them to a nice but cheap hotel. The hotel, really a guest house, was nice. The rooms and toilets were clean but basic. The shower consisted of an outside tub with a high-level tap over it. On the way to the hotel Hannah and Charlie were astounded by the sights they saw. As dawn began to break local people were getting up from the roads and pavements where they obviously slept. There were cows wandering around the streets and other animals running loose – it really was the real India they had imagined. At the hotel they managed to catch a few hours' sleep before the owner called them to say breakfast was outside. This was not expected – it was fruit and flasks of tea and was absolutely delicious and very much appreciated.

The rest of the day was spent wandering around the city, looking at the markets and trying the local street delicacies. Charlie had decided before they arrived that as they had suffered all the necessary inoculations for the countries they were visiting, she was not going to be fussy about food and water – that was not the purpose of backpacking to see the real life in the countries so she hoped Delhi Belly would not happen.

Later, on the same day, the Rickshaw driver who had taken them to the hotel came back to see how they were doing. He had brought some tourist leaflets for the sights in Delhi for them to look through and offered to take them to any they chose over the period they were in the city. It was too good an offer to turn down but was left as a casual arrangement with the Red Fort and Taj Mahal being on the list. The girls had a fabulous tea of Indian snacks in the hotel and a restful night's sleep.

The next day, they were taken to the Taj Mahal. They were lucky that the rickshaw driver had told them before they left that shorts were not allowed, and arms and shoulders should be covered up, so they were prepared. At the Taj, Charlie and Hannah met a couple from the UK who were also backpacking. Peter and Jane. They all spent some time together over the following few days and became friendly and started making plans together for the next part of their travels. The plan was to travel to Srinigar in Kashmir by train, and to stay on a houseboat. There were plenty of booking offices for such trips in Delhi, so the plans started to be put into action.

They booked a first-class sleeper train up to Srinigar, and a houseboat to stay in on the lake – there were various grades available but as the budget was limited, the cheapest option of houseboat was chosen. That left a few more days to explore the sights of Delhi with the rickshaw driver. This unveiled a fabulous surprise. The rickshaw driver invited them back to his house for a meal one of the days. It was fascinating for Charlie to meet his family. They all lived, cooked, and slept in two small rooms and the family were adorable and welcoming. The snacks and drinks provided were to die for and the rickshaw driver was full of gratitude that he had regular income from Charlie and Hannah over a period of time – it meant an awful lot to him. This was when Charlie also found out that the postcard, she was going to send home had to be taken to the post office to be stamped across the stamp before being sent. The reasoning behind this was because the stamp was worth a week's wages in India and there was a high chance of it being removed and sold on, and the postcard would not arrive in the UK.

Departure day for the North arrived. The train journey was not as smooth as planned. There were other people in the beds allocated to the four travellers on the ticket, and they would not move. The train conductor said they would have to pay to get the beds back, so the four friends decided to just sleep upright in the seats. Eventually they reached the last station and caught the local bus as they had planned in the travel agency in Delhi. This led to more adventure. The bus was packed with people on top of each other and on the roof and some of the passengers were carrying live chickens and other animals. After travelling only a few miles, the bus was pulled over by two cars travelling fast. There was a big commotion with the driver and other passengers and then a man came down the aisle and asked Charlie and her friends to follow him and get off. After nervous and heated discussions, they were convinced that as the man said, he was the owner of the houseboat they had booked, and he was taking them directly there. They climbed into the cars and hoped for the best. However, there was no need to worry as they arrived at the shore of the lake and were boarded onto a houseboat. It was glorious with a fantastic pot-bellied wood burner on deck and luxurious rooms.

By now, it was getting on for late afternoon. The houseboat owner had taken them out on the lake in a shikara. It was a fabulous and breath-taking experience. He then took them back to the houseboat and cooked a fabulous meal for the travellers of local cuisine and delicacies. Much fun and laughter were shared by the group before it was time to retire to their own rooms on the houseboat.

The next morning brought a turn of events. Charlie was awoken by shouting and arguing that sounded extremely aggressive. She went up to the deck of the boat to see a couple of other men sailing off from the houseboat. Their houseboat owner explained that it was another houseboat owner that was accusing him of kidnap and stealing his customers. During the day it turned out this was true and a common occurrence. They were due to be collected from the bus station by the owner of the houseboat they had booked, but the owner they were with now had stopped the bus before the bus station and taken him to their houseboat. He also showed them the one they had actually booked, and Charlie and the others were quite glad they had been kidnapped – they had definitely ended up with the much better option. No money had changed hands over the booking as only a small deposit had been paid in Delhi and the kidnapping owner only wanted the same amount for his much-improved offering, so it was an easy decision for the group of four where to stay.

During their time on the houseboat appreciating the hospitality and kindness of the owner and their tour guide, he also invited them to a Kashmiri wedding that one of his relatives were having. It was to last for a few days, and they had been invited on one of the spectacular days. He arranged traditional outfits for them all to wear and ferried them back and forth. It was another fantastic experience that Charlie and her fellow travellers would remember for life.

After Charlie and Hannah left India and their new friends the next country to be visited was Thailand. The girls were full of excitement for this trip and the sights and culture they were to experience.

On landing in Bangkok, they made their way to the youth hostel which was to be their place of stay for the duration of their visit. It was in Thailand where the differences in expectations and interests were beginning to show between Charlie and Hannah. After having seen half a dozen Wats (temples), Charlie was boring of them, but Hannah wanted to see more. Things were saved by a planned visit to the Bridge over the River Kwai and the prisoner of war camp at Kanchanaburi which was an emotional experience. Their days in Thailand also involved some time at a silk factory discovering how it all worked and ordering some handmade clothes. They visited and stayed in hostels near Pattaya and finally ended up in a cheap hotel in Phuket. This was a beautiful area and was full of holiday makers, some of whom they became friendly with. One particular group invited them to spend the day with them at their much posher hotel with accommodation huts by the sea and a beautiful pool. It was on one of these days that Charlie experienced her first bout of sunstroke which they diagnosed themselves after a day in the pool with the sun beating down on Charlie's neck and back followed by an evening of violent sickness. Luckily, she got over it by the next day.

The next leg of the journey involved a flight to Malaysia and a few days in a hostel and time spent round the local markets and sights. This was followed by coach travel down to Singapore. This should have been a smooth journey but at the border of Singapore the customs officers decided to go through the coach with a fine toothcomb. Unfortunately, due to heavy rains and floods on the route down all the luggage in the luggage compartments of the coach had been thoroughly drenched.

The officers wanted to trawl through the girl's rucksacks which was fine but very embarrassing when they were pulling out knickers and other underwear to inspect. Then there was a big delay. Hannah had some clothes washing powder in a small plastic bag and the officers insisted on taking it off for analysis for drugs, leading to a holding up of everyone on the journey. Eventually it was sorted, and the coach could continue, to the relief of everyone as it was a long coach journey.

When the girls got to Singapore, they asked for directions to the local travellers' hostel and headed off on foot with their soaking wet rucksacks. The hostel was lovely and buzzing with other travellers like themselves. They settled into their room and went out for an explore. Singapore was a complete change from all the other places they had been and seemed to be much more westernised.

One of the main places they wanted to visit was the Raffles Hotel, so this was done the next day. They tried some of the cocktails and enjoyed the opulence of the place.

Meanwhile, back at the hostel, they spent time with fellow travellers and swapped adventures with people from all parts of the world. It made them realise how lucky we are as English as everyone they met could speak a great deal of English, so communication was easy. In particular, Charlie chatted a lot with two lads from New Zealand who said she was welcome to come and stay with them when she arrived there. This was great news as it gave her a base to travel and explore from.

Before they knew it, it was time to pack up again and start to make their way to Australia. This was via Bali for a few days' stopover.

As usual, they were on scheduled flights with plenty of room to lie across the spare seats and get some sleep. A lot of their flights were night flights, so they were the only chance the girls had to catch up on some kip – that and in the airports whilst waiting for flights. When they arrived, they found it easy to get help to find a cheap travellers hotel to explore from. This time Charlie thought it was a clever idea to hire a motorbike to travel around. It was the best way according to everyone they had spoken to, and Charlie had her full motorbike licence, so it was no problem.

It was going really well getting around on the bike, with Hannah on the back until one day, when they were in the middle of nowhere, the heavens opened. It was not just a downpour; the rain was washing in floods down the road. They decided to be safer than sorry and found a roadside café to stop in whilst it calmed down. The rainstorm only lasted for a few hours, and they were able to get on their way. It was amazing weather, going from hot and sunny to extremely wet in a matter of seconds, but then they had arrived in the middle of the rainy season.

After a few days it was off to the airport again for their flight to Australia. Both girls had secured a work visa for Australia for 6 months. They had only left the UK with enough money to last until they got to Australia with a bit spare so they could not wait to get jobs and top up the funds.

Also, Charlie' mum had grown up with a best friend called Joyce who had moved to Australia many years before and had married a man called Jim. Charlie and her mum had managed to contact Jim before she left the UK. Unfortunately, Joyce and Jim had divorced many years earlier, but Jim was happy for the girls to stay with him when they arrived in Australia.

The flight took them to Melbourne on the Southeast coast of Australia and Jim picked them up at the airport and took them to his house in Geelong which was just over an hour's drive. Jim's house was lovely, and they each had their own rooms. The girls spent a few days filling Jim in on their travels and adventures so far and then started their job search.

Charlie had worked in bars in her university holidays and whilst at university so quickly landed herself a job in a local pub. She was amazed at the rates bar staff were paid in Australia as it was considerably more than at home. Hannah had no experience of working but managed to get herself a job waiting on tables in the yacht club. This was where the two girls really started to drift apart. The clientele of the two establishments they were working in were completely different.

In addition to their new social circles, things were not really working out staying at Jim's house. He turned out to be a bit strange and treated them more like teenage daughters than 21-year-old grown women. They moved out and rented off a lovely couple they had met in Geelong which meant life was easier all around. During her time working in the bar the other staff had told Charlie that she could take a dollar or two from the money from customers, whether or not they handed over the extra money. She thought this was strange and would mean the till could often be down, but she accepted that this may be the way things were done in Australia so started doing it herself. Unfortunately, she was to find out that it was not the way things were done and was caught by the bar manager putting money in her pocket.

She was mortified but luckily after a big discussion with the manager and a severe warning she was let off and did not lose her job although it made working relationships difficult, and she started to long moving on to different work.

She left the pub and started in jobs selling paintings door to door. That involved being dropped off in a residential area by a minibus that had similar door to door sellers on board. They were to cold call at people's houses armed with a portfolio of paintings and a storyline about how they were originals and tell the imaginary background on the artist. It was not a job Charlie was particularly good at – selling obviously not a forte. People either doubted her story or were just plainly not interested in her wares. She did manage to sell one painting on one evening and nearly another. Unfortunately, on the second near sale she was about to complete it when the customers friend came to call from a few streets away. This friend was keen to tell Charlie's potential customers that they had just bought the same painting, leading to the realisation by them all that the story about them being originals was not true. She was quickly ushered out of the door although at least the friend said he liked his painting so much he would not ask for a refund.

Following her failure in this task Charlie secured a job selling vacuum cleaners. She was horrified that they could cost so much but the commission was high if she did make a sale. The job involved meeting at the local office where all the salespersons had to sing a song together for motivation before they headed out. The appointments were made for them, but they were made for carpet cleaning.

The salespeople had to clean a carpet and then try and flog the vacuum cleaner demonstrating all its benefits. Needless to say, many of the appointments just wanted the free carpet clean and were not interested in a purchase.

Once the carpet had been cleaned, usually involving the moving of heavy furniture, the sales spiel began. The first was obviously the benefits of the shampooing attachments and the cleanliness of the customer's carpet. Before cleaning the carpet, samples had been taken using pads instead of the bag to show the amount of dirt in the carpet after the customers own cleaner had been used to hoover the same area. This often-brought shock and surprise. After the carpet shampoo the same routine was carried out on the customer's bed mattress using the same pads. A discussion – more like a lecture- was then undertaken to describe the bed bugs and skin particles and so on that had been hovered up. Finally, the attachments for the hoover were demonstrated. During her time selling the vacuum cleaners Charlie managed to sell one. Although the volume was low the commission that she earnt on the one sale was good and worth a week's wages. She persevered at this job until it was her time to leave Geelong.

Charlie became good friends with a group of locals that were bikers and petrol heads. One of the members of the group was called Finn and he took a close interest in her. As the days moved on and plans started to be made for her and Hannah to travel round to other parts of Australia, it was clear that their plans had diverged.

Hannah wanted to travel up to Ayres Rock and the North of Australia whereas Charlie had plans to go to Perth on the West Coast. Charlie, with the help of her new friends and Finn, had bought a minivan. It was fabulous and bright red with chrome detail everywhere including some fantastic bull bars. The inside of the minivan had been converted for travelling with a mattress inside and a canvas attachment so that when the back doors were left open the sleeping area was about a full-length double bed. Inside the back of the van were shelves and compact cupboards so that everything you could need for travelling could be stored.

Chapter Five – when it did not work out.

The decision was made to leave for Perth and Finn was to travel with Charlie and try and start a new life for himself in Perth. Finn had a criminal record, for fighting and violence, and wanted a fresh start. Charlie believed he thought this life was planned out to be with her although secretly she knew that was never going to happen. Ever since she had left the UK Charlie had stayed in touch with her boyfriend Daniel mostly by letter and the occasional phone call as mobile phones were not a thing back in 1985. She had also stayed in contact with her family and specifically her brother Stewart as they both had been given mini tape recorders by their father and sent each other recorded messages back and forth.

The day they set off for Perth was exciting. There would be new places to see, new jobs to experience and the round the world trip was moving on. The journey involved over two thousand miles so would involve some stops and sleeping in the minivan on the way across the Nullarbor desert. But things were not meant to go smoothly. The engine blew up near Adelaide and they had to find a garage in the town that could repair or replace the engine. A Mini was a rare car in Australia, so this turned out to be a mammoth task. Eventually a place was found, and with the help from some money from her dad as the job was expensive, the minivan was ready to move on.

The last section of the journey involved some very scary roads with the risks of Kangaroos running in front of the car, and massive gulleys at the side of the roads that would destroy any car that veered into them, especially when it was dark. Eventually they arrived in Perth and found a cheap hotel to stay in whilst they looked for more long-term accommodation.

In the days that followed they rented a one bedroomed flat in a nice block and looked for various job opportunities. Finn managed to secure a position with a firm of panel beaters as this was his job before he had been in prison. Looking for work turned out to be a revelation for Charlie. She was looking for bar jobs, and in her search found out that some bars employed topless bar staff that were paid at least double the going rate. Whilst the money was an incredibly attractive prospect, she also found out that there was a less exhibitionist option of a see-through bartender which paid around one and a half times the going rate. This was the job she decided to take as it involved wearing a top made of chiffon or similar so at least you could keep a bit of modesty. Charlie also convinced herself that it was no different to being topless on holiday and at the time she had a fairly fit figure and perky boobs.

As the weeks went by, they took on a rescue dog, Ditch, and settled into their new life. Charlie also found out that Finn was not the man she had thought he was. He drank a lot and used to come back to the flat in an angry mood. Charlie soon learned that she had to be careful what she said when he was in that kind of mood, and usually ended up taking Ditch out for a long walk to get out of the way. She also found out that Finn had an extremely jealous nature.

There was a particularly bad evening where Finn had accused her of flirting with the customers in the bar she worked in and wanted her to leave her job. This was not going to happen as she loved her job and was not about to be told what to do. A violent row followed with Finn taking his fists to Charlie and hurting her quite badly but not enough to warrant hospitalisation. He also went outside and kicked every panel on the minivan and then stormed off.

Charlie was so upset that she called the police, and after taking down all the details they informed her that even if she pursued the matter and he was arrested nothing would come of it as by the time it came to trial her visa would have expired and she would have left Australia. This was not what she wanted to hear.

After a few days, Finn turned back up with his tail between his legs, and full of apologies to make up for his behaviour. Charlie was not so easily fooled. She had already started plans to make her way to Sydney which was where her next flight was due to depart from. She decided it was in her best interest to play the game with Finn to meet her own objectives. He said he was going to repair the minivan – it was after all his trade – so Charlie agreed on the condition that as soon as it was back to original condition, she would sell it as even though she had become quite attached to it, it was not practical to even consider taking it back to the UK or anywhere else.

It turned out he kept his promise, the panels were fixed and resprayed on the minivan, and it was put up for sale. It sold quickly and Charlie even got her money back in full.

Plans were then finished for the trip to Sydney. Charlie removed her name from the rented flat and Finn decided to stay in Perth and start a new life there with Ditch, and the coach ticket to Sidney for Charlie was arranged. It was to be a long journey but meant Charlie could leave quickly as she was really not comfortable living with Finn the abuser.

Charlie packed her essentials in her rucksack and headed off on the next part of her journey. Once she arrived in Sydney, she had a few days to explore before the plane to her next adventure in New Caledonia (Noumea) was due. Even though she had managed to replenish her savings and some more whilst working in Australia Charlie planned to stay in traveller's hostels for the rest of the round the world trip. It was easy to find a taxi who took her to a hostel he recommended in Sydney, and he was a lovely driver. He chatted about the places she should see whilst she was in the city and what was really worth seeing and was cheapest. It was so nice that someone would take their time to help her so much.

Charlie checked into the hostel and was lucky enough to be the only one in the room they allocated her – it must have been a quiet time of year for travellers. Once she had sorted her stuff, she went down to the main reception to see what was going on. She was not in the least bit tired as she had managed to get some sleep on the coach journey and started chatting to some of the other travellers in the communal lounge. As had become typical of Charlie she veered towards a group of bikers who were staying there who were fascinated to hear of her travels so far. They were just 'doing Australia' in between their studies and finding careers – just like herself really, putting off the inevitable rest of life working role.

There were other travellers in the lounge and kitchen areas from all over Europe, and some from America. It always amazed Charlie how well all the Europeans she met spoke English. It really made it clear how lazy the British were with languages in general as all the other nations seemed to strive to speak her native tongue.

The next few days were spent visiting the sights with various members of the hostel she had met – it was great because they would all pair and group up the evening before based on who wanted to see what the next day. The day before she was due to leave for the next part of her round the world journey, some of the group jumped on the back of the motorbikes to go to a fairground that had set up on the outskirts of the city. That was a fabulous day but ended a bit sourly for Charlie. She was wearing as normal her homemade leather mini skirt and without thinking caught her leg, on the inside of the calf, on the exhaust pipe of the Harley she was on the back of. It was extremely hot, and the smell of burning skin was nasty, along with her scream. The skin went red, bubbled, and blistered and the overall decision by everyone was that whether she liked it or not, she had to go to the local hospital to get it checked out. Off she went and after various inspections from the medical team it was decided it was a second and maybe third-degree burn. Charlie did not know the meaning of this terminology, just that it looked nasty and hurt. Anyway, they treated the burn and bandaged it up securely and then they also advised that she should not travel the next day, so Charlie decided it was time to get out of there as she did not want anything holding up her plans and coming back the next day for a check-up was not part of those plans.

Back to the hostel she went – more carefully getting on and off the bike this time. The owner of the bike she had damaged herself on was mortified and it took all of Charlie's might to convince him that it was not his fault, and it was just down to her carelessness and natural tendency to be accident prone. A good night's sleep was needed after a couple of beers – the next day was going to be busy, and more painful than Charlie had first imagined.

In the morning, Charlie knocked back a load more painkillers, packed up her rucksack and spent some time saying her goodbyes to the new friends she had met in the hostel. The taxi to the airport was booked for just after lunch for Noumea and it was not too long a flight luckily. A fellow traveller who was staying at the hostel in Sydney had told her where she should stay when she arrived and how to get there. She was off on her travels again. The taxi was on time, and as the flights were all scheduled there were rarely any delays or problems with them, and they took off spot on time.

It was not a long flight and Charlie was full of excitement for the next leg of her journey. This was the first country she was going to visit as a solo traveller. She had not met up again with Hannah and had no means of contacting her. She knew her friend would be doing well and as they had booked the same flights originally there would be a chance that they may meet up again if neither of them had changed a particular flight, although deep down she knew this was unlikely. She held no ill-feeling towards Hannah and privately wished her the best of luck in her own travels in her mind.

On arrival at the airport Charlie was able to remember and follow the advice given to her by the fellow travellers she had met. There did not seem to be anyone else in her position on the flight or around the airport, but she was able to find a taxi and explain where she wanted to go. The journey to the hostel was not long and although they were driving further and further into jungle-like territory Charlie was not worried. She was already a confident young lady and her experiences in life so far had given her the strength and courage to know it would be safe and have a good ending.

The traveller's hostel was lovely – just like a colonial house with lovely rooms and shared areas. As she had found with all the other places she had stayed whilst travelling the hostel was comprised of people from all different nationalities and Charlie very soon managed to make some new friends to spend the hours with and explore. What was really different about this country was that the son's and male relatives of the tribal leaders from the local areas spent some time at the hostel speaking with the travellers which Charlie later found out was so they could improve their command of different languages and extend their own personal knowledge of the rest of the world. Charlie joined in with the chats with the local boys and it was during one of these occasions on her second day that the pain in her burnt leg began to get really intense again and the tears started to come. Her fellow travellers were concerned, and one went to find the manager of the hostel to find out about how they could get some medical assistance for Charlie.

In the meantime, three of the locals who had been part of these discussions and had heard about the burn and how it had come about, asked Charlie if she would trust them to try and help her with her agony.

They explained to her that the burn had started to fester and that they needed to do something before it became too infected to treat. She was in searing pain and decided she had nothing to lose. Charlie had no idea what they planned but put her complete faith in them on the basis that they had no reason to want to harm her. They warned her that it might hurt for a little and suggested she had a couple of shots of Brandy before-hand, so she did.

Then two of the lads sat her down at the edge of the garden area whilst the third quickly ran inside the hostel. He re-appeared next to her with something in his hand and a hosepipe in tow which was turned on. The lads all told her to look away from her leg and whilst the original two kept her still in a sitting position (although Charlie did not feel trapped) the one with the hosepipe produced an old-fashioned style scrubbing brush, the harsh wire sort that people used to scrub their porch steps with and proceeded to scrub away at the dead and damaged skin on her leg. It felt like it took a lifetime but in reality, was probably for no more than a few minutes. The water from the hosepipe was soothing on the now red flesh but all the gooey bits had been removed and it looked like a much cleaner wound.

The lad who had been doing the scrubbing then wandered off into the gardens and returned carrying a bundle of leaves and some fabric pieces. He explained that the first treatment he had to do was to bathe and soak the wound with the gel from the inside of the aloe vera plant, and then make a poultice with the remaining gel and leaves, finally secured with the cloth as a bandage.

It was all done and after a while the intense pain subsided. Charlie was not sure whether it was the Brandy she had downed or a miracle cure.

They all said they would be back the next day to check on the wound and see how it was progressing and at that point the whole experience hit Charlie, so she said her thankyous and took herself off to bed. That night was a much more peaceful sleep. The next day, true to their word, two of the three lads turned up and removed the dressing – the redness from the wound had disappeared and it looked nowhere near as angry. They redressed it with more aloe vera and continued to do this each day for the remainder of her stay in the hostel. She was able to still get out and about and enjoy the sights and surroundings of the beautiful country. One particularly memorable visit was to a small local zoo where Charlie and her fellow travellers all screeched in amazement at the sight of the native animals and beasts doing their male to female things whilst suspended in mid-air – it was certainly a sight to see.

Chapter six – getting back on track.

Eventually the short visit to the beautiful island was due to end and the next country to be visited was New Zealand. Charlie did have a contact from her mother's old best friend from Denton in Sheffield that she could look up but decided after the experience with this friend's ex-husband in Gelong, Australia, she would make it a brief visit. She also had the contact details of the two travellers she had met in Singapore and decided this would be a better arrangement for a bit longer term. As the prior arrangements had been made with her mother's friend Joyce, she decided that she would stick to that first and call her from the airport as had been arranged many, many months ago. The flight from New Caledonia to Auckland was only a few hours and Charlie was soon on her way in a taxi to the airport after bidding goodbye to her fellow travellers. Two of them were also due to fly out, although to Australia, so she was able to share the taxi fare and journey with them and they all enthused and chattered about the small and beautifully exotic island they were leaving.

    Once Charlie's plane had landed and she had collected her rucksack from the luggage carousel, she cleared customs and made her way to find a public phone in the airport in Auckland. Joyce answered the phone on the third ring and told Charlie where to wait and said they would be along in 30 minutes. Soon enough the time had passed, and Charlie was getting in the car with them on the next part of her adventure.

Their house was amazing, situated just in the suburbs of the city, and the front garden and patio were adorned with flowers in pots and baskets, and there were beautiful flower beds in amazing and vibrant colours.

She warmed very quickly to Joyce and her husband and was loving telling them all her travel tales whilst she settled in with them in the comfortable and spacious lounge for an evening of fun, food, and drink. It was fascinating to hear the stories of her mother as a youngster – she knew her mum would never have been a saint, but the tales of mischief and sneaking around behind their own mothers' backs were hysterical.

If Charlie did not change them the flight schedule originally booked allowed for 3 weeks in New Zealand altogether. The day after her arrival and after good discussions with her hosts it was decided that Charlie would stay with Joyce for 5 days and then head off for a week or more to South Island to meet the lads from Singapore, and then return to Joyce for a few days before flying back out of Auckland. This arrangement suited everyone, including the South Island contingent and Charlie spent a delightful few days being shown around parts of North Island. They went on shopping trips – mainly window shopping in Charlie' case - and went out for some fantastic meals at a wide variety of different restaurants be it for lunch or dinner. This was intertwined with barbeques, one which was particularly fun where Joyce and her husband had been invited to a pre-wedding barbeque at one of their friends and took Charlie along to meet everyone. Other exciting visits during the day included a trip to Rotorua. Here Charlie was able to see the delights of the geothermal mud pools and geysers and experience the cultural side and history of the Mauri population of the country.

When the five days were up and it was time to move on to South Island, Charlie was quite sad to leave Joyce and could fully understand why she had been such good friends with her mother all those years ago.

It was sad that they had not kept in touch all this time but luckily for Charlie her own mother had stayed connected with Joyce's mother who was now in a residential home in Sheffield and had managed to get the contact details for her old friend. The journey to South Island was planned and was to be by coach down to Wellington, and then a short flight to Christchurch where she would be met by the South Island boys Dave and Chris at the airport. Charlie packed her meagre belongings – replacing a few personal items with the new ones from the shopping trip with Joyce and packed some extra essentials she had added and jumped in the car for her lift to the coach station. She found it the saddest of her goodbyes so far on the trip when she climbed out of the car at the coach station it had almost been like being back at home with her mum and dad. She was also looking forward to the next adventure, at the same time as thinking how soon the whole journey would be over. Charlie had mixed feelings about it – she longed to see her family and friends with desperation, but on the other side knew that it would signal the end of her year of adventure and welcome her with a shock to life in the real world.

It was set to be a good 8 hours' drive, but as it was already evening time, Charlie figured she could get some sleep on the coach as it was nowhere near full, and she could curl up in two seats easily. Once on the coach and out of the city it was clear that the other travellers on the coach had the same plans as it was the quietest journey she had encountered to date.

There was a short stop about halfway along the journey at a clean and tidy roadside café. Most people disembarked for toilet and food and drink breaks but within 20 minutes of the coach setting off again everyone had quietly gone back to sleep. Charlie liked this kind of travelling as it meant she would be fully alert for her next leg of the journey and able to take in everything she saw and did.

At the airport in Wellington as it was only an internal flight, and as she did not have much baggage the check-in process and boarding went fairly quickly. Boarding was a walk across the tarmac and Charlie was a little surprised to see that the plane she was boarding was ridiculously small and old fashioned looking, with a propeller on the front. It had to be safe she thought to herself as everyone else looked happy enough to get on. The flight was only around an hour and as smooth as any other she had been on with the big jumbo jets and long-haul planes.

Disembarking was just as quick in Christchurch, and she was soon out of the airport and spotted Dave standing by his car waiting for her. She had wondered whether she would recognise either Dave or Chris as it had been a while since she had seen them and did not really spend much time with them in Singapore. Dave was lovely and welcoming and gave Charlie a big hug before throwing her rucksack in the boot. He explained he had today and could have tomorrow off work so would be able to settle her in and see to anything that she needed. Charlie felt so lucky to have met such genuine and nice people on her travels. As ever she was probably too trusting, but it had not caused her any problems so far.

When they arrived at Dave's house it was a lovely bungalow on a typical residential street.

He explained that Chris lived just round the corner and would be joining them later for tea when he had finished work.

Dave showed Charlie to her room – it was a small single bedroom but had more than all the comforts she could need. He also showed her the bathroom and how the shower and stuff in the kitchen worked. He said he had a spare key for the front door should she need it. Then they settled down to relax and chat. Best of all, he said before they went any further, she could use the home telephone to ring her mum and dad and have a good, long, and free catch up. That was the best present she could have been given. During the whole of her travels Charlie had only managed to have fairly short and infrequent catch-up calls due to the costs of the long-distance calls even though her mum and dad had got her to do reverse charge calls sometimes, and due to the fact that it meant finding and often queuing for a phone box. She quickly took advantage of the offer – it was late afternoon in New Zealand which meant it was incredibly early morning at home and she knew her Dad would be up, and her Mum would not mind. Dave said he was going into the kitchen to continue prepping the food for tea and would be back with her shortly. She must have spent over half an hour on the phone filling her family in on her adventures and finding out all about happenings at home. It was so comforting and filled her with joy as well as some sadness to chat for so long and hear their voices clearly and feel the love coming through. Eventually they said their goodbyes and Charlie promised to call again as soon as she could and said she could not wait to see them and get back to her home. When she had finished and put the receiver down with mixed feelings Charlie went to help Dave in the kitchen.

As it was winter in the country a barbie evening was out of the question, so Dave had prepped some Indian dishes and Chris was coming round with his girlfriend Tracy to share in an Indian buffet. When they had sorted and plated up everything ready for reheating where necessary they settled down in the lounge with a glass of wine.

Dave and Charlie chatted for a couple of hours like they had been life-long friends. Charlie found out that Dave had been engaged with the wedding planned and everything just over a year ago. He found out his then fiancée had cheated on him with one of her work colleagues, so he called the whole shebang off and threw her out. There were no legal problems as the bungalow was still in his sole name and they manage to get the money back for most of the wedding arrangements. The parents on both sides were disappointed and tried to get them to make up, but the trust had gone and what she had done did not bode well for the future. Dave said he had only had casual relationships since. It also affected his best mate from school, Chris's plans, as Chris and Tracy decided it was best just to stay as 'living in sin' for the time being and not to tempt fate by going through to marriage and permanent commitment. It was working well for them so far.

Then Dave explained the jobs they did. He drove coaches for a tour company so in the winter months drove groups from the towns up to the ski resorts and winter sights, and then in the summer he might do longer sight-seeing and airport runs across both Islands. It was regular work and paid well so it enabled him to have a roof over his head as well as enjoy some of the finer things in life. Chris was a fitness fanatic and worked as a ski instructor and guide in the winter months, and anything to do with tourists and school and college pupils during the rest of the year.

They were both prepared to turn their hand to anything if they needed work and had been best friends since junior school. The trip on which they had met Charlie involved years of saving up for a year off work and had been talked about and gradually planned since they were young. It was always a dream, and they were able to fulfil it and visit all the countries they originally had on their list as well as some others. Dave raved about how much he loved the United Kingdom. Even though London was exciting and buzzing he felt it was really like many other cities and being more of an outdoors type he loved the Lake District, Scotland, and parts of Wales best so they talked about some of the places in these areas that Charlie knew with excitement and happy memories. Charlie talked about her many camping trips with her dad and brother, and sometimes close family friends, and how this developed into going away with her own friends to the same areas in the Lakes once she was over eighteen, and the fun they had on those trips.

The plan was also hatched for the next day – subject to the approval of Chris, Dave was to accept a job to take a coach up to a ski resort where Chris was working, and Charlie would go with him and spend the day with Chris and Dave and have a go at skiing, before returning on the coach with Dave. When Chris and Tracy arrived at the house it was again like seeing an old friend with Chris, and Charlie warmed to Tracy really quickly. She worked in the hotel and events industry and was a couple of years older than Charlie. She travelled quite a lot with the hotel chain she worked for and really loved her job.

It made Charlie wonder whether her planned career would excite and interest her enough. Charlie already had secured a position with a large accountancy form in London to start a training contract to qualify as a Chartered Accountant in the September following her return to the United Kingdom. She thought to herself that she was lucky to have a job arranged to go home too, and as with everything she did she would put her heart and soul into it and see how it panned out.

Chris was quite happy to agree to the plans for the next day, so they continued the evening with drinks and food, laughs and stories and had a thoroughly enjoyable time. Unfortunately, by the time Chris and Tracy left, Charlie had drunk a few too many glasses of wine – she was not really a big wine drinker and it had really hit her quite obviously, with her staggering around the lounge and kitchen collecting dishes and glasses with many near misses and lots of slurring. Chris offered to help her through to the bedroom and plonk her on the bed to sleep it off – he said she would need all her strength the next day as she had never tried skiing before, only occasionally on a dry ski slope in Bartondale. The thought of lying down felt very appealing although she did suggest he brought her a bucket. One of Charlie' issues with excess drinking was that when she lay down and her head started to spin, it was usually followed by vomiting so being prepared was best. Dave took her through and said he would finish the clearing and washing up and then come and check on her before going to bed himself.

Good to his word, a couple of hours later he checked on Charlie. She had gone out like a light as soon as he had originally left and slept soundly for the whole time without the need for the bucket.

Even when she stirred when Dave came into the room, she felt surprisingly clear, due to the pints of water she had downed before retiring. Dave sat on the edge of the bed and Charlie asked him for a hug, telling him how grateful she was for his kind and welcoming manner to her and what a lovely evening she had spent with them all. needless to say, the hug led to more – first a kiss, and then the start of a fondle, and then to full blown sex. It was fun because it felt naughty and unplanned and had been a long time, certainly for Charlie. Afterwards, Dave fetched his alarm clock and stayed holding Charlie in her bed for the evening and they both slept peacefully until the alarm clock went off at 7 the next morning.

Dave said he would get himself showered and ready for work. They both agreed that last night was a drunken (on Charlie's part) one off, and maybe best put to one side. It was not as if there were any regrets, but it was not what either of them had in mind and certainly had no plans for a relationship like that going forward. Dave said it would be a few hours by the time he had checked his coach and collected the skiers from the various hotels. He had to pass by his road at the end of his collections so would swing in and pick Charlie up about 9.30 and she was to be ready outside the house. This was great news as it gave her time to wash and freshen up after an evening of alcohol and fun.

She was ready on time and the ski wear that Tracy had dropped off for her that morning fitted and was sure to keep her warm. The ski boots were even the right size although she decided she would not try and put them on until they arrived at the resort and Chris could make sure she did it right. She locked the bungalow behind her and jumped in the coach, passing the house keys to Dave.

He had kept the front seat free for her and Charlie laughed with him that she hoped she did not have to do the announcements and Dave reassured her that it was part of his job, so she did not have to worry.

The journey to the ski resort was over an hour long and there had been really heavy snow fall over night. The roads, as Dave worked his way higher and higher into the mountains, were getting scarier and scarier, with snow and ice everywhere and big drops down the cliffs at the edges. It reminded Charlie of the Italian Job where the coach teeters over the edge of the cliff with the weight of the gold, and all the hairpin bends in the film. At one point Dave pulled the coach over to the side and she got off the coach although the other passengers were told to stay inside. Charlie watched him fitting snow chains to the tyres which she had never seen before but was reassured by Dave telling her that it was an everyday occurrence at certain times of the season, and really just added as an extra safety precaution.

Once up at the slopes, Charlie followed the group to the building near the bottom of the lifts as instructed by Dave. After a bit of looking around she found Chris who was just finishing with a young couple on their lesson. She waited patiently until he came over to her. Dave was following over once he parked up the coach and gathered his ski stuff. Chris took her into the ski building and sorted her out with skis and poles and checked she was properly kitted out with gloves and hat and sunglasses. The sun was beating down even though there was a cold bite in the air, so it was a lovely day. Then they made their way back outside, with Chris carrying her skis for her. He said he had a few hours in between lessons to dedicate to her and the plan was to at least get her up and sliding.

They chatted about what skiing she had tried before and Charlie explained apart from grass skiing in the Lakes years ago and one attempt and dry slope skiing, she had not done any. It was obvious this was going to be a challenge.

Charlie sat on a bench whilst Chris fitted her skis and then Dave came swishing over all cool in his ski gear. She was amazed at how easy he made it look but doubted it really was. Once up on her feet, Chris guided her to a small incline at the top of the slope. This was where the fun – if she could call it that – started. Dave moved down to the base of the small slope and to Charlie it looked like there was a big drop behind him, but she knew she had to trust them. Dave showed her how to position her feet in a snow plough shape, a V with the skis digging in on the edges. Then he told her to put her hand on his shoulder and let herself slide forward naturally. As soon as he moved his skis from blocking hers, they were off down the slope. Dave stayed in front of her and slowed her from getting out of control. They did this a few times down to Chris and then with Dave dragging her back up the small slope using his ski poles.

Then it was time to try it on her own without the cushion of Dave in front of her. He set Charlie off at the top of the slope and she tried hard to keep her skis parallel as she headed to Chris. It was terrifying as all she could think of was the what if Chris did not stop her and she went flying past or off the edge. She amazed herself and pulled it off, although she was prepared to fall down in a heap into the snow if she went too fast or too far. They continued doing this a few more times before it was time to return the gear and head back to the shop for Chris to take his next student.

Although Charlie had found the whole experiencing exhilarating, she was exhausted and the muscles in her calves and thighs were already starting to ache. She wondered how it was going to feel the next day if it hurt now. In reality she was relieved to get the cumbersome skis off her feet and put some normal footwear back on. It was like floating on air being able to walk again. She had an hour or so to entertain herself until the coach was departing back down to the town. This was good because it gave Charlie time to grab a drink and something to eat and contemplate her new experiences whilst watching the world go by. She was amazed at the skills of the skiers that swished and swooshed past her and had some regrets that she never went on the school ski trips and learnt at an early age. Although Charlie had parents who were comfortable financially, extravagances like expensive school skiing trips were never an option. At an early age she had forgone her pocket money for the chance to have a pony and was grateful for all the joys horse riding had given her over the years. On balance, she decided that if she ever wanted to start skiing or any other new sports, there was plenty of time in her life to learn.

Once Chris and his passengers were ready to leave the ski slopes, they all climbed back on the coach and began the scary descent down the windy, icy, and snowy roads. Chris dropped Charlie near the house and gave her the house keys back. She hobbled to the front door and once in flopped on the sofa. Although she had promised herself, she would find something useful to do in the house whilst waiting for Chris to return, she just could not muster the enthusiasm or energy to do anything. She helped herself to a cup of tea and eventually fell asleep on the sofa until Chris woke her around an hour later when he returned from the coach depot.

They made plans for tea, the remainder of the week, and the plans for getting Charlie back to the airport later in the week, the day she was due to go back to Joyce's house.

Her last evening with Chris and Dave was really good – they chatted for hours about everything and promised to stay in touch. The boys had already visited the UK as part of their earlier travelling spree but said if they were ever back in the North of England they would be in touch. Charlie said her goodbyes to Dave and Tracy that evening as they were both in work on her departure day. Chris was only driving part time that day, so he was able to give her a lift to the airport. It was quite a sad goodbye, mainly because she had enjoyed her stay so much and because she had a lot in common with the boys.

The journey back to Joyce was just a mirror image of her journey out, luckily with no delays or disasters on route. Joyce collected her at the coach station as agreed. Charlie chattered away in the car about all that she had been up to. The muscles in her legs were about beginning to ease after the attempts at skiing for the day and the initial exhaustion from her efforts had long since subsided. It was nearly teatime by the time they arrived back at the house, and it was nice to be able to relax and share all the tales of her most recent adventures. Joyce and Charlie laughed about how Charlie would have a lot of stories to tell her own family, both her mum and dad and brother on her return, and any future children she had and partners she met. Charlie wondered whether she would ever be able to remember everything as it had been such a whirlwind since finishing at university.

The next few days involved a few visits to some more local attractions and wandering around the city and before Charlie knew it, it was time to move onto her next, the second to last, destination. This was to be short visit to Tahiti, before flying on to Los Angeles. The original booking had involved a plan to arrange separately for travelling across America and then flying back to Heathrow from New York. Charlie had changed these tickets whilst she was in New Zealand. America was so vast and even with the travelling coast to coast, there was nowhere near enough time to see much at all. On top of that Charlie felt that she had seen and done enough for one year. She was not physically tired, but the longing to see her own family and get settled back in the UK before relocating to London to work pushed her decision. She changed her return flight to be from LA instead of New York and resolved to 'do' America at some future time.

Chapter seven – a welcome relaxation

At the airport, Charlie said her sad goodbyes to Joyce and headed off for the 5-hour flight to the exotic island of Tahiti. She had reduced her stay on the island to 5 days, and that included the arrival and departure days. As she was travelling on her own and wanted to cut down on spending her savings, 3 days exploring seemed to be plenty of time to relax and enjoy the sites. Charlie had made no plans to do anything in particular whilst there and was just going to go with the flow so to speak. As she had found out at all of the previous destinations there were plenty of people, guides, and taxi drivers, who were happy to help and advise her on where she could stay. The taxi driver she chose took her to a lovely traveller's guest house near the beach roads. She thanked him and checked in. It was really reasonably priced, including breakfast with other canteen style meals available if wanted, and her room was just lovely. Quite luxurious she thought, when compared to some of the places she had stayed in on her travels. Charlie unpacked her essentials and stretched out on the bed taking in her surroundings. The room was small, functional, and even had a small ensuite. She could see across the road to the beach from her window and there were street stalls lining the pavements and a real buzz in the air. Before she knew it, she had nodded off and a couple of hours had gone by.

Charlie was woken by a soft tap on the door. She pulled herself up from the bed wearily and opened the door. Standing on the other side was one of the members of the staff at the guest house.

He explained that he was the manager and was just letting her know that in a couple of hours' time some of the guests were heading off to a beach party down the road and he wondered if she was interested in joining them. He also said that there would be barbeque and snack style food at the party and drinks available and the whole thing was for a small ticket price, less than £3 equivalent. Charlie bought a ticket from him, and he said he would be back at 7pm to take her down to the gathering. This gave Charlie enough time to have a wash and get changed. It was still warm into the evening, so Charlie had to root through her clothes to find something suitable to wear. Party gear had not been high on the priority list when she had first packed her rucksack all those months ago. She had picked up a couple of items from the countries she had visited and decided on a bright blue silk shirt she had bought at the silk factory in Thailand, and a pair of jeans she had brought from home.

The evening was a laugh – lots of chatting and dancing and Charlie kept the alcohol consumption down. By midnight she had run out of steam and her and a couple of the others in the same guest house meandered their way back down the road. She had found out lots about all the places the other travellers had visited and had some useful tips for her stop in America and recommendations of where to stay. Luckily, she always carried a mini pad and pen so was able to jot down some notes during the evening as there was no way she was going to remember all the useful information she had been given.

After a very relaxing and restful night's sleep Charlie helped herself to some of the delicious buffet breakfast that was on offer. She opted for a selection of beautiful and fresh fruits and some hot fruit tea.

There were very few people around as it was after eight by the time she had sauntered into the breakfast room, but she had a good chat with the waiters who spoke perfect English. She explained that she was just going to wander around the area on foot and the beach for the day and take in the local surroundings and atmosphere. They recommended a particular beach bar that might be a good place to stop for some lunch or a drink as the prices were good and the snacks tasty and value for money. After breakfast, Charlie popped back to her room to collect her bag and put her comfortable shoes on and headed off towards the beach.

Immediately opposite the guest house she was in was a large complex of hotel rooms and beach bungalows. They were the type you see on films and in posh holiday brochures where the bungalows or huts stick out from piers into the sea. It was luxury everywhere. As she wandered around the complex, with no one stopping her, she was amazed at the size and clever design of the swimming pools that had swim up to bars, waterfalls, jacuzzies, and everything else you could think of. There were posh sunbathing areas with beds and swinging sofas, massage, and gym areas, but surprisingly not many guests. Charlie thought that it was off season. She had lost track of school and other holidays as most of the last year had been like one long holiday. She contemplated how lucky she was to have such an opportunity. As she walked along the beach, she spotted the bar the waiters had told her about. It did look enticing, but she decided to carry on walking down the beach.

She went past beach sellers with all sorts of wares from fresh fruit, snacks and drinks to clothes, toys, and gifts.

There were lots of places trying to encourage her to try water-skiing, scuba diving and many other water-based activities, and she stopped and chatted with some of the sellers to pass the time and be polite. She was careful to not get herself signed up for anything.

After meandering for a few hours, Charlie made her way back to the road. The pavements were filled up now with street sellers offering food, gifts, clothes, and everything else you could think of. Many of them were very keen to attract her attention and she did feel sorry for them as it was still relatively quiet customer wise although it was slowly getting a bit busier as it neared lunchtime. The people she was seeing around the stalls looked more like they would be the locals than tourists and many seemed to be picking up something to eat. She decided to stop at one of the food stalls that had a particular buzz around it. They were selling peppers with meatballs and a sauce, and she was persuaded to try some by the stall's owner. It was really delicious, so she ordered a portion to take away and asked for chilli flakes to be added. Charlie had always liked spicy food, and this was an opportunity to assess her resilience to the local spices.

She took her food a few strides down the road to a bench that was at the corner of a little triangular park. From here she could still feel and see the buzz of the street markets but could also see the beach and the sea. It was idyllic and Charlie wondered if she could do this for the rest of her life, or even after she eventually reached retirement age.

The rest of the afternoon was spent wandering around some more, picking up some bottles of soft drinks and snacks for her room and then heading back to the guest house. When she returned there a couple of the other travellers were by the small bar and stopped her on the way past.

Three of them were planning to book a taxi for the following day to take them to a couple of the sights on the island that were not too far away. They had worked out that four in a taxi would work out half the price each over booking an official tour or trip, and Charlie would make the fourth. She readily agreed to join them and said she was looking forward to the trip. Charlie chatted some more with the group before taking her stuff back to her room and having a lie down. Within minutes she had nodded off and did not wake up for over an hour. She had a quick wash and went downstairs to see what was on offer for tea in the guest house.

She found some delicacies off the canteen buffet style offerings that looked delicious and sat down at a table with a few others to tuck in. The food was very satisfying, and she drank plenty of bottled water to rehydrate herself after all the, albeit mild, exercise of the day. The group she had chatted to earlier were in the canteen and they decided on a handy start in the morning, so after a bit more chatting with her fellow travellers she took herself off to her room for a good night's sleep.

Charlie was up and ready for breakfast in the morning, feeling refreshed and eager to go. She had her breakfast and met the others outside the guest house to wait for the taxi. They did not have to hang around long before their transport arrived, and they all climbed in.

The first of the adventures for the day was to some spectacular waterfalls and when they got there Charlie was glad she had put on suitable footwear as there was a bit of a climb up to the best bits. The rest of the day took in more sights and showed them how beautiful and unspoilt most of the island was.

They grabbed some lunch at a local roadside bar during the day and eventually arrived back at the guest house feeling exhausted and culturally uplifted.

The next day was her final full one and she did more wandering around and taking in the atmosphere. She had an early flight to Los Angeles the following day so when she returned to her room Charlie decided it was best to get packed and ready to set off in the morning. She chatted with the other travellers in the canteen at teatime before retiring to her room.

The next morning the taxi was there at 5.50 am prompt to take her to the airport. She had settled up with the guest house the previous evening so was able to get straight off. Check in at the airport as always went without a hitch. All the flights that had been booked were scheduled flights and made life so much easier than the holiday charter flights. The journey to Los Angeles from Tahiti was around 8 hours and although she was not tired, Charlie decided it was better to get her head down for a few hours as she did not know how long she would take to find the travellers hotels when she landed in the evening. She was woken up by the cabin crew a couple of hours later for her airplane meal.

These were all included in the price of the flight and were all very pleasant. This meal was equally as nice as Charlie opted for a chicken in cream sauce with veg and potatoes. It was only a few hours to landing so she chatted with the man in the next but two seat after her meal for the rest of the journey. As they were scheduled flights, they were also often not full so there was plenty of room. The man was called Ken, and he was a barrister based in London. He had been to visit family in Tahiti and was on his way home via a meeting with a client in Los Angeles.

They chatted about London and Charlie told Ken of the training contract she had secured with the accountants in London. She explained that apart from the odd school trip and one with her parents, that she knew nothing of the city. Her boyfriend before she had left on her travels had been to university there and had promised to help her find somewhere to live in London, even if they did not hook back up together. They talked about the various commuter areas for the city and the pros and cons of the travelling in and out. It was the first time that Charlie had really thought about the vast size of the city, and how far out she was likely to be for a reasonable rent. Most of the travelling she had done in the past was on the local trainline between her home village and Hull, and that was no more than a half hour journey.

When they landed in Los Angeles, Charlie collected her rucksack from the carousel and headed outside the terminal to find a taxi. She was not surprised by the size of everything – from buildings to car parks, as she had always thought that America had to do everything bigger and better than everywhere else. She quickly found a taxi rank and chatted with one of the drivers about the hostels she had been given the name of. She had them written down with the most recommended two at the top of her list.

The driver suggested the second one on the list as it was easier to get around from there and had more bars and cafes nearby. They agreed this was where she should go, and they headed off on the half hour journey.

The hostel was lovely as had been all the others she had visited. This one had its own bar and restaurant come café, and a few communal lounges. All the rooms were double and ensuite which was heaven and Charlie quickly checked in and made her way to her room.

She had run out of energy and even though there was a real buzz in the bar and communal areas, she was all talked out. There was a public phone booth in the foyer, so she decided to call her family after she had unpacked and then retire for the night. Half an hour later she was making the reverse charge call home and was delighted to hear the voices of her mum and dad. She filled them in on the last week or so and discussed plans for her return to the UK. Her dad was insistent that he would collect her from Heathrow even though Charlie was quite happy to jump on a train. She said she would dig out the revised flight time from Los Angeles to Heathrow as she had changed it from the original flight home from New York and said she would ring them back in a couple of days.

After a good night's sleep, Charlie went down for breakfast and opted for the continental selection off the buffet. It was lovely and refreshing and set her up for the day. She wandered into one of the communal lounges to meet some of the other guests and look through some of the leaflets of activities and things to do that were on display. She collected a couple for later reading and then settled down into an armchair. She found out from some of the other guests that Santa Monica beach was within easy walking distance from the hostel and was a really lively area.

Charlie resolved to take a walk down there and wander around on her own. Her fellow travellers were right, it was less than 20 minutes away. The beach itself was a few miles long and interspersed with people sunbathing. There was a pier which Charlie headed for first. She chuckled to herself as she walked alongside the beach, that everyone that was in swimwear, male or female, seemed to mimic Baywatch.

She found it funny that the beautiful, tanned bodies that were on the TV programme really existed in abundance in real life in places like this. She was glad she had normal, although summery, clothes on, and had not worn her swimwear to be able to show off her not so beautiful, untanned body. There were people playing volleyball and other ball-based sports, and water sports everywhere. People were surfing, parasailing, water-skiing and much more. It was a lovely atmosphere seeing everyone having so much fun. She walked to the pier and was amazed by the amount of fairground rides and attractions they had manage to fit into the area. The place was remarkably busy even though it was a normal weekday and Charlie wondered whether it was school or national holidays in America, or in Los Angeles in particular.

On her travels she found a small, slightly hidden, beach bar to have a toastie and drink at, and sat peacefully taking in her surroundings. She enjoyed the food and the peacefulness of the place and watched all the people coming and going on the beach, smiling to herself at how happy and relaxed everyone seemed. After a while she forced herself to move on and slowly made her way back to the hostel. On her return she sat down in the communal lounge and started looking through some of the leaflets she had started looking at the day before. There were activities galore to do in the area – all at a cost if you went on the guided tours.

Charlie decided the things she would like to do if she had time were to visit Universal Studios, drive round the posh housing areas of Beverley Hills and Hollywood and see the star name signs on the pavement.

There were many more attractions and places to visit and if you wanted you could fill weeks and weeks with things to do. Universal Studios in 1986 was not a theme park, more a visit of various movie sets and similar displays. The price of the trips for the ones she had picked were quite high and some of them included things she really was not interested in at the moment, but fortunately for Charlie, a couple in the lounge who were also looking through leaflets had been remarking on the same thing. They were called Ben and Jane, and they had looked into hiring a car that afternoon to see if it was any cheaper and more flexible. Unfortunately, Jane did not drive, and Ben did not have the international driving permit that was needed to hire a car in America.

Whilst Charlie was chatting with the couple, she explained she had her permit if they wanted to think about sharing the costs. She had done this with fellow travellers in other countries and it had always worked out all right. They planned and chatted about what they wanted to see. They were happy to go along with each other's suggestions as they planned to have the car for a couple of days to get the best deal from the company – they were doing a three for two offer, so 3 days was decided upon. The three of them popped down to the car hire company that Ben had found out was the best around and booked the car in Charlie's name but split the cost three ways. The company would even deliver the car to the hostel at 8am in the morning, and then pick it up 3 days later.

They headed back to the hostel and grabbed themselves some tea – it was only a few dollars in the café, and they sat at a table to discuss the rough plans for the few days.

Ben and Jane were a happy and chilled couple who although a few years older than Charlie had both recently finished degrees in Physics type disciplines, but unlike Charlie, had not managed to secure a job yet for their return to the UK. They still had 3 months of travelling to do, and when they returned home had a busy time ahead. As well as finding jobs in the same or nearby towns, they had a wedding to plan and book and had to find a place to live. Shortly after tea, Charlie went to her room although she realised once there, she had forgotten to ring her parents with the flight details. She hoped there would be enough time to do it in the next day or two. Los Angeles was 8 hours ahead of the UK time wise, so she decided to call them when she returned to the hostel the next evening.

The car was delivered exactly on time after all three of them had eaten their breakfast. They were ready to go and had decided the first place to visit was Universal Studios. This was on the basis that it was midweek, and they thought it would be quieter in the earlier morning before the majority of tourists were up and about. Ben directed and Charlie drove. She was glad she had someone to direct her as driving on the wrong side of the road as well as all the strange ways of American signage and lights would have driven her to panic on her own. They found Universal Studios and parked up before heading inside after paying the small entrance fee.

They wandered around the sets and Charlie loved the cowboy sets – they had been her favourite type of films from an early age – more to do with the horses in them than the actors, and around various other well-known sets. Charlie could not work out when they managed to use them for filming as there were tourists all around, but figured they must have set opening hours or days, or these were just old sets.

They spent a few more hours looking around and grabbed a burger and drink from a snack bar before heading back to the car. That afternoon and the next few days were spent driving around the area, stopping to see free sights as they went. They saw the Hollywood sign, some of the fabulous houses of the stars – albeit only from the end of gated drives, trees and hedges and took a walk down the pavement of the stars looking for names they recognised. In addition to the original places planned, they also drove to some of the other beaches and took in some of the famous buildings. They had decided they were not going to any other pay for attractions but had a fun time just looking around at a wholly different world to home. As Charlie had always thought, everything seemed bigger and more extravagant, including the people she saw, and it made her think about how relatively shy and reserved the British were. It also made her happy to be British in some ways.

The next day was her last day in the city before heading off to the airport for her trip back to Heathrow the following early evening. She spent that day with Ben and Jane and a few others they had met wandering around the city and local beaches.

One of the really wonderful things Charlie had found about travelling was that there were always many stories to tell and experiences to share as she was constantly meeting new people, so she knew she was not repeating herself. She also loved hearing all about other peoples' experiences and lives and the way the travellers she met enthused about everything they had done.

She had also remembered to ring her parents a few days before and give them the arrival time of her flight at Heathrow. The flight was the best part of 11 hours, and she was due to land at 13.00 UK time with the time difference. Her father said he would meet her outside the arrivals area shortly after she had landed and collected her baggage.

Chapter 8 – the homecoming

Finally, it was time to head home. Charlie had booked a taxi to take her on her last journey and said her goodbyes to her new friends as she headed out of the hostel to the waiting car. She had decided to wear her staple homemade leather miniskirt, an item of clothing that had been a godsend throughout her travels as it was all weather, needed no washing, and took up little room in her rucksack. The journey to the airport did not take long and check-in was as smooth and quick as it had been on all the scheduled flights. Charlie dropped her baggage and headed for the gate. There were a few cafes by the gate so she thought she might as well get a drink and a snack as there was over an hour to boarding. The flights always included a meal, but she had skipped lunch and was feeling a bit peckish. She chose a toastie and a coffee and sat down to wait, watching the other flights coming and going through the window, wondering where everyone was heading.

Eventually it was time to board. Charlie had a whole row of seats to herself as the flight was quite empty – this was good as it meant she would be able to lie sideways and get a quick nap. Charlie spent some time during the flight updating her diaries with her latest escapades. There were lots of details to fill in as she had been a bit slow at doing it in recent weeks, but she knew if she did not do it now, she might forget some of the details and some of the names of the lovely travellers she had met. There were some films playing on the TV and she watched one, dozed for some time and enjoyed the evening meal that was served.

She was flying with KLM this time again, an airline that had been used for quite a few of her flights, and the service and food was excellent.

Before she knew it the captain was announcing their descent to Heathrow. Charlie was so excited about seeing her dad and the rest of her family and close friends again. After they had disembarked, she was quickly out of the terminal looking for her dad – she spotted his car straight away as luckily, he had not changed it in the time she had been away. She ran to her dad and hugged him so much he eventually had to step back. They put her rucksack in the back and headed off out of the airport to start the long motorway journey back to Hull. Her Dad told her he planned to stop around Stoke-on-Trent at a restaurant he knew well so they could have a nice meal before carrying on with the journey. Charlie was not really dressed for posh restaurants, but her dad reassured her it did not matter. She thought if he did not mind, she did not. They chatted non stop on the journey and arrived at the restaurant at teatime. They enjoyed a lovely meal together before returning to the car for the rest of the journey. Her Dad laughed that the staff in the restaurant probably though Charlie was his young girlfriend and she found this very amusing. On the final leg of the journey Charlie asked if they could drive past the old port buildings in Hull. She could not explain why, but somehow it had an emotional pull to her and a feeling of being home. As they drove past the grand buildings, Charlie felt a lump in her throat telling her she was home. She was also excited as it meant she was even closer to seeing her Mum and brother.

Within half an hour they were pulling up outside her home – Mum and Stewart had heard the car and were at the door to greet her.

There were tears, hugs, and laughs and lots of joy before they all went inside to sit down and have a cup of tea. It was quite late so after a couple of hours of chatting they all retired to their beds.

It was heaven for Charlie being back in her own room, in her own bed with all her old things around her. She knew she was going to sleep well, and she did. Charlie did not wake up until gone 9am the next day – the latest she could remember sleeping for a long time. In the next few hours, she had phone calls from friends and family welcoming her home, and her long term and childhood friend Abigail was round early to see her. Daniel rang, the boyfriend she had been with before she left on her travels, and said he was on his way up from Worcester. Charlie was pleased he was coming to see her but was completely unsure about how she felt about their relationship right now. She had been away a long time now – longer than she had been with him – but she was very fond of him before she set off and her Mum just suggested she let him come and see how it went. So, it was decided, he was to come to Hull.

Whilst Charlie was away, she had taken an Olympus SLR camera with her and had frequently sent films back to home from various countries for them to be developed. The family spent a few hours looking through these photos with Charlie explaining where they were and what she had been doing at the time. They also talked about the next chapter in her life – before setting off on her travels Charlie had secured a job with MTB accountants working in London. This meant that in the next month or so she had to find somewhere to live in London and get herself all sorted for this next adventure. Luckily, she did not have to start looking for a car, even though they thought it was unlikely she would need one in London.

Charlie valued her freedom and hoped she would find somewhere to stay that would have parking for a car. Her Mum was planning to change her car so she said Charlie could have the Fiat 127 she was going to get rid of. It was roadworthy and cheap to run so this seemed a marvellous idea.

Later that day Daniel arrived. He was full of emotion and love and told Charlie how he never wanted to be parted from her again. She found it very overwhelming although very touching. They went for a long walk on the sandhills and chatted about the future and London and everything else. Daniel had been to university in London and still had a lot of friends there so said he would help her find somewhere suitable to rent. He planned to stay a few days if that was all right with her family, and suggested they start looking in the newspapers for rental adverts. That evening they strolled up to the local pub and Charlie was able to catch up with other friends she had grown up with and share some of her stories. Even though she had been nervous and worried how it would be with Daniel, she need not have worried, they hit it off and got on like they had never been apart. It was comforting although a bit daunting at the same time. There was so much left to sort and do in her life, Charlie was not sure that she wanted to be locked into a permanent relationship just yet.

London was to be another adventure for Charlie, because apart from the odd school trip visit, she knew little about the Capital. She found a place in a block of flats that were all rented or owned by metropolitan police officers near to Grove Park in London. It was only a few minutes' walk from the two bedroomed flat owned by police officer, Mark, to the station so was convenient for work. Mark had a lovely Burmese cat called Sandy which Charlie was overjoyed about as her mother had always had cats at home.

Surprisingly, Charlie continued her relationship with Daniel. Worcester was only an hour and a half on the fast train from London, so either Charlie would get the train up to him, or he would drive down to London at weekends. He had a lot of university friends still in London, so the couple had an active social life in both cities. Charlie found it really different being in the Capital. She worked with a wonderful team in the business services department, the department which looked after the smaller business audits in the firm. Small to the London office was not the type of company most people would deem to be small and involved audits on a lot of large companies where the audit work could entail adding up a computer printout, the type that was about 3 inches thick and bound in a plastic cover with white plastic ties. More exciting work involved vouching or checking numerous invoices to similarly bound printouts or vice versa, and the occasional attendance at stock takes. Making the tea and coffee was also part of the first-year trainees' duties, as was photocopying and filing. The accountancy firm sent all the trainees on courses fairly regularly, mostly external with a training organisation on block release for exams, but also some internal development training courses. There were students from other accountancy firms on the external training and there was one in particular, one of the 'big four' like her own firm, who had all been issued with the same brown clasp-over leather briefcases, and Charlie could not help laughing to herself how silly and old-fashioned they looked, it was almost like they were clones, and the trainees she had spoken with certainly seemed to be lacking in exuberant personalities.

It made her glad she had chosen the firm she was with as even at the recruitment events her firm seemed more interested in whether you had a personality than whether you had perfect grades.

One part of living in London that Charlie really hated was the travelling. Because of its vast size and the spread of locations around the spokes of the transport wheel to the North, South, East and West of London, and all points on the compass in between, there was no-one she worked with that took the same route home each day as her. It was not a vast distance, but Charlie had to catch the tube to London Bridge from the office or training company, and then change to an overland train at London Bridge that was passing through Lewisham. Everywhere was crowded, the tubes, the trains, and even the platforms and staircases and nobody spoke or even smiled at each other. In fact, it was clear that even eye contact was a no-no which was so different to what Charlie was used to when she used the local train service at home and most people you sat next to would start up some type of conversation.

She remembered vividly one particular episode on the packed overland train. The train was the sort that had the old-fashioned heavy swing doors. Charlie was squashed up near the entrance with many others and for some reason at one of the train-stops she had ended up with her hand near the hinged side of the door to stop her losing her balance. As the train prepared to pull off from the stop and the last passenger to embark slammed the door shut behind him, Charlie's thumb was in the gap between the door and the carriage on the hinge side. She screamed in pain as the door crushed her thumb as it was swung shut.

The passengers next to her asked her if she wanted to sit down and in a less than grateful manner, she shouted expletives to indicate it was not her arse that she had hurt, but her thumb. It was really a bit unfair of her as the concerned passengers were only trying to help. But she did not care, she just wanted to get off the train as quickly as possible. It was her stop next, and she sheepishly disembarked, and scuttled down the platform to make her way back to the Grove Park flat. By the time she arrived at the flat her thumb had grown massively and was pulsating. She was concerned she was going to have to go to the emergency department at the hospital but luckily her police landlord, Mark was in, and had a good look at it for her. He had completed basic first aid training and decided that it was not broken, and just bruised. He found some bandages and strapped it up tightly for Charlie as she gulped down a cup of tea and some painkillers. That night she found it really hard to get comfortable in bed as whichever way she tried to turn, she ended up banging or squashing her thumb.

Over the next few days, the swelling slowly went down, and the pain became more bearable, and Charlie continued going into work every day. She was actually on block release for exam training and did not want to miss anything, so she battled on. She could move her thumb increasingly each day, so Mark had been correct, and nothing was broken. Luckily, she also did not see any of the poor passengers on the commute that she had sworn at because she would not have known what to say to them and hoped they would forgive her in the circumstances.

As the months went on, Charlie continued with her usual routine of travelling to London to the office or the training company during the week and either travelling up to Worcester to see Daniel, or him driving down to see her at weekends. It was becoming obvious that they were going to have to make the arrangement more permanent in one location or the other. As Charlie was keen to get out of London it was clear to them both that Worcester was to be the home of choice. By this time, it was Easter 1987 and Charlie was due to sit her first set of accountancy exams, the graduate conversion course, early that summer. The plan was made, and Charlie spoke to her manager in the London office and the partner in charge of her department. They said they would be sorry to see her go but put in place the arrangements for her to transfer to the Worcester office. Charlie thought to herself how amusing it was that she had accepted an offer from one firm of accountants in London and turned down another much larger firm. This was nearly 2 years ago now, but when she returned from travelling around the world the two firms had merged so she effectively ending up working for the one she had turned down as it had a much bigger presence in London.

In contrast, the Worcester office had been dominated by the original firm she had accepted, so Charlie thought it would be amusing to see the difference in culture of the two offices, as it was the feeling when she had attended for interviews that had formed her original decision.

Chapter nine – starting a new life together.

Once her first year exams were completed, Charlie moved to Worcester. Daniel was living with his friend from work, Dev, at the time, and Dev was happy for them both to lodge whilst they searched for a house. Daniel had finished his final exams to be a chartered accountant, but Dev had recently left as he had decided accountancy was not for him. He had taken up a job as a management trainee with a well-known burger chain and was loving it. Charlie and Daniel had already identified the house they wanted to purchase. It was a new build Wimpey house, and they were going to buy the two bedroomed semi off plan for £30000. Every time they went to see the progress of the build in Narborough they laughed as it always looked so tiny. When the foundation walls and concrete floors and groundwork were done, the whole ground floor of the house looked no bigger than her parents' lounge.

    Between them they had saved enough for the 5% deposit required and the various fees and costs. Auditing involved a lot of travelling out to clients in the region and they were both paid mileage for the travelling. They had opened a joint building society account for this to be paid into, originally with the plan of using it as holiday money, and now it was only any remainder that would be used for holidays. Around the same time as they moved to their new house, Daniel decided he wanted to work as an accountant in industry and not in practice and moved to a crisp manufacturer as an internal auditor. Their new house was fairly tiny but was plenty big enough for the pair of them and was after all a starter home.

You walked straight into the lounge, and the open staircase was also in the lounge. The kitchen diner was behind the lounge although there was barely enough room for a table and chairs in the dining room part. Upstairs the two bedrooms were doubles, just, and there was a small bathroom. Charlie's dad helped them fit a shower over the bath and do various other bits around the house, teaching them DIY as he did so. This was the first time that Charlie was to be told about men's toilet habits. As her dad squashed in between the toilet and the bath, on the floor, to sort the plumbing for the shower, he pointed out to Charlie that the carpet around the loo smelt of pee. He explained to her that men often dribble a bit before or after peeing and it was best to have a toilet rug or hard flooring. The whole house, except the kitchen, had come carpeted by the builders. The garden was a job and a half to tackle. The builders had turfed the main area and put some flagging outside the patio doors, but planting anything was proving to be difficult. The soil was thick clay, and under it was just rubble, as though the builders had demolished a building and just left the bricks and stones under the soil. Charlie ordered one of those packs from a magazine which contained one hundred or more shrubs and was quite amazed when it arrived and looked like a box of sticks. She persevered though and planted all the sticks in accordance with the instructions in the flower beds that her and Daniel had attempted to make.

They spent a year getting the house the way they wanted it. They had formed new friendships in the town and at work, and along with the existing friends Daniel had made before Charlie moved up, they had a good social circle.

By summer of 1988 Charlie had finished her second-year professional exams and after a lot of discussion they decided to move and upgrade the house.

There were still three main house building companies in the area and Daniel and Charlie walked around in their spare time to look at where they wanted to live and what style of house. They had a lot of laughs at the way some of the salespeople in the sales offices treated them. They were young, in their mid-twenties, and often went into the sales offices in their casual clothes, usually tracky bottoms. It was as if they did not look like they had any money and were treated as such. They ignored the ignorant salespeople and eventually decided on the Wimpey show home round the corner from their own house. It was a four bedroomed house and had a reasonable plot as it was a corner house. It was for sale for £95000, but as the two bedroomed semi they had been living in had increased in value by £25000 in a year, the jump in mortgage was not going to be as much as it could have been. Charlie was also due a significant pay rise if she passed her final exams and qualified in 1989.

The sale and purchase went through quickly as the builders had someone to buy their existing home already. The house was so much more spacious, and they were back to square one with the garden. The worst thing was that a week or so after moving in there began to be a smell in the bathroom, followed by excrement coming back up the bath drain. It was not pleasant but luckily the builders sorted it quickly. They had to dig up the front garden and it turned out that because it was the show house, they had forgotten to connect the main sewerage drain from the house to the sewers. They sorted it out and repaired the damage to the garden.

The next few years were to prove quite eventful in Charlie and Daniel's life. During 1989, they had moved into their new house and Daniel had proposed to Charlie.

She was over the moon and accepted, but they both agreed he was to do the old-fashioned thing and officially ask Charlie's Dad. Knowing what an independent woman her mother was, Charlie suggested it had better be an ask mum and dad thing, rather than only the male parent. Both sets of parents seemed over the moon and an official date for the Wedding was set for summer 1990. Neither of them wanted a lavish affair, or to spend their own and parents' money on one single day of their life. They had informal engagement parties with Daniel's parents and Charlie's parents which consisted of a nice family meal out for both occasions. At the meal with Charlie's parents, her old boyfriend, and particularly good friend Brett, came to see them at the restaurant in Bridlington. He Invited them back to his house, where he lived with his wife Penny and newborn baby Olivia, for an after-dinner drink. When they all left the restaurant, Brett had left first followed by the rest of them with Charlie's dad driving. They arrived at Brett's house, but Brett was nowhere to be seen. They waited half an hour but still he did not appear. Eventually they went back home and found out later that day that Brett had been stopped on his way home for jumping some lights, breathalysed, and was over the limit, so he had spent the night in the care of the local police.

After the engagement celebrations, Charlie sat all her final exams, PEII as they were known then. She passed them all and became a fully qualified accountant.

There were some secondments that she could have asked for on qualifying within the firm and she decided to have a secondment to the training department.

This department dealt with all the recruitment and in house training and coordinated the external training for the firm. Daniel also decided that auditing was definitely not for him. Having been an external auditor, and now an internal auditor, Daniel applied for and was offered a role as financial controller in a design consultancy in Worcester, reporting directly to the financial director.

Life carried on fairly normally for a while. Charlie was loving her job in the training department, even though presenting to a large group was very unnerving to start with. Daniel was also loving his new job and the team he worked with. At one point, Charlie was sent on an outward-bound course in Wales. It was a sort of trial for a team building course for the firm, and there were colleagues there from other offices. They did all sorts of activities such as building a raft, following a leader whilst they were all blindfolded, and abseiling and climbing. Charlie had abseiled and climbed a little as a child with her mum and dad so although a bit rusty, she enjoyed the challenge. The bit she did not like was having to trust in someone she did not know as the anchor but was happier knowing the course leaders were always on hand to advise and support. It made her laugh to herself, that whilst climbing she could hear her dad in her mind telling her not to spread out or reach too far and it really helped her progress this time. One activity really tested the team spirit and nearly led to Charlie pulling out of the activity.

The group was split into two smaller teams, and each team was led up either side of a gorge. The challenge was for the teams to swap sides. They were provided with ropes and a pulley system and a few other bits of tackle to complete the challenge.

There was no way of communicating with the team on the other side except shouting, which occasionally worked, and hand symbols and signs. They worked out that they needed to get the rope from one side to the other, so using stones and string they managed to achieve this part of the challenge. The next stage Involved securing the rope around something on either side. Some of the louder members on Charlie's side decided to tie the rope around two trees that were at right angles to the gorge, one closer and one little further back. Charlie was not an engineer, although she had been brought up in an engineering family, and she did not think the two trees, in linear formation and quite young and hence thin trees, would support the weight of the humans across the gorge. Strangely, there were three thicker trees conveniently placed in a triangular layout also within reach of the gorge, and Charlie considered these much stronger and safer. She sat herself down on the floor and watched and listened in silence to the rest of the group. One of the instructors came over to see what Charlie was thinking. He said to the group 'I think Charlie has got a suggestion' so Charlie told the group her thoughts. It was clear to the rest of the group that the instructor wanted them to take heed of Charlie's suggestion and thankfully they followed it. After that, they managed to successfully transfer the teams from one side of the gorge to the other and safely return to the accommodation. During the year up to Charlie and Daniel's wedding in June 1990 the couple attended many other weddings as all their friends were of similar ages.

It gave them a really good idea of what they did and did not want at their own wedding. One decision they made which was slightly controversial, was that there should be no children invited apart from Charlie's niece who was to be a bridesmaid and only twelve.

They had been to enough weddings where children or babies had shouted or cried just as the vows were being repeated and could not see why the parents would not want a day and or night free of children. Luckily, on both their sides, there were small families and hence no lists and lists of relatives to invite. This meant they could invite more of their own friends and their parents' friends whom they had grown up with.

It was a combination of being accountants and the desire to not waste money that made them plan the wedding for a small group of family and close friends to attend the church and wedding breakfast, and more friends to be invited just to the evening do. The wedding breakfast was arranged to take place in a local restaurant, and the evening do in the lounge of the local pub with a buffet, both locations near to Charlie's home. With the help of Charlie's mum, they chose a local photographer and booked one wedding car for the day. The groom and best man were to arrive in the two cars that Charlie and her brother owned, old Porsche 924's, which were to be decorated with ribbons. The flowers were from a local florist and Charlie committed to make the dresses. The male contingent was to wear dinner suits as they all had them from the various functions they had attended over the years.

Charlie and her three older bridesmaids decided on the bridesmaids' dresses. They were all her childhood friends and Charlie knew they would not be happy about the thought of wearing over the top meringue dresses.

It was decided that Charlie would make three dresses in raw silk from Worcester market. They were to be simple strapless dresses with bolero jackets, and the three friends chose their own colours – a teal blue, bright red, and a bright purple. They also chose a lovely pale blue for Charlie's niece's dress which would be more befitting to her age. Charlie chose the material for her own dress with her mother. It was white silk satin in the same style as the bridesmaids. They found some matching material that was beautifully embroidered to make the bodice part and the bolero jacket. Charlie's father helped her cut out the train for the dress using engineering knowledge to make sure it hung and flowed beautifully. Once it was finished Charlie attached tiny little lilac bows to the dress to match the lilac in the wedding flowers and her wedding shoes. As they had kept the costs of the wedding itself down, Daniel and Charlie were able to book a fabulous 2-week honeymoon in Jamaica.

The months running up to the wedding flew by with work, visiting family and friends, and attending other weddings. On the day of the wedding everything went off with very few hitches. Charlie was a bit put out before she left the house to go to the church. The photographer was taking pictures of her and her bridesmaids in her parent's house and her Aunty and Uncle on her father's side appeared at the house. Charlie screamed at her mum and dad to get rid of them. She was not superstitious but did not like the idea of them seeing her before she arrived at the church. The next bizarre happening was when she arrived at the church. The church in the village had no permanent vicar at the time, and the one that was covering from nearby could not do their wedding date.

Charlie's mum had found a solution, one of her co-workers was allowed to conduct weddings in churches. Charlie had known him as 'Geoff the deaf' for many years, as helping hard of hearing was his key responsibility in social services. What Charlie was not expecting was that as she entered the church on her father's arm, Geoff would be standing at the front in a monk's habit with the hood up. She could not help herself, she burst out laughing, followed by the rest of the guests. As Daniel and his best man took their places they too joined in the laughter. This set the tone for the rest of the day and made it a most enjoyable occasion. Even the strong wind whilst the photographer was taking his pictures with people holding on to their hats made everyone chuckle in the garden outside the church.

The wedding breakfast was similarly light-hearted, with the restaurant owner taking on the role of master of ceremonies. The speeches went down really well, especially when Charlie's father included in his speech that Charlie was 'brought up with a tool in her hand.' That raised raucous laughter from every corner of the room, including the bride and bridegroom. Once the celebrations were over, Charlie and Daniel headed off to a hotel in Bridlington for the night. The next morning, they drove back to Charlie's parents and collected their belongings to go straight off to the airport for their honeymoon. The hotel in Jamaica was fabulous and as it was an adult only hotel was full of other honeymooners as guests. The hotel had even set up one of the outbuildings with chairs, sofas, and TV's as it was right in the middle of the World Cup, and even though she considered it a bit of a sexist thought, there were prolonged periods where there were only brides around the pool.

Chapter ten – when things started to go wrong.

On their return back to the UK, life continued as normal. Many weekends Involved visiting friends and family, work was good for them both, and home life settled and happy. Then another disaster hit – Daniel was to be made redundant. The design consultancy was not doing very well, as he knew, so it was back to the job search. Many opportunities were available, and the one Daniel chose was a vending company based outside Sheffield on an industrial estate. This meant a move for them both and Charlie had to consider what to do with her career. She discussed with her line manager and the partners in the firm her options. She could transfer to the Hull or Sheffield office, but Charlie had worked hard to prove herself in the firm and it was clear that by transferring she would have to do this all again which was not fair. She decided instead to take a position with a medium sized accountancy firm in their Doncaster office.

It made her laugh to herself when she thought about this – her beloved mother had told her that with two professionals following careers there would come points at which one of them would have to make a career sacrifice for the benefit of the other, and as usual, mum had been right.

Charlie and Daniel really did not have long to sort all of this and so the house was put on the market and arrangements were made for them and their cats to stay temporarily with Charlie's parents.

By the time moving date came there was already another lodger at her parents' house – another childhood friend, Dylan, had taken up her mum's offer of hospitality whilst he looked for a house of his own. Once they moved their weekends were taken up house hunting. They had decided on the area of Auckley and nearby as it was equal distance for them both to get to work from there.

Dylan was also looking in the Doncaster area and this would be his first house purchase. The couple helped him look for a house as well, he would really have loved a house in Auckley, but it seemed to be out of his price range. In the end Dylan found a lovely, terraced house just outside the town centre. It had been well looked after although the carpets needed replacing as the owners had two large long-haired dogs and the smell of dog was overpowering. They all decided Daniel and Charlie would move in with Dylan whilst they continued their search. In lieu of rent they gave him the deposit he needed and purchased all the crockery, kitchen and household bits that were needed when setting up your own first home. Charlie and Daniel had two cats, Bubbles and Bruiser, and the cats were to stay at Charlie's mums where they had become settled until they could move to a new permanent home.

The arrangement between the three adults worked well, Charlie's mum had her house back, and Charlie, Daniel and Dylan were all much nearer to work. In the meantime, Charlie and Daniel accepted an offer on their house in Worcester. It was £20k less than they had paid as the economy was poor and interest rates were peaking at 15% so it was costing them a fortune to pay a mortgage on an empty house.

They found a house in Auckley they could afford – it was an ex-prison officers house. They had been built for the officers for nearby Haxey Remand and it needed some work but was liveable in. It seemed like an age before the sale and purchase was completed, but eventually Charlie and Daniel had their keys. They went to the house as owners for the first time with Charlie's brother and were astounded to find that the previous tenants had taken all the light fittings, most of the radiators, and anything else that could be removed.

Apparently, there had been some sort of disagreement between the prison officer tenant and their employers and this was their way of getting revenge. Within the week Charlie and Daniel had arranged for these things to be resolved, and moved their furniture, themselves, and the two cats in. It was heaven to have their own place again. Even though it had been fine staying with others, it never felt as comfortable.

They gradually started doing the house the way they wanted it. Charlie had always been a practical person and Daniel had learnt bits and pieces along the way, so they attempted a lot of the work themselves under Charlie's father's guidance. This included crawling under the floorboards running extra electric cables to put in extra sockets where they wanted them although the complicated connection bits were left to experienced professionals, including the fitting of a new boiler and associated work. There was a semi-outside toilet by the back door – it was in a porch area in between the kitchen and the garage. They decided to alter the layout of this area to make the toilet part of the inside of the house and more easily accessible.

They bought a reasonably priced kitchen from one of the big DIY stores and with the help of friends and family, fitted it and the new worktop and appliances. Charlie then tackled the task of tiling the whole kitchen with her mum to guide and help her. She had done little bits of tiling before, but never on this scale. She learned to cut tiles in curves, to cut shapes out of tiles, and a lot more. Both her and her mum were knackered by the time they had finished working evenings and weekends on the job as it was a good-sized dining kitchen.

They had the windows replaced on the whole house and redecorated throughout to match the curtains that Charlie had made. They did manage to find some time to socialise although too much of their free time was taken up with DIY.

She should have known how work would pan out. At the interview Charlie had been asked if she was planning to have a family – she had been married for less than six months and the partner interviewing her had obviously thought this was a red flag for breeding. Even in the 1990's this was not an acceptable question, but Charlie decided to take the role as there were carrots offered in the form of a future partnership. Why she believed this was also a mystery as the particular firm had no female partners, and she was the first qualified female manager. Even on her first day Charlie should have realised what she was getting into as the partner in the Doncaster office introduced himself as Mr Moorhouse. She tackled this head on and said 'am I ok to call you Bernard' which was luckily met by a positive response. Having worked in a much bigger firm for a number of years where all the partners were known by first names, Charlie was not about to take a step back in time.

Unfortunately, she could not convince any of the other staff in the office to use his first name.

The first year was a steep learning curve at work. Charlie had worked with a number of medium sized businesses, but the diverse needs and issues that arose with the small businesses and one-man bands required her to develop a completely new set of skills. Networking was also another responsibility which was new to her although she drew the line at becoming a golfer. Once she had settled into the role and knew the clients like old friends, the challenges began to wane, and she was bored.

Charlie found herself begging the larger Hull office to let her run some of their larger audits just to keep her busy. She frequently sat at her large desk in her lonely office and dreamt of new prospects. The desk itself was like something out of an antique shop. It was massive, sturdy, and impossible to move. It smelt of old wood and had a green leather inlay across most of the desk surface. It was grand but was not practical, and cost Charlie a fortune in laddered stockings that she constantly snagged every time she sat down. She had worn stockings since early in her business career as she hated the feeling of tights and found they were a pain every time she needed the loo. She frequently put her fingers through the fine tights when pulling them back up, and it always resulted in a massive run down one or more of her legs. There was one particular audit that the Hull office sent her on that stuck in her mind. It was an abattoir, and the offices were two storey portacabins. Some of the men who worked in the factory took their breaks in a seating area underneath the open stairs to the top portacabin where the accounts office was based.

Charlie was not sure whether it was the fact that their eyes moved to look upwards when she was up and down the stairs, or the fact that they were covered in blood, which unnerved her more but in true Charlie fashion she ignored her thoughts and concentrated on the job at hand.

It was 8 O'clock and Charlie was on the last minute for work as usual. She had been up early with her husband Daniel as had become the norm these days and seen him off to work already. He had been moved to Wakefield as the offices near Sheffield had been closed and had a longer drive to work.

They were both professionals and Charlie did not engage with the idea of making him packed lunches or any of that domestic bliss – she had her own career to contend with.

When she arrived at the office Charlie gave a long sigh. She had been working for this practice for nearly two years now as a 'small business manager' and was becoming increasingly bored and despondent as the weeks went on. She had been forced to leave the large firm of international accountants she had been working in when Daniel had been made redundant from the design consultancy where he was Financial Controller.

It was not long after this Charlie had a discussion with her father's old accountant who also lived in Auckley. He was retired now but during one of her university holidays she had done some work experience in his practice. She also knew him well because him and his wife had been quite good friends of her mum and dad. He suggested she start up her own accountancy practice and even said he had a few clients he could pass her way. He also suggested that she look for part time Financial Director type roles whilst she was building her client base.

After discussing the idea with Daniel and her parents for a few weeks and researching how to go about it, Charlie decided it was a good route for her. It was clear the firm she was working for was not open to the idea of female partners, and there was nowhere else she could go with her career with them. Daniel was earning enough to support them for a temporary period and so the decision was made. Before she handed her notice in Charlie secured a position with a management consultancy in the centre of Sheffield.

They were originally advertising for a bookkeeper for £100 per week for a few days a week. At the interview Charlie told the female boss of the company and her colleagues that she would do the job in one day a week for the same amount of money and to her surprise they agreed. This meant that she would at least have some guaranteed income. Charlie managed to secure this position. She also became involved with volunteering at Doncaster Business Venture. This was an organisation set up to help and advise business startups and could potentially lead to new clients. She had already registered as a practitioner with her Institute and arranged the necessary professional indemnity insurance. She had also subscribed to payroll, accounting, and tax software on the advice of her father's old accountant, Fred. Fred had also been good to his word and passed on a couple of small clients to Charlie.

In the meantime, she handed in her notice at the firm of accountants in Doncaster she had been working at. They informed all the clients she was responsible for that she was moving to work in management consultancy, to save the risk of any of the clients moving to use her as their accountant.

It was funny that she was asked repeatedly by some of them where she was really going and what she was doing, and although there was no restraint of trade clause in her contract, Charlie knew it was not professional or ethical to take any clients with her. Over the next few years, a couple did track her down and become her own clients, but it was certainly not due to any solicitation of her own. Gradually her client portfolio began to build from the various contacts she had made and through referral. She had tried putting an advert in the local paper but that just led to calls wanting a quote over the phone.

It was exceedingly difficult to do this as everyone's idea of bookkeeping was vastly different, some excellent and some absolutely terrible, but they all thought their own record keeping was fabulous.

Whilst Charlie was busy building her empire, Daniel was travelling to Wakefield as they closed the Sheffield office. It was not too much further distance wise, about an hour, but because he had to travel across the M62 Pennine route, it could be much longer. Charlie's mum also decided to take early retirement from her position as Deputy Director of Social Services. She had secured a freelance post working for the National Lottery. This was to involve visiting and helping organisations that were bidding for Lottery funding, helping them both in their original bids and in applying any awards in the best way. Over the next year Charlie worked hard with her mum to teach her the monetary value of time. Having worked in Local Government most of her life, it was hard to convince her mum that it was not efficient to spend 30 hours on something she might only ger paid £30 for.

Between Daniel and Charlie, they managed to persuade her to keep some sort of time records and use it to create bills for the lottery and any other consultancy work that was to come her way.

In the meantime, one evening when Daniel came home from work, Charlie was bimbling round at the front of the house. As he stepped out of the car, Charlie spotted lipstick kiss marks on the driver's window. She asked him why it was there, and he dismissed it as the girls in the office in Wakefield messing around. In her usual trusting way Charlie just accepted it, laughing, and they carried on with their evening as usual. One of the clients Fred, her dad's accountant, had introduced her to, was a small hotel in Holmes Chapel, run by a husband-and-wife team.

Charlie had set them up on an accounts programme and payroll and visited at least once a quarter to do the VAT and help with other matters. They had to report management accounts to the bank as part of the conditions of the loans and mortgages. As a bonus they offered her and Daniel a cheap meal in the very nice restaurant and a discounted stay in the hotel.

They took up the offer a few weeks later and it was during the meal that Daniel dropped the biggest bombshell Charlie had ever heard. He told her that he did not think he loved her anymore. To Charlie it was completely unexpected – she had no idea or recognised any signs that anything was wrong. The rest of the evening was awkward between them, but they persevered for the sake of appearances and returned home after breakfast the next morning. As the week went on it was becoming more obvious that the relationship was going to end. Daniel expressed his main reason was that 'he could never live up to her brother and dad.'

Apparently by this he meant that because they were clever and practical, could turn their hand to anything, he seemed to feel that he would never be able to do everything they could. Charlie did not understand as she had never expected him too. She was fairly practical herself and was quite happy to do things herself, or even pay for someone else to if they could afford it. Over the next few days Daniel moved out to stay in a hotel in Wakefield and Charlie felt her entire world had been turned inside out. There were no mobile phones and they spoke occasionally. Charlie's mum and dad were a great support, and a childhood friend, Abigail, who was cabin crew out of Sheffield came to stay and cheer her up.

Over the next few weeks, the two girls got up to all sorts of adventures and chatted into the long hours about anything and everything. Charlie laughed so much about Abigail's story about making a weed cake with her flatmates and ending up at the supermarket in her nighty, not knowing which planet she was on. Abigail encouraged Charlie to go out to town, Doncaster, and they also went to a few of the clubs after the bars closed. What was so amusing to Charlie was the realisation of the expression 'like flies around …..' They were constantly approached wherever they went by men trying to pull them. Even some of Charlie's single clients started hitting on her and one particularly unpleasant episode was from another accountant. She had to have an alternate as part of her practicing certificate and had made such an arrangement with another accountant in Sheffield who was a sole practitioner like herself. She agreed to go to the theatre with him, his reason was to get to know her better, and in hindsight Charlie thought she should not have been so naïve.

He came on to her after the theatre and somehow Charlie managed to make it clear that their relationship was purely business and platonic without offending him too much. It was at this point that she realised that it was necessary to be more street wise, alert, and cautious of other's intentions towards her. There were a couple of her clients that had also managed to woo Abigail, although Abigail did not seem too bothered and took it in her stride.

Charlie tried her hardest to save her marriage. Through her phone calls it was becoming obvious that she might be fighting a losing battle. Daniel told her that he had ruined everything, but in the end, he agreed to meet up with Abigail for a sort of impartial chat and mediation.

Poor Abigail offered to drive all the way across the Pennines to meet up with him and they spent a few hours together chatting and discussing what was going on. Abigail had been the chief bridesmaid at Charlie and Daniel's wedding and sort of had a personal stake, and she knew what a terrible state Charlie was in. The outcome of this meeting was that Daniel agreed to come over and meet up with Charlie for a sensible discussion.

Charlie had never been famed for her culinary ability. She had been lucky that all the men in her life, both family and partners, loved cooking. Her mum had taught her some basics so she could adequately feed herself and others, and since university she had been a whiz with mince and could make anything with eggs. The eggs skill did not include desserts – the few times she had tried baking cakes, even ones out of a packet mix, they had turned out more like clay pigeons or frisbees. One of the first evenings after Daniel had left, and Abigail had been staying, Charlie attempted to make them both a garlic bread using a pitta base.

Unfortunately, it turned out more like the sole of an old shoe and she was subsequently banned from experimental cooking. On this same evening Abigail and Charlie were chatting about old friends or people they had not seen for a while. They started talking about Brett, and both wondered why they had not seen him for a few years. Charlie had dated him for a few months in her early teens, and since then he had been a large part of their friendship group, and he developed a close relationship with Charlie's brother, Stewart. It was all very peculiar and when they spoke to Charlie's mother, she also had no idea why. The last time they had all seen him properly was at Brett's baby daughter, Olivia's, christening.

Chapter eleven – rekindling old relationships.

The girls decided to try and contact Brett, mainly Charlie's doing, and eventually managed to track down his home phone number from friends. Much to their surprise, he turned up the next day. It was so lovely to see him again, and Brett was equally astounded as others that Daniel and Charlie had split up. They all had a good catch up and filled each other in on what they had been up to over the last year or so. Over the next week Brett kept popping by and it was during one of these visits, when Abigail was away flying, that Daniel had agreed to meet Charlie at the Saddle, one of the pubs in the village. Brett dropped Charlie off at the pub and waited for her in the carpark in the second-hand Jaguar Sovereign he had treated himself to for his 30th birthday and with his voluntary redundancy money from Allied. Allied had been bought by the Alliance and Worcester and there were lots of changes ahead. Brett had chosen to leave the bank and was working with a mate who owned Hornsea Coaches driving the coaches and doing part time taxi driving.

Charlie felt very apprehensive as she approached Daniel in the lounge seating area of the pub. It had been a while since she had seen him and she had no idea what to expect, or where this meeting was going to lead. She did not even know what she wanted anymore. It was a very strained talk with Charlie trying to establish where it had all gone wrong, and Daniel proclaiming that he had ruined everything.

He expanded on this to say that it had been a non-sexual relationship with his secretary Naomi at the point he had moved out, but since then it had developed, and he had slept with her.

He then put the icing on the cake by telling Charlie that Naomi had herpes so there was no going back now. He could never 'be' with Charlie again because he would be infected. Charlie could not believe what she was hearing and ordered another drink to try and drown out what she was hearing. By the end of this short meeting, it was clear it was all over, and Charlie said she was going to see a solicitor and start divorce proceedings on the basis of his unreasonable behaviour. She left and went back to Brett in the car park. He took her the short ride home and as soon as she got in the front door, she grabbed a few cans of the strong white cider she had turned to in the last weeks, drank, and sobbed uncontrollably. Brett was there to console her, hug her, and make her feel loved and things very quickly moved on to more than a hug. It was not her intention for this to happen, far from it, but it felt right and comfortable.

Over the next few weeks Brett came and stayed increasingly often. Abigail moved back home and said she was no longer needed and although this saddened Charlie, it was true. It was a really challenging time for Charlie emotionally because although she knew of Brett's wife's affair, she had a fairly good idea that Brett had not been the most faithful husband, and the last thing she wanted was to break up someone else's relationship after what had happened to her. When Brett dropped the bombshell that Penny was pregnant this hit her hard. It was the usual story you heard about – she does not have sex with me, the relationships over, and even the added bonus of she is pregnant because she virtually made me have sex when I was drunk.

Charlie did what she could to try and get Brett to go back to Penny, even sending him over to Yorkshire where she had gone to stay with her sister at one point.

One day whilst Charlie was on her own, shortly after the meeting with Daniel, and after a few too many white ciders, she decided to send Daniel's boss, the Financial Director, a fax. She was annoyed with him too as Daniel's affair or whatever it was had been carrying on right under his nose, and it had not been long before Daniel's revelation in the hotel, that they had all been to various company functions and the fancy piece, Naomi, was there as well. She decided to call her 'that tart from Wakefield' and consoled herself with the fact that Daniel did not know what was coming, out of the frying pan into the fire, and supposed Naomi was only after his money. The fax was a bit of a shocker. She had drawn a sketch of a stick man and a stick woman but with various privates drawn on the picture and bubble speech and arrows referring to herpes. She sent it to David, Daniel's boss, before she could change her mind. Later that evening Abigail came back to stay for a day or two and could not believe that Charlie had actually sent it but the two of them did have a laugh for days and more about it. Needless to say, Daniel rang her the next day extremely angry about what she had done – the whole office had seen or heard about it. All Charlie could do was laugh to herself – after all it was him who was up to no good. She also received a call from David telling her that he was having to reassign Naomi in the company under the circumstances and made some sort of attempt to say he was sorry although she did not believe a word of what he was saying.

This was the start of Charlie's ability to move on. The next period of her life involved building up her business – she was getting regular referrals and secured another few clients to visit weekly, monthly, or quarterly.

She also sorted out the divorce with Daniel by using a local solicitor at a knock down price. Apart from the mortgaged house and fairly new endowment policies there was nothing else of importance, and luckily children were not part of the equation. There was little equity in the house and Daniel and Charlie agreed that Daniel should just walk away and sign it over as it was Charlie's home, and it would save legal wrangles over his pensions and any inheritances in which only the solicitors would have benefitted. Unfortunately, the bank would not release Daniel from the mortgage as Charlie's fledgling business did not earn enough to take it on, so she agreed to put the house on the market in due course.

The last bit of administration that needed sorting out was the joint bank account. They had one with an automatic ten-thousand-pound overdraft which although had never been used, the bank manager was concerned that either one of them could have run up the debt in spite more than anything. Charlie found this amusing as it had never occurred to either of them before the bank had mentioned it. To solve the issue, they had to meet at the bank in person to close the account. The branch was in the next town to Charlie's home village and as they came out of the meeting Daniel handed her a CD, telling her to listen to the words. She waved him off and put the CD in the car player. How she managed to drive the few miles to her parent's house after that she would never understand as the CD was Whitney Houston, 'I will always love you.'

She bawled her eyes out all the way home before bursting through the door into her mum's arms. She just could not understand – one minute 'I don't think I love you anymore' and divorce, and then the next 'I will always love you.'

Over the next few months Charlie managed to secure a buyer for the house that gave her a little bit of profit to carry forward to the next one. The house she had with Daniel was a 4 bedroomed detached on a nice estate in the village, and the one she eventually found, with the help of Abigail and Brett, was an early 1900's end of 3 terrace which had a long back garden that backed onto the fields, and an old workshop attached to the back which had been a blacksmith in years gone by. It had a lot of character including cast iron fire surrounds and sash windows, the only drawback was that it was on a quite busy road into the village. Charlie secured her mortgage, worked out her finances and made an offer and it was not too long before the move was completed and plans for a jig around of the house to meet her needs and desires could be made.

Charlie had already booked a week's holiday in Lanzarote for them both and although it was probably the wrong thing to do, they agreed to carry on with the holiday. Brett's wife either had them followed to Lanzarote or it was a coincidence, but somehow, she ended up with photos of Charlie and Brett on their holidays. It turned out it was a couple from Bridlington who had befriended them on the week's holiday and even convinced them to go to a nudist beach with them at one point. Charlie found this extremely uncomfortable and neither of them took their swimwear off.

It was quite amusing to see the not so beautiful bodies flopping around the beach, and the dug outs in the sand that some of the other European holiday makers seemed to enjoy lurking in. It led to Charlie been named as the co-respondent in Brett's divorce papers.

By 1995 Brett had become a permanent fixture in her life and was going through his own divorce with Penny. Again, it was a fairly amicable divorce with the usual hiccups over finances. He signed their house over to Penny as was only fair because there were children involved. He did not earn a vast amount from his coach driving and taxi work, but they agreed between them an amount he should contribute for the kids. He was more concerned about losing his greenhouse than his house for some strange reason and being able to see the kids.

Work began in earnest on the new house. Finances were tight for Charlie, and the priority was to create an office space in the workshop area for Charlie's business. Much of the main house had been updated, the bathroom had been recreated in the second bedroom. It was a fabulous bathroom with a massive walk-in shower, a jacuzzi bath and grand and enormous black and silver tiles on the wall portraying sketches of ladies. Apart from the work on the office areas, they updated the décor throughout, replacing the weirdly positioned picture rails with ones that befitted the lofty ceilings and adding dado rails in the downstairs rooms as these were all the fashion. The kitchen was fairly new although an old-fashioned style, and Charlie painted the wood doors a creamy yellow and replaced the handles. She bought a range cooker, and they created an island style worktop around. One of Charlie's clients, Norman, was a 'time-served' joiner with many years of experience.

He made and fitted new double glazing for the house – the original windows were sash windows and drafty – and the new ones he created looked like imitation sash windows made from wood as the age and style of the house really would not suit UPVC and he created a beautiful stained-glass window with a peacock for the side of the lounge where the view was of the neighbour's wall.

Charlie and Brett stripped all the rest of the wood and fireplaces in the house and had the old doors dipped. Brett also decided to knock the plaster off the back lounge wall where there was a chimney breast. He was sure he would find something as the house originally had a back kitchen which was now the smaller second lounge or dining room and a new kitchen had been created in between this room, the outside loo, and the workshop. He was correct and uncovered an old and original brick fireplace which was nearly big enough to be called an inglenook. He tidied it all up and they installed an open fire in the newly created space.

Chapter twelve – starting a new life.

Charlie and Brett continued with the alterations with their friends, Stella and Dylan helping. They would often be working late into the night, playing music, drinking, and fooling around in between. The workshop was just a bare and uneven concrete floor so after some research they ordered a bitumen covering to be put down. It was delivered hot and barrowed in but was the best option for insulation and damp proofing. After that the foursome, with any other help they could muster, plaster-boarded the walls and put up the partition for the office. The layout from the front door was now lounge, back lounge/dining, kitchen, outside toilet now inside and back door, office, big playroom, patio, and garden. It was still not the way they wanted it, so Norman gave Charlie a reasonable quote for adding a conservatory style extension onto the kitchen. This enabled the whole house to be completely connected and the toilet to become a proper downstairs toilet. They finished off the masterpiece with a stable door as a back door, something Brett and Charlie had always wanted on a house, for reasons she did not really understand herself.

Over the next few months Charlie sorted some office furniture – filing cabinets for her growing number of client files, and desks, chairs and other bits and pieces. She had painted the office a bright green to make it nice and bright and a complete contrast to the rest of the house. Brett put in a new loft hatch with a decent ladder in the small bedroom and boarded the floor of the loft and panelled the rafters with insulation.

They managed to get a wooden bed set up there to give more room to Brett's kids when they came to stay, especially when Noah was a bit older. It was a bit eerie when they found chains secured to the rafters in part of the loft – it was as though someone had been chained up there in years gone by. They began to wonder if the house was haunted. Even though neither of them believed in the paranormal, there was one particular picture on the stairs that kept falling off, but as though it had been chucked down the stairs, and with the picture hook still secure in the wall.

Whilst all this was going on Charlie's mum had secured a contract for the Social Services Inspectorate and Northern Regional Health Authority and other big organisations to monitor the effect of 'Care in the Community' on the residential and nursing home sector. The reason was to monitor how much business the homes were losing with the implementation of the guidelines to encourage the care of the elderly in their own homes. The project was massive, included all types of elderly care homes from all the Health and Local Authority regions in the North of England. The methodology involved getting completed questionnaires from them all the homes, various face to face interviews, reviews of other research and reporting on the findings in written form, supplemented by graphs and diagrams, every 3 months. The report itself was due annually for as many years as the funding could be obtained.

Charlie and her mum tackled the challenge with enthusiasm and skill. Charlie's mum knew the background and business of the elderly care sector very well, and Charlie was there to help with the donkey work, data collection, statistics, and diagrammatical side of the work.

They worked very well together – Charlie fitted in her accounting clients around the project and her mum continued with the lottery work, although that was starting to dwindle by now.

It was challenging work getting the surveys back from some of the homes and either together or on their own Charlie and her mum had to visit them to collect them in person or encourage them to complete the survey. It was not of course a priority for the care home managers and many just saw it as an additional administrative burden. Charlie's mum used her people skills in dealing with the more reluctant homes, and this meant they had an excellent overall rate of return in the end for each period. There were a couple of other projects that her mum was asked to take on. One involved a study of wheelchair usage using one of the large wheelchair distribution centres in the North as the starting point, and another involved secure units. This last one Charlie did not have much involvement with but did go on one visit with her mother. The banging and locking of doors behind them as they walked through the building scared Charlie and made her think of the TV programme Prisoner Cell Block H she used to watch with Daniel.

Meanwhile Charlie's client base was growing quite fast. She now had a number of clients she went to regularly, either weekly, monthly, or quarterly. She had also purchased a small parcel of fees from another accountant who had decided to change career and become a recruitment consultant. Some of these clients were stable or growing slowly but a number of them were on the verge of collapse so it turned out to be an average investment. She reckoned she had her money back within the year but had obviously worked the hours to be able to charge for them.

One client was a children's crayon and paint manufacturer, and this turned out to be one she became more heavily involved in, taking the role of Financial Director.

This meant she could not be impartial anymore and sign off or audit the accounts, but she managed to arrange for her old employer in Doncaster to take on this task for a reasonable fee.

Over the next few years everything was going really well in her life. Business was good, they were financially comfortable, Brett had taken and passed his class 1 HGV licence and was busy working for another of Charlie's clients, a driver and warehouse agency for temporary staff. This agency was run by two women of similar age to Charlie and Brett. They were making a great living from the business but at her weekly visits to do the accounts Charlie was becoming increasingly concerned that they were draining too much cash from the business. It ended up with one of the ladies leaving to pursue other avenues as the business could not support two large salaries, company cars and other benefits from a cash perspective.

Another opportunity crossed Charlie and Brett's path in the next year. The shop and post office in their village had been closed and was being made into a house. This meant that the shop in the next village was the nearest to go to for essentials, bits, and pieces. Brett found out that the owner wanted to sell up and Brett was really keen to take on the business. After all, there was the security of Charlie's income, the owner was selling the whole property, and he was determined he could make a good profit out of it and improve takings considerably.

Charlie arranged a meeting with her business bank manager –they actually came out to you for meetings in this era – and after discussions about it and the forecasts Charlie had produced, it was all agreed.

They had obtained a mortgage and loan to buy the property and business and it was all steam ahead. The whole deal seemed to go through fairly quickly. They kept the full-time member of staff, Delilah, and the part timers from the village. Neither of them had ever run a corner shop and off licence beforehand so it was going to be a big learning curve. Before the deal completed Brett had to obtain a personal license to sell alcohol which meant he first had to attend training on the laws and regulations surrounding selling alcohol and appear before a magistrate which he completed with flying stars.

It was now 1997 and their life was full. Noah (now 3) and Olivia (8) thought it was fabulous that daddy had his own sweetie shop when they came to stay. Brett and Charlie had a good circle of friends, and they had the shop how they wanted it. Charlie's dad had helped them with the refit of the shop, along with some of Charlie's clients. One of the best ideas her dad had was to position the counter where the till was higher than the rest of the shop floor. It made such a difference, and all the staff thought it was great being that little bit higher than the customers giving them a feeling of control. They also installed new CCTV and Brett created a 'wine cellar' effect area with wine racks stocking a good variety of brands and prices of wine. There was a new estate that had been built on the old Armthorpe hospital with big, detached houses, and these customers, along with the locals, were attracted to the extensive and fair priced wine selection from a local shop.

They also installed a commercial sunbed in the back room of the shop as the locals seemed to have a demand for this.

The premises itself owned the hairdressers next door and she paid monthly rent, and the whole of the upstairs of the building was a massive three bedroomed flat that they rented out.

They had to 'let go' of one member of staff. Charlie had suspected something was amiss for a while and had discussed it with Brett. There was one button on the till, which was for payment top-ups for electric, gas, phone and so on. The total on this from the Z read quite often was round sums out from the z read from the payment machine. Charlie was a stickler for Brett keeping his books and he had to cash up, balance and record every night. It got to the point where it only took him less than half an hour with the record sheet Charlie had created. At one point they looked at the recordings on the camera and saw this particular lady member of staff not only topping up her own electric and phone card, but then she helped herself to some cigarettes and shuffled out to the staff kitchen with the camera behind her and put them in her bag. The cameras were not in the kitchen, but it was clear what she was doing. In the end they gave Vanessa a choice as to what to do as they were going to bring in the police, but she rightly decided to leave. Charlie and Brett knew that there were other bits and pieces that could be slipping into the bag unpaid for of at least one member of staff, but the incident with Vanessa would hopefully stop anyone else risking it.

As an extra precaution Charlie looked into an EPOS system and found the best deal going.

It was a lease arrangement with support and updates included. It took a bit of getting used to, but Delilah was quick to learn and master the system with regarding to booking in and pricing stock and she was the one, along with Charlie, who taught Brett how to work it.

The new system meant they could do spot stocktakes on key and expensive items like tobacco products and spirits, and also added to the security of the stock from pilfering.

Everything was bimbling along very happily except Charlie kept getting pins and needles in her hands and fingers, and sometimes her feet. It was gradually getting worse, and the GP said it would be due to the contraceptive pill and she was to come off it. Charlie also had a client, Sharly, who was a masseur and Reiki specialist. She had massaged Charlie's back and shoulders in case it was some sort of trapped nerve, and recommended she take spirulina tablets as they are high in vitamin B12 and may help. In the meantime, Charlie's mum had accompanied Charlie to her next doctor's appointment. Her mum was furious with the GP that she had not taken Charlie's problem serious enough, and basically insisted the GP referred Charlie for a scan. This was great but did make Charlie feel like a child again and not thirty-four.

It was early of summer 1998 when Charlie was given an appointment for her scan. She felt fine now, and the tingling and pins and needles had stopped but her mum insisted she went anyway. As it was to be a full body scan, she had to answer various questions beforehand. One of the questions was 'when was your last period' and Charlie had to think hard about this.

Since the GP had stopped her taking the contraceptive pill, she had hardly been regular, much to her annoyance, but she managed to work out it was about 5 weeks earlier. This worried the radiographer as he explained they did not conduct this sort and area of scan in the first trimester of pregnancy.

Charlie laughed this off as a near impossibility, but he was adamant that she should do a pregnancy test and rebook the scan for after her next period. This sent her head into a whirl and on the way home she bought a home pregnancy test kit. It was positive and she was terrified. Having children had certainly not been in her plans at that time of life, and she was thirty-four after all. The next day, a quick visit to the nurse at the doctor's surgery confirmed the home test and over the next few weeks it was estimated that she would be giving birth around the end of November.

Over the next few months Charlie went through all the emotions and thoughts that maybe every mum-to-be goes through. She wondered whether she would be able to cope, would she know what to do, would she be any good at it and so on and in addition she was concerned about whether she would still be able to work. She was self-employed as a sole trader so maternity pay and leave was out of the question. She only got paid for the hours she worked. In the meantime, Dawna, the girl who was virtually running the driver recruitment agency started to work from Charlie and Brett's home. The agency business was dwindling and remaining director was looking for work elsewhere and was closing the office to keep overheads down. Charlie and Brett agreed that Dawna could work from their house as a temporary arrangement.

There were still contracts in place and agency staff in various locations. It was also beneficial to them as Brett shared the 24-hour on call duty with the phone with Dawna and got paid for his time.

Chapter thirteen – bringing in new life.

Over the summer and autumn as Charlie's bump grew, she was very well and happy. Her parents, and most obviously her mum, was over the moon at the thought of her first grandchild. Her brother was in a permanent relationship in Scotland and his girlfriend Grace already had a toddler from her previous relationship and in usual mum fashion, Charlie's mum had welcomed Grace's daughter with open arms. Charlie completely calmed down her lifestyle to give her new son the best chance he could in life. She had asked the sex of the baby at the scans as although many people liked to have a surprise, Charlie had always been too organised to not know although she would have been thrilled whatever sex her baby was, as long as it was healthy. When she was 6 months pregnant, she was still riding on the back of Brett's motorbike and at 5 months they took a holiday to Rhodes. This was when the baby really started to let his presence be known as she was starting with horrendous indigestion and lived with a packet of Rennie's permanently by her side and in her bag.

    Her son was due according to the experts around the 22 November 1998. Charlie had worked out her own dates and reckoned this was a bit early. Her and Brett also reckoned he had been conceived in Kitzbuhel on the skiing holiday with her brother and Dylan. As it got past the expected date Charlie started trying all the old wives' tale's methods of getting her lump out. She was still working full time, helping with the shop, and was very tired. She tried standing on her head, long walks, curries, and anything else people suggested.

One day when Brett was out on the wagons, he went into panic mode as he could not contact her.

Mobile phones were still not a common thing – more of the brick style with a big battery you carried around and often sported by car dealers. Charlie had just gone for a long walk and eventually he managed to find her through calling their friend Stella. A week or so later it looked like the baby was thinking about showing himself. Charlie had had quite bad stomach pains for a few hours which she believed were contractions, but when she phoned the maternity department in the hospital in the early hours, they told her to take some paracetamol and go back to bed. Eventually, by that morning, Brett and Charlie decided to go to the hospital. Charlie was checked in and Brett was sent home with the message that it would be hours yet. He had only just got home when he was summoned back. Charlie had been on the ward for an hour or so when one of the midwives came to see why she said she was in pain, and it turned out she was already 8cm dilated. It was not long after this that her baby arrived. She coped on gas and air and a touch of pethidine, and she already knew that an epidural was out of the question. She had been told that there was slight curvature at the base of her spine and had heard horror stories about the injections causing issues so had ruled out an epidural early on.

Throughout the last few months of pregnancy Charlie had a constant worry that there may be something wrong when he was born. Due to her age, she had also been told she was at higher risk of a baby with Downs syndrome but at each stage this would involve a test and a decision, and she had decided she could not cope with these decisions and would hope for the best. When he arrived, he was perfect.

She had originally thought about the name Anthony Sebastien, but luckily for her newborn son she had changed her mind, influenced by Brett, his mum, and everyone else, and they decided on Jack Stewart. He had a flurry of black hair which was most peculiar as Brett was blond and Charlie was naturally a mousey brown-blond although she died her hair lighter. The next 24 hours were more painful than the birth itself, both emotionally and physically. It was the era of 'breast is best' and whilst Charlie was happy anyway as long as he fed and had discussed with her mum the benefits of breast milk, Jack was having none of it. She had various nurses and midwives trying to force both Jack and Charlie to comply, including holding his head and holding and squeezing her breasts to the point where mum and baby were both screaming and crying in pain and frustration. Luckily, they finally relented and gave Jack formula milk. Later that day Charlie's mum brought her in a manual breast pump which she took to like a dream after a bit of practice, so the issue was resolved. Charlie was kept on the ward for another 24 hours and then allowed to go home. Brett picked her up with the baby seat all secured perfectly and they headed home to where he had got everything ready.

The next few months were turmoil as both Charlie and Brett adapted to their new life and new member of the family. Brett knew what he was doing, but apart from her attempt at being an au pair when she was 18, Charlie had no real experience of babies, especially new-born ones, but the couple coped well and had the support of Charlie's mum regularly and their friends, especially Stella who had 4 children of her own.

Charlie's mum helped her find a nursery for Jack. The plan was to put him in nursery Tuesday to Thursday, and mum would have him on a Monday and Charlie would have him Friday's and keep that as her day off. Charlie managed to fit working around her new responsibilities, and it was about 4 months later that exhaustion hit. She had given birth on a Tuesday and been back out working the following Tuesday. She would go to clients, more of which she was acting as Finance Director for, with her breast pump in her briefcase. Luckily, they all knew her well and had a good rapport, so it was a topic of amusement. Sometimes if she was in a meeting one of them would say 'Charlie, I think you need to go to the bathroom' if it was becoming evident that she needed to use the pump.

To give her a break and a much-needed battery recharge, Charlie's mum arranged for Charlie and Brett to spend a long weekend in a cottage in Higham. The cottage was owned by her mum's old boss from Social Services, and Charlie's mum was having Jack for the duration. Charlie returned from this break like a new woman, rejuvenated and ready to tackle the world head on. Over the next few years everything in their life was good. There was a minor hiccup when they were burgled on the village carnival night whilst they were asleep. They and everyone else in the village knew who was behind it and Charlie verbally tackled one of them when she bumped into him in the village. Nothing major was stolen, it was the inconvenience of the handbag and wallet being taken and having no access to cash, but their friends helped out until they could get new cards. What was more upsetting was the thought that someone had been in the house, a sort of personal violation.

There was another upsetting moment when the husband of a lady in the next village, a lady who advertised her services for men, turned up on Charlie's doorstep and told her that Brett was having an affair with his wife. This was a revelation that did not sit well with Charlie and whilst it was a peculiar one because that was the lady in questions business, the thought of it whilst Charlie was at home with their baby made her quite sick. Brett protested it was all a lie and was made up because the bloke did not like him, but Charlie knew of Brett's past from long ago and also considered it was quite possible. The lady only lived near the shop and used the cheap rooms at the back of the next-door pub to conduct her business.

Charlie decided to put it to the back of her mind, and they continued with life as normal. Business was good with her regular visits doing bookkeeping and accounts, annual accounts, and the work she was doing with her mum. The shop was paying for itself although it was clear that it was never going to make them rich. They had a good team of staff and Brett had built up the business well and was great with the customers. It was a bit of a catch twenty-two as he needed to work longer hours behind the till for them to make decent money from it, but if he did that it limited the amount Charlie could work and time with Jack was the priority for them both over money. They had tried someone new to help with minding Jack. She was the girlfriend of one of Charlie's clients. Dawna had to leave as the driving agency was being shut down and Charlie really only needed help when she was busy, so it was difficult to commit to a permanent arrangement.

This trial did not work out as the new lady seemed to know less about childcare than Charlie herself and was no good at answering the phone nor completing any accounts, so it was back to square one.

Charlie's mum would step in to help extra times when needed but they really had to make a more permanent arrangement. Charlie was getting busier and busier and needed someone to help in the office even if she had to train them up. She was conscious that when she was at clients all day no-one else could get in touch. There were some clients that were quite far away and especially when the weather was bad, Brett would take her to these and find something to do during the day whilst he waited for her.

Brett had got to know the bartenders, and everyone else, in the local pubs well. There were two pubs in the village and at the time, one was more of a posh eating pub, whereas the other one, opposite the primary school, was a drinking pub with snacks. It was in this latter pub that Brett had been chatting to one of the bartenders, Gretchen, who had recently had a baby girl and had a daughter of 6 years old who was at the primary school. She was telling Brett that she needed to find something better than the pub to work in. Her husband was a drayman, but she needed to work herself both for the money they wanted and for her own fulfilment. Charlie went to see Gretchen in the pub and explained what she wanted and needed and that she would train Gretchen up on all the software and how to do any basics, they agreed a start date and a rate of pay and they were all set to go.

The new arrangement worked really well. Gretchen and Charlie hit it off really well together and Charlie's mum was also pleased with the arrangement.

Many hours of Gretchen's were spent on the floor in the office with papers spread out everywhere sorting and cataloguing the survey returns from the care in the community research Charlie's mum was doing. This worked really well regarding Gretchen's work time.

It meant between Charlie and her mum they were able to keep her busy for the hours that she wanted, and also freed up Charlie to visit clients without the hassle of the phone going all the time. Mobile phones were not really commonplace yet and were still fairly brick like in design.

Charlie's business was growing well but she tried to keep to the plans she originally made with mum having Jack on a Monday and Charlie dedicating Friday to doing something with him. Over the next few years Jack progressed from nursery to primary school and began to develop his own confidence. As a family they decided to include a dog in their family with the cats. The final decision was for a Doberman as their research had shown that they were very loyal and temperate dogs that also did not have a big moulting issue when the seasons change. In due course Duke was chosen as the family dog. He came from a litter in Anglesey and when they all went to the breeder to choose their puppy Duke seemed to choose Jack in a strange way – he kept going over to him in the lounge of the breeder and so the decision was made. Charlie still had cats but unfortunately had lost two to the speeding traffic on the road outside their house since moving there.

The road was one of the reasons they decided to move. Charlie needed more room for her business, there was nowhere in the two bedroomed house for her mum, Brett's other kids or anyone else to stay except the sofa in the small lounge, and Charlie's business was doing well and could support a bigger mortgage.

And so, the search for a suitable house began. By mid-2004 they had found a dormer bungalow down a quiet cul-de-sac which backed on to the fields. It needed considerable work and updating but Charlie and Brett were not afraid of that idea and knew they could add value.

Their house was put on the market and a sale was agreed within a week and the arrangements for completion and the move began. The bungalow they had chosen had a kitchen diner, a big lounge and three other rooms downstairs. One of these was right next to the front door and the plan was for Charlie to use this as her office. This would save her growing number of clients trapsing through the house and enable her to see when clients were arriving. It was a good-sized room, with plenty of space for Charlie and Gretchen to have big desks, a small meeting table, and all the file storage she needed. In the meantime, there would be a makeshift office as the various trades did their work.

Charlie had some good clients and had made friends with other tradesmen in the village. There was work that Charlie and Brett could do themselves, but it was finding a balance between speed, loss of earnings from not working herself, and paying tradesmen. The house luckily did not need a rewire but needed new central heating, windows, bathrooms, kitchen, and a load of plastering. They also decided as part of the modernisations to take a few feet off the end of the garage to include it as a room off the kitchen as a utility room and mini kitchen. Gretchen had started making sandwiches to be sold in the shop and by doing this in a separate room it would keep everything separate for hygiene reasons and away from the animals. Over the next 6 months Charlie lived and worked in a building site.

They found rats nest under the bath in the main downstairs bathroom, and dead rats with their mouths around electric wires when some of the ceilings came down for the various work. They laughed about the fact that the rats must have been running around the feet of the old chap who lived there before.

Eventually they had a beautiful house and were able to order floor coverings and finer details. Charlie did all the tiling in the kitchen, the downstairs bathroom, and the Jack and Jill ensuite between the two dormer bedrooms on the second floor. They fitted a new banister on the stairs and an air conditioning unit for the main bedroom in the dormer as it was extremely hot up there and with the windows only being on one side there was no through draught. In Jacks bedroom, the other one in the dormer, they opened up more of the loft space to give him a play area, and had a circular window put in the gable end to provide some light. The finishing touches to the inside were to set up Charlie's office properly. Charlie and Gretchen did a lot of research into the best priced office furniture and settled on 2 L-shaped desks, a round table and chairs for sitting with clients, and some fantastic cupboards for Charlie's client files. Charlie was adamant she did not want the old-style drawer filing cabinets for her hanging files, and these cupboards, with all the names on show when you opened the doors, were fantastic. One of Charlie's clients, and close friend Webby, networked the two computers together and sorted out automatic backups for all of Charlie's work.

After the house was finished to the way they wanted it, Charlie and Brett started work outside. They had already bought and assembled a wooden climbing frame set up for Jack and his friends to play on.

They sorted out the patio in the back garden as it was a bit messy and mismatched, and bought a second-hand pool table to put on the side patio. The garden still needed more. They had had a small above ground pool at the last house but as it was at the end of the garden under the trees, apart from the kids in the summer it had not proved very popular.

This time they decided to go one step further. The cost of a proper fitted swimming pool was far too much so they settled on burying an above ground pool from a major DIY chain in a hole in the garden. A mini digger was brought in, and the relevant sized hole was dug. With the help of Brett's friend, Tommy, they erected the pool as much as possible, along with the filtration system that came with it, and dropped it in the hole. The sides were backfilled, and suitable paving put around the pool. They bought a cheap little shed for putting the system in out of the weather and had the necessary outdoor electrics put in.

The moment of truth in filling the pool came around very quickly, and in time for the school June half term. By this time, Gretchen and Grunter and her girls were frequent visitors to the house, outside of Gretchen's working hours. The first weekend that the pool was filled was a popular event, and other friends of theirs from the village and local pub came round for a barbeque. Both Brett and Charlie had birthdays in the middle of June, and it had developed into an annual barbeque party. To ease the pain of the chilly water, Charlie had filled part of the pool with hot water straight off the kitchen tap and it certainly took the edge of it for the adults. The children did not seem to care.

Chapter fourteen – life is good.

As a family and with Brett's 2 other children, they had camped many a time in Wales. At one point Brett decided it would be much better to get a caravan and so a second-hand twin axled six berth was purchased. On the first journey to their usual site near Caernarfon, Brett was on tenterhooks the whole way as it was not towing well at all. He had previously had a caravan with Penny, his ex-wife, and was a lorry and coach driver so if he was worried Charlie knew there was a problem. Eventually it turned out it was the chassis that was not correctly attached to the body, so they made the decision to site it permanently at their regular site in Wales. Leaving it there meant their journey was much quicker and without the danger of a caravan towing disaster.

This plan did not last for very long afterwards. During a visit in easter, a particularly wet and windy one, it took four adults to hold down the awning whilst they tried to attach it and set up the frame. The weather was completely against them as even after they had the awning in place it ripped down in the wind. Totally frustrated and fed up they went to the club house on the site to regain their composure. Whilst in the clubhouse they were chatting with Mark and Dave the site owners who happened to mention they had a couple of second-hand statics for sale. They would give Brett and Charlie something for the tourer and only charge them the difference in the annual site fees for the first year. It was a done deal. Brett's mum had cashed in some small investments she had built up and shared the proceeds between Brett and his sister.

The next morning Charlie, Brett and Jack had a look at the options, decided on the best for them, sorted out the paperwork, and headed back home. They had chosen one which was an older model because with the dog and the kids, there was no point in trying to be posh and wasting money on something that did the job no better.

Life back at home appeared to be really good. They had a big circle of friends, work was good but their work life balance, certainly with Jack, was not as good. Their house had become a permanent party house and drinking parties were becoming increasingly the norm. It was all getting a bit too much. Between the shop and Charlie's self-employed accountancy business it seemed like they were never off the hook from someone demanding their attention. The shop was only breaking even, and making a loss when the loan and mortgage payments were considered. Getting decent tenants in the upstairs flat was a constant headache and after much thought and discussion they decided to put the shop on the market with the plan that Brett would go back to driving, part time.

Things really came to a head at Christmas 2005. They had been out in the local pub for drinks early on Christmas eve. Brett's two other children were staying and late in the evening Charlie walked round to the pub to collect her car as she was opening up the shop on Christmas day. They had been arguing and as she walked out of the door, she swigged the drink left for Santa and took the carrot to throw away. She thought as she had not drunk any alcohol since they had returned home that she was fine to drive, but as she pulled out of the pub carpark in her car, the police followed her.

They pulled her over around the corner and she was absolutely hysterical and in no fit state to blow properly on the breathalyser.

After a big commotion she was taken off to the police station where she was put on the proper breathalyser machine. Eventually they managed to get some readings off her and they were way over the limit. Charlie was in a terrible state as they asked her to change into a paper suit. Even though she was hysterical, she remembered being watched by male police officers as she changed and was then banged into a cell and told she would be processed in the morning, Christmas Day. Once the door banged shut on the cell Charlie broke down into uncontrollable tears. She might have been over the limit, but she was still aware of what she had done, the implications, the embarrassment, and potential repercussions. At some point she must have fallen asleep on the wooden bench as the next thing she remembered was being woken up to be processed. She had her fingerprints taken, her DNA taken, and all other personal details written down. When they had finished, she had no way of getting home except in a taxi.

When she arrived home for Christmas Day, she felt that she would be better off if she had been kept in the cell. Brett told her she got what she deserved and even though she tried really hard for the sake of the children, the day was miserable. It was an episode in her life she knew she would never repeat, Charlie had learned a lesson the hard way. The next few months seemed to go with a whirl. Charlie received a 2-year driving ban, reduced to 18 months because she attended a drink driving course. She had to plan for visiting the clients she travelled to on a regular basis. She started off by making an agreement with a local taxi driver who used a small minibus come people carrier.

It worked ok for a number of journeys, but Charlie queried some of the routes he took.

As she knew the quickest and best way to get to all of her clients it was clear that these extra miles added on extra money. After a while Charlie discussed with Gretchen the possibility of her driving Charlie to the clients. Gretchen could take work with her and work in a spare office or at a spare desk and even though it would mean the phone at home was unmanned, they could get around this by diverting the phone to the mobile. Gretchen was an incredibly nervous driver and had not really driven much except the few miles around her house to the local shops.

The arrangement worked well. Once Gretchen had built up her confidence, especially on motorways, under Charlie's guidance and direction, it was clear it had benefits for them both. During this year, the sale of the shop went through. It had been bought by a Chinese chap who planned to make it into a local food and booze franchise and to live in the flat upstairs. Charlie and Brett managed to make a small profit from the sale but at least it was not a loss after all the improvements they had done to the premises. Brett had built the business up whilst running it and so the turnover when they sold was quite a bit more than when they opened. Unfortunately, it was never going to make them a living unless Brett worked in the shop full time. Although he could have done more hours rather than paying staff, it was a bit of a catch twenty-two as he needed to go to the cash and carry most days, and to be there for Jack and to support Charlie so she could work enough hours. Brett found himself a part-time job with a local bus company so that they could work around various commitments. His hours were the school runs, collecting and delivering pupils from housing areas to the local schools.

In the meantime, Charlie had also started exam marking for some of the accountancy organisations. This functioned as a fill in for when business was quiet and although she was never guaranteed a contract each sitting, it would be a fairly reliable source of income. Things at home were still not right. They were still caught in a trap of entertaining constantly, drinking with friends and Charlie felt they were not giving enough attention to Jack. After a discussion with one of her old neighbours in Skipsea, Gabriel, which had taken place whilst they still had the tourer and were on a site in the Lakes, she decided to get back in touch with him. They had spoken briefly about Gabriel buying Charlie's fees off her and taking over her clients. Charlie had been chatting with her mum and Brett about a career change for a while. Mathematics had always been her favourite subject at school, and by retraining as a teacher Charlie considered she would be able to move away from the stress and ties of being self-employed, as well as have more holiday time to spend with Jack.

After much more discussion and contemplation, a plan was made. Gabriel was going to buy Charlie's client base, the house was going to be sold, and Charlie would start teacher training. The chances of the timings of these all falling into place were very slim, but as usual Charlie had a backup plan. In the meantime, Charlie applied for teacher training, a PGCE in secondary mathematics. Even though she had maths A levels and there was a considerable amount of maths in accountancy training and exams, she was requested to complete a mathematics enhancement course at the university for 6 months before starting her teacher training.

As there was a shortage of maths teachers there would be a bursary for the enhancement course and for the PGCE although she would need a student loan for the tuition fees for the latter.

As it turned out, the timings fell fairly well together. They had a buyer for the house quickly and completion of the sale and the transfer of the business to Gabriel was scheduled for July 2007. Charlie's mum had been doing research on schools around where she lived. Mum and dad still lived in Skipsea where Charlie had grown up, and Brett's dad, sister, ex-wife, and children all lived in Hornsea, the next town to the village of Skipsea. They had been searching for a suitable home in the area, and in the end decided on a four bedroomed traditional semi, right in the middle of the village. It was not their ideal move and the choice of houses caused friction between Brett and Charlie, but the important thing was to find somewhere, cheaper, and smaller, until they were in a position to move again. In the period between July and the start of the mathematics enhancement course in January 2008, Charlie was to start working for Gabriel to ensure a smooth handover of her client base. She was also to continue with the monthly accounts and quarterly VAT visits and work for her bigger clients. Luckily, the month of the move and everything else was the month that Charlie got her driving licence back and was able to purchase a car. They had sold the Mazda she was driving when she was banned 18 months earlier and Charlie decided her new car was to be a Renault Megane convertible. She bought the car as an import to save money and was so pleased with it when it arrived. The fact that it would rarely be sunny enough to have the roof down in the UK had not occurred to her.

Moving day arrived. They had packed everything up in boxes and gathered up the cats and dog. The removals company arrived and loaded up and then it was just the wait to get the go ahead from the solicitors to say the keys could be handed over. It seemed like an age and the buyer arrived with their removal's vans. The solicitor confirmed the monies were in from the buyer, so Charlie handed over the keys to the lady who was buying their lovely bungalow. There was a moment of worry when she expressed concern at the garage not being full length as they had the main garage door open. Charlie said it was exactly the same as when the lady viewed it and as detailed on the house brochure prepared by the estate agent, she also said it was only a partition to make the utility area if the lady wanted to remove it. After that Brett, Charlie, Jack, and the animals shot off to Skipsea to get the keys for their new house and to beat the removals vans to the house.

Unfortunately, when they arrived, it appeared the solicitors, in this case Charlie's solicitors, had messed up. They had not transferred the funds to the owner of the house they were buying and everything was a nightmare. The sellers had to arrange a bed and breakfast for their family as all their stuff was packed in the removals van and the house was empty, Charlie and her human and animal family had to go and stay with her parents, and the removals companies had to take everything back to their respective depots. Charlie was furious but there was nothing she could do. It was a Thursday, and it was clear the deal was not going to be finalised until the following day. It ended up being a very peculiar 24 hours, and nothing like they had originally planned, but they got through it, and completion soon came round, and they had the keys to their new house.

The furniture and belongings all arrived, and they spent the next few days settling in and for Charlie in particular, enjoying seeing so much of her mum and dad who were just down the road.

The house they had bought was another do-it-upper. Gradually, as the days went on, they worked out what they wanted to do, what was affordable and necessary and made plans. One thing that really stuck in Charlie's mind in that period was the filthy built-in oven. Her mum spent an entire day cleaning inside the oven as it was covered in baked on fat and grease and heaven knows what else. The woodwork throughout the house, skirtings, doors, and frames, were painted white but with years and years of layers of paint, including the old black layer that was like bitumen. It took a long time and lots of effort to strip everything down to bare wood. Brett had the doors dipped which although it saved a lot of effort and made them back to the lovely original finish, they found out later that the dipping process had slightly warped some of the old doors. They decided this just added character to the old house.

Chapter fifteen – a turn for the worse

It was not long into the new house that Charlie's mum had a quiet word with her. She explained that whilst sitting on the lounge floor with her paperwork and her cat, as she had done for many years, she had found a lump in the side of her breast by her armpit. She had been for scans and so on and they had confirmed it was cancerous, an extremely aggressive form, and she was to have a mastectomy as soon as possible and a treatment plan would be made afterwards. Charlie's mum for some reason did not want to tell her husband, Charlie's dad. Charlie convinced her she had to tell him. At the time Charlie did not really understand why she would not want to. She knew her mum had always been a very independent and strong woman, but surely this was something that she needed support with. The mastectomy came round really quickly, and mum made a fantastic recovery. Charlie went shopping with her to look at bras for survivors. Her mum had opted to have a prosthesis instead of an implant as she thought at 72, she was not really that body proud. Mum started chemotherapy quickly after the surgery and between family and friends they all helped to take her to and from the sessions. She was still driving but the treatment left her very tired for a while and they all had to make themselves useful. It never occurred to Charlie at the time, but when her mum had appointments with her oncologist, she always went into the session on her own.

All was going well with the new house and the renovation works. It was great to have Charlie's mum and dad nearby to help and her mum and dad were really enjoying having Jack in their life so much.

It was lucky that Brett had bought the caravan in Wales as there were quite a few weeks where they had no bath or shower but could luckily go up to the caravan for a night or two and use the shower there. In the house the bathroom and kitchen were redone, the walls all replastered, electrics repaired or improved where necessary, and a whole new central heating system installed. The previous owners had put in double glazing, and although it was fairly old and not very efficient, it was not an extra cost they considered at the time. As the school summer holidays ended it was going to be a time of change for them all. Jack was coming up to 9 years old and was due to start a new school in Bridlington. Charlie's mum had done all the research and there was no guarantee Jack would be given a place in one of the schools in Hornsea due to them being oversubscribed and it being a few years further on than normal junior school starting age. They agreed on a small private school in Bridlington that was only a primary school but was also a feeder school for the private senior schools in Tunstall, subject to passing entrance exams. This route would probably not have been the first choice but there were not many other options, and Charlie's mum said she would pay a substantial part of the fees. Brett had also secured himself a job driving the school coaches back with the firm he used to work for 12 or more years previously. Charlie was working more than part time for Gabriel who had officially taken over her clients at the same time as they moved in the beginning of July. She really had to do her best to ensure the clients stayed with Gabriel as the sale of her business was on an earnout basis over 2 years and depended on clients staying. Charlie had already received some phone calls on her mobile phone from her clients, ex-clients, who were not happy as Gabriel rarely answered his phone or returned their calls.

Life was good, the house was nearly the way they wanted it, Jack had started in his new school, Brett in his job, and Charlie was holding together as much as she could of her business. Charlie's mum was doing well until the October half term. She was entertaining Jack and his friend from across the road, actually she had them polishing her brass trinkets at the kitchen table. Completely unexpectedly she rang Charlie. Brett answered the phone and said her mum said they were to get round there as soon as possible. He said he could not really make out what she was saying, just that they needed to go now. By the time they did the 5-minute journey down the road, the kids were in the kitchen and Charlie's dad was up in the bedroom with her mum. According to her dad, Charlie's mum had literally crawled up the stairs on all fours and dragged herself to the bed. Brett took the kids home and after a few minutes and the realisation that there was something seriously wrong with mum, they called an ambulance. Charlie and her dad followed the ambulance to Bridlington hospital, a mistake as it was to turn out as where they lived in Skipsea, the ambulances could take you to Bridlington or Beverley. After various tests mum was admitted to a ward. This was Tuesday, and it was Thursday before they got round to sending mum for a scan. The scan showed that mum had suffered a massive stroke and there was nothing they could do to help her. Even though this was before the adverts were shown on the TV to act FAST in cases of a suspected stroke, Charlie and her dad knew that mum should have been accurately diagnosed as soon as she was admitted when there was still a chance that they could have done something.

The days on the ward for Charlie's mum went on. Mum and dad had their 50th wedding anniversary whilst she was in hospital and Charlie's dad had chosen a beautiful earring and necklace set for his wife. Whilst she was still herself and thinking normally, Charlie's mum was having difficulty speaking clearly and using her left arm and leg. What was blatantly clear was that she wanted to get out of the hospital as soon as possible. Charlie and her dad had meetings with the consultant and the various members of the discharge team. A physio was arranged for home for helping mum get independent and mobile again. Charlie found it heart-breaking seeing her mum so frustrated once she was home. She frequently lifted up her left arm and dropped it again saying how useless it was. Her speech had improved and was nearly back to normal, and she was beginning to be able to walk short distances unaided. Charlie, her dad, and Brett all worked hard with the physio to help her mum regain as much movement as possible over the next few months. They took her out to places whenever they could and kept her as active and involved as possible. There were two things that really concerned Charlie's mum, one of which Charlie would not realise the implication of until many years later in life. This was the fact that her mum was really concerned that they would not restart her chemotherapy treatment. It was never actually confirmed but there was some suspicion that the stroke might have been brought on by the treatment itself. The second thing that really upset Charlie's mum was that she had been told by the optician that it was unlikely that she would drive again, due to the way the stroke had affected her vision.

As Mum gradually made progress and became more mobile Charlie started her Mathematics Enhancement course in January 2008. This was a 6-month precursor to the PGCE in secondary mathematics and was meant to boost the maths skills of people like Charlie who although had A level maths and had done a lot of maths in her accountancy training, did not have degree in maths. The course was split between Mere University in Hull and Short Hill university in Nafferton. It involved some hard maths, Decision, Statistics, Pure and Mechanics. Charlie enjoyed it all, well except for the Mechanics. She had done Pure and Stats at A level and really hated Physics, the core of Mechanics, but muddled through it. In the middle of the course, they had a placement in a school. Charlie was given a Catholic school in Tunstall. This part of the course and some of the taught aspects were more about the teaching side of mathematics, the pedagogy. They were not expected to teach unless they chose to take part of the class but were expected to watch and learn.

They had school holidays off, so this fitted in really well with Jack, and in between the course hours Charlie continued doing bits of work for Gabriel, building up exam marking for accountancy exams, and helping her dad care for her mum. Charlie, Brett, and Jack managed to steal some time away to the caravan in Wales. Her Dad also took Jack to the caravan whilst Charlie stayed with her mum. Sometimes, when Charlie and Brett took her mum out, her mum was acting a bit strange. The consultant at the hospital put this down to ministrokes and said it was to be expected but Charlie and her dad were not convinced.

It had also become apparent that Mum was needing an increasing amount of personal care. At one-point Charlie remembered her mum asking her to end it all for her if she got worse and this really scared and hurt her. As was her usual persona, Charlie worked hard and carried on. It was soon September and her PGCE course was starting in Short Hill.

Throughout the summer Jack had been complaining his ankles were hurting. The GP assured them it was just growing pains but when it did not seem to improve, and was affecting his knees as well, Charlie and Brett decided to take Jack to Elm Hey hospital and get another opinion. The consultant they saw was brilliant. The A&E doctor had his suspicions as to what it was and called a specialist Professor to look. After some discussion amongst his team, and some blood and urine tests, The Professor Consultant informed Charlie and Brett, and Jack, that he was fairly sure Jack was suffering from Juvenile Arthritis. He explained it was a chronic condition but was treatable and so Jack was booked in for some scans and a treatment session.

The results of all the investigations proved the suspicions and he had steroid injections in his ankles. They worked very quickly and relieved the pain a great deal and reduced the swelling. He was scheduled to go back for more injections and more scans and consultations with the plan that Charlie and/or Brett would continue giving him methotrexate tablets for a while.

The PGCE course had three teaching periods on it. The first one was in the October, the second one spread throughout Christmas into the new year, and the final one, the longest one, was from spring through to June. The times before, after, and in between were spent in the classroom at the university.

Charlie's first and second placements were to be at a boy's school in Wilsthorpe and it would open her eyes to the difference in classrooms from when she had been at school 44 years earlier. It was however a career change that she had made with open eyes. She was fully aware of what to expect and had seen the modern-day classroom on her brief placement on the Mathematics Enhancement Course. By the time they were let loose as trainees in the classroom they had been allowed to spend time in college practising on each other and the lecturers, getting to know how to use the modern whiteboards and some of the basics of class management. Charlie had learned new (to her) ways of teaching and helping understanding of certain topics. It was also clear that differentiation and inclusion were key parts to a successful lesson. A lecturer from the University would be coming to observe her teaching, the preparation documents and paperwork for the lesson, and would be awarding a grade. Charlie had always strived to do her best in everything she tackled and was determined to try and get outstanding grades.

On top of the teaching practice and time in the lessons, they were expected to complete and submit assignments, and complete a key assignment or thesis at the end in order to gain the level 7 in the PGCE, a master's level. The trainees also had to pass the QTS (qualified Teacher Status) tests which involved Maths, English and IT online tests as well as being signed off for their teaching practice. Charlie was assigned a mentor at the boy's school where her first and second placement was based. She was excellent as a mentor and a teacher and inspired Charlie to try and be as good as her. The children all seemed to want to learn from her and her passion and enthusiasm for teaching were so evident.

Charlie was to take some classes from Clare, her mentor and one or two others from others in the department. Charlie got the teaching bit; she could even differentiate her lessons and keep most of the students engaged. She never really cracked the classroom management as well as she had hoped. Charlie had tried all the techniques that were in her toolbox, and the new ones she had been introduced to. She tried, not very successfully, to learn all their names. She did seating plans according to the advice of their usual teachers, she wrote names on the board, but nothing seemed to work very well. It was obviously good enough to get her through teaching practice and Charlie knew herself that to be the successful teacher she wanted to be engagement of the class was key.

Overall, the placement went well, and Charlie seemed to be getting the hang of this teaching thing. She soon realised that there is nothing more satisfying than that penny drop moment when students suddenly realise how to do some maths, or how easy something really is. The initial phase involved observing and learning how to teach whilst building up the number of lessons taught. After the October half term, the developmental phase involved about half a teaching timetable of the classes she had started in. This phase would go through to around February at which time Charlie would return to the university for academic work and consolidation, before going to a different school for the final placement from around March to June where she would build up her teaching practice to around two thirds of a full-time teacher alongside completing the academic work and portfolio.

Unfortunately, things were not going quite so well on the home front. Mum had deteriorated.

She was behaving strangely, shouting at, and hitting the carers Charlie and her dad had arranged to help him, Charlie and Brett would take her out somewhere and she would throw her food on the floor. Mum had been set up in the dining room with a hospital bed but was really not very mobile anymore. They would help her out into the lounge and kitchen for short periods of time, take her places when practical, but it pained Charlie so much to watch her deterioration. At one point mum developed fluid on the lungs, pulmonary oedema they were told and ended up back in hospital. After much pressure from Charlie and her dad, the hospital agreed to give Mum full scans. The results were not good and showed that her breast cancer, although she had the mastectomy, had metastasised to her brain. She had a massive brain tumour that was inoperable. The news was so hard to take, especially since Charlie and her dad had been telling the hospital teams, attended an MDT session, and pushed for the fact that something was wrong. It was also clear that had the teams listened to them there would have been a chance of operating but now it was too late.

In the middle of this the methotrexate Jack was taking for his arthritis was causing him to be violently ill so the only option was to inject the drug into his leg or buttock. Charlie was told and shown how to do it but hated having to chase him round the house every night and inflict pain on him by stabbing him with a needle. The benefit was that it did seem to be making a difference to his mobility. He had put on some weight as it had been too painful in his ankle and knee joints to do sports either at school or at home, and this had resulted in him being bullied and teased at school.

Just to finish off the problems going on in life, at the end of October the family Doberman, Duke, collapsed at the front door after returning from his usual walk on the sandhills. Charlie was doing mouth to mouth, Brett was pumping his chest and Jack was screaming, but there was nothing they could do, and he died there and then. Charlie rang the vet who told them to take his body to their associated practice in Nafferton – it was of course a Sunday, whilst Brett fetched a blanket to cover him and lift him into the car and they tried to comfort Jack. Eventually they managed to get themselves calm and sorted and Brett took Duke off in the boot of the car to be cremated.

Keep calm and carry on was to be Charlie's motto for the rest of her life. Charlie's Dad started to intervene in the bullying issue at Jacks school. He had taken over the paying of the fees for the small private junior school and was having meetings with his form teacher and headmaster, but things were really getting no better for Jack. He was struggling with his own arthritis, the loss of his dog, and the fact that his Gran, who had been his world, was not the same, and Charlie did not push him to see her in her current state as she knew it would be just to upsetting for him. Charlie also continued to attend MDT meetings with her dad at the hospital when they were allowed and between them, they pushed the consultant to recommend mum for hospice care. She was becoming worse, and it pained them to watch the centre of all their lives, their rock, mentor, and hero deteriorating mentally. Luckily for them all, Charlie's mum had some incredibly good friends from her career in Social Services and between these friends they managed to secure her a place at one of the really respected hospices for end-of-life care.

Over the next month or so Mum was moved to the hospice and Charlie tried her hardest to continue improving her teaching and classroom skills, whilst at the same time keeping a close eye on Jack. There were three boys that had been worse to him at school and under Brett's influence Jack began to fight back. Charlie and her dad went into school on a couple of occasions. The first was because Jack had stabbed one of the bullies with a pair of compasses in the arm. Luckily, there was no damage as compasses had a very shallow point and the boy concerned had his blazer on. The second made Charlie, Brett and her dad laugh uncontrollably, the worst of the bullies had been 'accidentally' locked in one of the sheds in the school gardens for most of the day and no-one had even missed him. Even though they were clear with the school that the boys concerned deserved it, Jack was duly reprimanded at home as even though they all agreed his actions were justified, they could not condone them openly with him.

It was around the same time as all of this was happening that Brett started to drink a bit too much and lied about it. It was becoming a frequent cause of arguments between Brett and Charlie. Charlie had bought a home breathalyser for the 'morning after' after her drink driving incident but whenever she asked Brett to blow on it, he would claim it was not working properly. It was all getting too much for all of them and they made the decision to pull Jack out of the private school as soon as he had completed the entrance exams for the senior schools in early December.

Charlie had her teaching practice and coursework to deal with, helping her dad, problems with Brett, Jack's arthritis, and her best friend and mum's worsening state and she felt like she was going to explode if something did not give.

In the background Gabriel had been losing her clients by the week, including some of the bigger ones, due to lack of communication with them and not returning their calls. It was obvious that she was never going to receive the full earnout payments they had agreed as the total payment was based on clients retained. On some occasions she regretted her haste and trust in not using a contract law solicitor for the arrangement, but it really was the least of her worries.

Things were not all bad though. The teaching practice that Charlie was on for her developmental phase in her PGCE was with a talented team. Her mentor and head of the maths department Les was excellent and supportive as were the rest of the teachers. There were other students with her at the school, PE, and English students, and although significantly younger than Charlie, they were a great support to each other. She was gaining more confidence in her teaching and although her classroom management skills were still not what she and others hoped for, she was learning new ways of dealing with it. The actual subject matter and her ability to get it across to the students in a way that they could mostly understand was doing well and her academic work, which ran alongside teaching practice, was also doing well.

Visiting her mum in the hospice was really emotionally difficult. It was obvious that she was fading away, more mentally than physically, and it pained Charlie so much to see this once brilliant woman like this.

They decided that they would not push Jack to see mum as it would break his heart and he had enough going on in his own life as it was. They also decided to get another Doberman puppy.

This time from a different part of the country, from near Sheffield and before long Buddy had moved into their home. It was a pleasure to have something in their lives to take away from everything going on, although the cats were not best pleased with the new arrangement. The cats had spent some time getting Duke to behave as they wanted, and they really were too long in the tooth to start training a new member of the family as both Saffy and Holly were getting on in their years. Jack was getting on a bit better at school although Brett and Charlie knew he was not in the best place. His juvenile arthritis seemed to be getting under control. The swelling and the pain had reduced considerably but it still involved Charlie having to administer weekly methotrexate injections to him which she hated doing and he certainly did not enjoy.

When it was approaching Christmas, as a family they decided they had to continue despite mum getting weaker. They decided Brett would cook Christmas dinner and dad and his sister, Aunty Alice, would come for the meal. When it got to Christmas eve Charlie went to see her mum again, but she was really distant and not making sense. Charlie chatted away to her as if everything were normal and she did respond to some extent. When Charlie returned home, she busied herself with helping Brett sort everything for Christmas day and got on with wrapping presents and keeping Jack happy.

For a couple of years now Charlie had been marking over Christmas. It was intensive although only for a short period of time, but Charlie felt she should continue to do the December sitting of the exam as the exam was quarterly and she felt if she started turning it down when she was offered a sitting, they may not ask her again.

The good thing was she was off from the school due to the Christmas holidays, so did have more time on her hands.

On Christmas day morning, quite early, her dad called and told her that the hospice had just rang. They did not expect mum to live much longer but Charlie could not bring herself to see her mum die. She agreed with her dad that he would see mum and then meet them at Charlie's house with Aunty Alice around 3pm for Christmas lunch. It was around 11.30 when Dad rang from the hospice to say mum had passed. Charlie was beside herself with sadness and had an overwhelming feeling of abandonment but had to stay strong for Jack. Dad said he wanted to keep to the plans for Christmas lunch as there was nothing more he could do at the hospice after the next hour or so. The day seemed to drag on for ever whilst Charlie, Brett and Jack were waiting for their visitors. They had told Jack about his Gran; he had spent so much of his early years with her, and she doted on him whenever given the opportunity. It surprised Charlie and Brett how well he took it – they all knew it was coming but that did not make it any easier. Charlie did worry that Jack was hiding his feelings too much, but she was no psychiatrist, it was just motherly instincts. Once dad and Alice arrived, they all tried to enjoy the day as much as possible. The food Brett had made was fabulous and they all had far too much to drink.

Whether it was to say goodbye to mum or to drown their sorrows, Charlie would never know, but it seemed right at the time. It was late by the time Charlie's Dad and Alice toddled off back home and Charlie tidied up and fell into bed exhausted. She had planned to get another hour or so marking in but was really not in the mood anymore.

The next 2 weeks were a bit of a whirlwind. Charlie decided not to visit her mum in the funeral home as she wanted to remember the fun, loving and lively mum who had been there for her all her life. Her dad was ever so conscious of Charlie's new career as a teacher and his practical side took over as usual with him arranging mum's funeral for as soon as possible, a day which after checking with Charlie, was an inset day at the start of the January school term. Dad arranged everything, the funeral, the wake, the paperwork, and it was not until many years later that Charlie realised, she should have done more to help at the time and take some of the burden off her dad. In hindsight she supposed it suited him to keep busy and concentrate on the future.

On the day of her mum's funeral Charlie had arranged for Jack to go and spend the day with Brett's older two children and his ex-wife as even though they had discussed it with him, he was only just 10 years old and really did not want to be there. The service was short at the crematorium and Charlie's dad gave a really moving speech. As they came out of the crematorium Charlie asked her dad where his sister, Alice, and brother Theodore were as she understood they were coming. Just as they spoke dad received a message from the undertakers at the crematorium to say that Alice had had a fall and Theodore and his wife Ava had gone to the hospital with her.

Dad said they should carry on with the wake at the Skipsea Hotel as people had come a long way to say goodbye to Mum. It was a lovely get together of all mum's good friends with just the small immediate family.

During the afternoon dad went home for a while to make some phone calls and came back to say that Aunty Alice had died in the ambulance, she had a massive embolism and there was nothing the medics could do to save her. It was a shock to everyone at the wake who knew Alice, but they all tried to continue with the purpose of the day, to remember Charlie's mum.

Chapter sixteen – battling on with life.

The next few months were very strange for Charlie. She had lost her mum and best friend but had been brought up to believe life must go on. Jack had to be her priority so she carried on supporting him as best as she could, working on her teacher training, and finishing off the house they had ripped apart to renovate whilst they lived in it. Luckily, they still had the caravan in North Wales and at one point when the bathroom in the house was out of action, they were travelling up there for the weekend just so they could all have a proper wash in the shower. Dad was busying himself doing as much as he could with Jack at the same time as applying for planning permission on the garden at the side of his house. Mum and Dad had always intended to get planning permission and sell the plot next door but there had been a moratorium on building in the area that had now been lifted. He also collaborated with an architect on some plans to put a roof on his own house. The house had a flat concrete roof and the leaks had been getting worse over the years.

Dad had kept on top of it with his friend, but it was too big a job and needed a permanent fix. Whilst all this was going on it was obvious by the February half term that Jack was not happy in his school and things had really not got any easier for him with the bullies. The headmaster and his team were less than supportive, and it was clear that they had to find a new school for him quickly.

He had passed the entrance exams to the senior school and been accepted for the September intake into year 7 but no matter how hard Charlie tried she could not get him into one of the local primary schools straight away.

Eventually, one of the larger primaries in the next town agreed to take him for the summer term, after the easter holidays. With her dad offering to home teach him for the remaining half of the spring term, they took him out of the small private primary school in Bridlington with immediate effect.

After the final weeks of her own placement Charlie spent some weeks on academic studies back at the university before moving to a different secondary school for her final, or synoptic, teaching placement. This was a much bigger mixed school than her previous placement and it took pupils up to A levels at 18 although Charlie was only assigned classes in the 11-16 age group as this was the area of her PGCE. The maths team at the school was vast but as seemed to be the norm for trainee teachers and was often the case for new teachers, she was assigned mostly lower-level classes. Her mentor at the school was great. He was really supportive and was himself an excellent and innovative teacher and she knew she would continue to learn so much from him.

The next few months seemed to fly by. Jack did lots with Charlie's dad – they went to London, they went to Paris, and all the time Charlie's dad was teaching him in a practical, doing, kind of way. They were not concerned about the academic side of schooling so much as Jack had no problem with his knowledge for his age academically, and afterwards he settled into his temporary primary school really well.

Charlie was busy looking for jobs as a fully qualified maths teacher, alongside still carrying on bits of accountancy work and her marking. When she was really busy her dad would take Jack to the caravan so that she could knuckle down in peace. Eventually Charlie managed to secure a role at a school in Bridlington.

For both her and the new science teacher it was only a one-year position as the school had received extra funding to boost maths and science, but it was a job, in what seemed like a nice school.

By the time September came everything had settled down in Charlie's life. The house was finished, dad was doing well on his own and Charlie and Jack started their new schools with enthusiasm and excitement, tinged with a reasonable dose of nervousness. Brett was working on the coaches and although the pay was not great, he enjoyed the jobs he was doing. Charlie knew he was still drinking when he was not working but had resigned herself to the fact that there was not anything she could do about it and any confrontation just led to an argument. They had friends in the village, friends from Doncaster they saw often, and Jack was making new friends at school. As it approached the Easter term of 2010 Charlie knew she needed to start looking for a new, more permanent teaching job. Her confidence had grown over the academic year under the watch of her head of department. She felt so blessed to have another excellent teacher to guide her – one that would think out of the box and use any method she could to help the students in their learning. Charlie achieved her qualified teacher status which gave her a little advantage over the PGCE students that were due to qualify that summer.

Eventually, after some failures, she secured a place at a secondary school in Carnaby. It was an easy enough commute on the motorways and the head teacher and maths team seemed really pleased to have her on board. Charlie knew she still had not mastered classroom management as well as she would have liked but felt her actually teaching was not bad. She was given the lower sets as usual, including one class of highly demotivated year 11's.

As a family they continued with the same arrangement – seeing and visiting friends, staying at the caravan, and her dad staying at the caravan with Jack now and then. Jack loved going there as he had a completely separate set of friends that were there, who like him went on most school holidays and some weekends. Buddy the Doberman was used to the journey backwards and forwards and they could always find someone to feed the cats whilst they were away. On the whole life was good although unfortunately Charlie was having some what she liked to call women's problems and it was causing her issues during the teaching day, meaning she had to go to the bathroom frequently. It was made worse by the fact that the school she was in had what they termed 'wet break' which effectively meant that the teachers had to keep the students in the class throughout break when it was raining so a non-stop period of not being able to leave the classroom could be for all morning or all afternoon. Charlie went to see the headteacher about her issues but there was not much they could do to help, and Charlie was scared she would end up having an accident in front of the students.

Chapter seventeen – building the dream.

One day, in the Easter school holidays, Charlie and Brett were swapping over from Dad at the caravan. Because Jack was in a school with longer holidays to compensate for the longer school day, it meant Dad would entertain him whilst Charlie and Brett were still at work. On this particular occasion they all sat chatting in the caravan before Dad headed back off home. Dad had obtained the planning permission for the land next door to his house and had plans drawn for a four bedroomed detached house and had been trying to find a buyer through estate agents for the plot. Charlie had an idea – she said to her dad – 'can we build the house.' All of a sudden it seemed doable. She had bought houses to live in that were in various states of disrepair and neglect. The degree of DIY that her and Brett had done together was way above the normal a couple would tackle as they were both so practically minded and determined. They had created some lovely houses together on this journey and Charlie knew she had the skills to project manage the build. She was organised and astute enough to manage the finances and deal with paperwork or any issues that arose.

In the months that followed they talked more with Charlie's Dad about the possibility and agreed with her brother a value for the land. This was important as using the land at the side of the house to build on would reduce the overall value of the house should anything happen to their dad.

It was at this time that Dad received some not very wise legal advice to break the trust arrangement Charlie's mum had set up years earlier, whereby half the value of her Mum and Dad's estate passed to Charlie and her brother should one of their parents die, with the remaining parent having full use of it. Charlie and Stewart went along with Dad's wish to remove the trust – he said it was the only way the land could be transferred to Charlie – although Charlie knew this was not legally the case. It was however what her dad wanted so her and Stewart duly signed the relevant paperwork and a charge equal to the agreed value of the land was established on Dad's house in Stewart's favour.

Once the decision was made, Charlie handed in her notice at the school she was working in. As it was getting near to the GCSE exams she offered to stay until the exams started even though she did not need to. She had one particular year 11 class who she had worked extremely hard with to improve their confidence and to reduce their demotivation and disillusionment with maths, and she believed that if they were to have a supply or change of teacher at this late stage it would really undermine her hard work. It was agreed that she would leave the day before the first maths GCSE paper was to be taken. Throughout this time and in the months since she left the school Charlie began her spreadsheet mania. She had worksheets with minute detail for the cost of the build. They had to choose the brick and roof tiles and submit a sample to the planning office for approval so once they were approved Charlie used her maths skills to work out exactly how many bricks and roof tiles would be needed to build the house.

Similarly, she collaborated with a local builder's merchant, an independent and not a chain merchant, to detail and cost everything else that would be needed for the house.

Charlie and Brett planned to do as much as they could themselves once the structure was up. The main issue now was finding someone to build the house, and this proved to be a challenge in itself. She had a couple of quotes from local builders that were ridiculously expensive. Charlie knew this as she had costed the materials in so much detail and even as a one-off customer, they were receiving a generous discount from the local builder's merchant. She used extensive research from self-build websites to estimate the labour element and even asked on old client of hers who was a retired quantity surveyor to cost the project based on the information Charlie had provided and current market rates using specialist software. Eventually she was satisfied she had a reasonable idea of how much the house was going to cost and factored in 10% for contingencies as was advised. It was to be funded initially through some cash from her dad, Brett had received some money following the death of his father, and credit cards. The grand plan was to obtain a bridging loan once the structure was up to clear the debts and then convert this to a mortgage once the house was complete. Charlie knew a bridging loan was not the cheapest option, but it was cheaper than credit card debt and at least would be a fixed amount of interest, rolled up for the twelve-month period.

Over the summer Brett and Charlie started on the finer details of costing and planning the house. They wanted to alter the stud walls that were in the original plans for the bathroom.

Her mum had always teased her dad about his wish to make bathrooms as compact as possible and the plans for their new house were no different. Considering the fact that the house was planned with four large double bedrooms, the main bathroom was pokey, so they altered photocopies of the drawings to make the bathroom a couple of square metres larger. They also jigged around the layout of the kitchen diner to make it more like their dream layout. None of it would be structural and after a meeting with planning to discuss an alteration to the dormer in one of the bedrooms, it was agreed that no revised plans were needed for the internal revisions. Brett had also quit his job driving coaches and spent the months after the summer holidays upgrading and decorating her Aunty Alice's house with her dad so that he could put it on the market. Dad was paying him an hourly rate for his time, so they had some money coming in and Charlie was carrying on with her marking work that she was building up and doing some private tutoring.

By the time the school term started in September everything was coming together. Jack seemed to be much happier in school and had started to develop some new friendships. They had managed to find a very experienced brickie, Leo, to complete the main structural build. He was a fabulous find after they had been let down by other tradesmen over and over again, and they spent time with Leo discussing finer details. He would help them get the foundations dug out and then start on the block and brickwork. They then had to find someone to clear the site. It was covered in sycamore trees and small sandhills. The planning department had insisted that any of the trees that had a diameter of 100mm or more had to be replaced.

At one point they were asking Charlie to pay £12000 to the council so they could plant these replacement trees across the borough. The only option to remove this penalty was to provide a planting diagram to show where they would plant the twenty replacement trees themselves. It was decided and agreed with the council that they would be mainly planted on Dad's side along the boundary, along the front boundary, and with a few dotted around in the rear garden. Charlie used the opportunity at meetings with the council to have the drive layout approved as well as her drawings of the planting for the site included and extra wide driveway entrance and the brick wall running across the front of the property.

By December they had managed to engage a brother of the owner of the builders' merchant to come and clear the site and work began in earnest. As well as removing all the weed sycamore trees and surrounding scrub, the land was cleared with twelve enormous lorry loads of sand being taken away and disposed of, but finally they had a level site with just some of the nicer sycamore, beech and holly trees left in the back of the garden. These would be trimmed to a much tidier state in time. The company that had done the clearance then delivered loads of crush and run for the front of the plot as this would be where the drive was to be as the whole plot was on sand. The original plan was to hire a mini digger and dig out the foundations themselves but after a lot of careful thought and discussion they decided that it was better to hire a driver with the digger. Digging out the foundations was a difficult job. Not because the ground was hard, but the exact opposite. Every time a trench was dug out the wind would blow the loose sand.

The rain did not help either and the sides of the trenches had to be kept away from as any undue pressure would cause the sand to collapse and fill the trench. As they were digging Charlie, Brett and Leo fitted wooden boards to the sides partly to stop the collapse and also to make a neat surface for the concrete to be poured for the footings.

Before the concrete could be arranged and poured, they spent days cutting and fitting steel reinforcement into the foundation trenches. Charlie's dad had insisted they make all the foundations one metre wide and with reinforcement. Although the soil survey had only indicated one or two points of soft ground, they had to do it her dad's way, but Charlie knew that as an engineer he was giving good, if not labour intensive, advice. Eventually the foundations were finished and the building inspector from the council gave his go ahead. The house looked like it was going to be so tiny based on the current appearance, especially the cloakroom that would be by the main front entrance. Charlie remembered thinking something similar when her and Daniel had been to visit the start of the build of their first Wimpey house together. When the concrete arrived someone had to be in charge of the massive pipe that would be at the end of the pump on the wagon. Charlie drew the short straw, with Brett following behind with the back of a rake patting and smoothing the pour down. It was a very delicate operation as Charlie had to walk round each foundation channel with her feet over one metre apart, being careful not to disturb the sand or boards at the sides, whilst manoeuvring a massive pipe into the right places. Surprisingly, the whole operation did not take too long – it was over in a few hours.

Charlie was glad it was over and knew that her leg muscles would ache the next day, if she could walk at all, and felt like she had been doing the splits or riding a very wide horse for a long time.

They then had a few days break from the build whilst the foundations set, and the blocks were delivered. As was her dad's way, the foundation blocks and any blocks for the walls had to be upgraded to extra strength but again Charlie trusted and respected her dad's advice. Leo began laying the blocks the day they were delivered. He had brought his own cement mixer so at least that saved them the cost of buying or renting one and he had previously given Charlie a list of what to order regarding sand and cement and any other bits he needed. As the days went by Charlie and Brett could not believe how quickly the blocks were going down. Once the first few feet of blocks were laid there was to be another concrete pour, this time for the ground level floors. But first, there was more work to do. They had to lay a damp-proof course and cut and fit deep insulation material for the floors. They went for deep insulation to keep the house as well insulated as possible, and in due course the concrete floors were set, and the house was beginning to take proper shape.

Whilst doing all of this an opportunity for a part time teacher had come up at a local FE college so Charlie had applied and been offered the role. It was to teach functional skills mathematics to adult learners and could develop into a more full-time role over time. It was a completely different set-up to teaching in schools. There were no specialist maths trained teachers and the teachers for functional skills seemed to be more variable in their skills, some teaching mathematics and English, classes with learning difficulties, and a wide variety of ages.

The few hours a week Charlie had been given built very quickly into twelve and then 20 hours. The house build was going well and by the end of 2012 the shell of the house was complete, and it was time to arrange the roof and windows. Over the rainy months of the autumn season, they had needed to hire a number of submersible water pumps. The rain had been atrocious, and the concrete floors were open to the elements and sealed in at the sides by the brick and blockwork, so the water was pooling very deeply in the middle, sometimes up to their ankles. It was a priority to get the house weatherproof and after many attempts at trying to find someone to do the roof Charlie ended up doing the drawings herself, using her mathematical skills and with her dad checking her drawings and calculations. The roof was not a straightforward shape, but she managed to find a firm in Yorkshire who would make the roof trusses to the drawings and deliver in a relatively short time. Charlie and her dad worked closely with the firm to make sure the final trusses would be the best fit possible. Leo had to do some last-minute alterations to the walls of the dormer to be able to take the roof trusses as the original architect who had designed the house seemed to have designed what they could only describe as a floating roof as it had no way of being supported.

The windows were an easier arrangement. Leo had a close childhood friend who had his own window company and he agreed to supply all the windows and the conservatory. Both the main roof height opening at the front door and the dormer could not be manufactured until the roof was in place, but the rest could.

Eventually, by Christmas 2012 the roof was on and waterproofed and the windows were in. Charlie and Brett had helped Leo lay all the flooring boards for the first-floor bedrooms and any other help Leo needed, even if it was just holding something whilst Leo secured it. He was now also doing all the joinery as well as masonry work in the house. Over the next few months Leo completed the stud walls upstairs and the door frames throughout the house whilst Brett and Charlie worked on the first fix electrics. They had agreed with a local electrician that they should do all the running of the cables for the electrics and tv aerials and then the electrician would fit all the sockets, lights and connect up the switchboard. Charlie had purchased all the socket fronts in bulk off a supplier on the internet at a substantial discount and they were all a crisp brushed steel finish. Both Charlie's dad and her brother helped advise where needed on the wiring and doing it themselves meant they could have plentiful sockets in the places where they would be needed and not end up with extension leads across all the floors once they moved in.

There was a never-ending list of things to do. Whilst the foundations were being dug the necessary wastewater and sewage drainage had to be put in, a sink hole dug and filled with rubble in the front and back gardens for the surface water from the roof of the house and all the fittings needed to be purchased and fitted for the whole of the outside guttering and drainage. There were also all the connections to be sorted for electricity, gas, water, telephone, and drainage. When the roof tiles arrived, Leo took it upon himself to fit them.

It was amazing watching him walk on the roof trusses as if he were on solid ground. He would sit on the slope of the roof fitting tiles as if it were a level surface and was up and down the scaffolding like a ferret. Charlie had also found a plumber who was working on the internal first fix. It was all with plastic pipes which was a new one for Charlie as she had only ever seen copper pipes used before by the plumbers in the houses they had renovated and by her dad. Keeping track of all the different trades, the finances, and scheduling deliveries and workers was a full-time operation on its own.

During the Easter holidays Charlie, Brett and Jack went for a well-earned break at the caravan in Wales. Whilst they were there Charlie received a phone call from her manager at the college. The department was going to start running access to HE courses, and her manager wanted to know if Charlie would run an Access course for business. It would mean more hours for Charlie if it happened but would need at least six students to make it viable. Charlie had never taught business before but as an accountant she decided it was a challenge she could take on and succeed in. It would mean she would have to be in college more over the summer holidays to design the course, meet with the awarding body, and recruit students for the course. The last term of college and school seemed to fly by. Charlie was doing her teaching hours, starting to plan for the new course, being a mum, and managing the ever-growing number of trades at the build. At one point they had Leo in doing the joinery, plumbers doing second fix and fitting bathrooms, plasterers, electrician, fence men, people fitting internal doors and on and on. It tested Charlie's ability to project manage endlessly.

By August 2013 they had moved in and had the certificate of completion from building control. They had used the services of the Local Authority for the building inspections throughout the build and it had been the best decision. Their allocated building inspector had been excellent at providing advice and guidance. They had a big housewarming barbeque and party and proudly showed off their magnificent achievement to all their close friends and family. They had accepted an offer on their house in the village, but it had fallen through as the couple that were proceeding split up. The market for selling was not good and Charlie's childhood friend Abigail had sold her flat and needed somewhere to stay. It was a fantastic opportunity for both of them so Abigail rented their old house on a short-term basis until she could find something more long term with her new boyfriend who was also one of their childhood friends and married.

Chapter eighteen – the bullying was back.

The next few years were fairly uneventful for Charlie and her family. Jack was doing well at school; Brett was back working on the school coaches and Charlie was doing more for the college. In addition to running the access course for business, being effectively head of mathematics and leading on the development of the teaching of GCSE maths to the 16-18 cohort, in September 2014 Charlie had started running a new PGCE specialist mathematics course. She was really enjoying all these challenges although it was incredibly stressful and demanding work. Jack was also sitting his GCSEs in the summer of 2015 and Charlie enlisted the help of one of her fellow teachers who was an English teacher to help Jack with the English Language exam. Luckily, it looked like the mathematics GCSE would be fairly straightforward for Jack. In September 2015 Charlie found herself a position as Associate Tutor for the PGCE in Further Education and Training for the local university and had negotiated a reduced timetable with the college. The college were not providing a second PGCE and there had been insufficient applicants for the access to business to run a third year and so it seemed like a suitable time for Charlie to extend her skills and widen her horizons.

It was during the first Autumn term that things started to get really difficult for Charlie and her team of maths teachers, and for the English team. Some idiots in top management in their college had decided that the 16–18-year-olds would sit in 3-hour lessons of maths and English each week.

The government had decreed that all 16–18-year-olds who left school without a grade 4 in maths and English had to continue working towards their GCSE in college. Working towards could mean completing functional skills maths and moving on to GCSE but the college Charlie worked in decided to put them all in for GCSE classes for 3 hours despite the fact that they may have already failed the GCSE at school two, three or even more times and they were being set up to fail again. It was all about getting more funding as far as the college was concerned and had no benefit to either the teaching staff or the students. Consequently, the maths and English team were having to deal with a lot of behaviour issues, abuse, aggravation and even bullying by students.

In addition to her part time teaching hours at the college, part time tutor at the university, Charlie also designed and delivered a course to enhance maths teaching in Further Education which meant visiting other FE colleges and demonstrating ways to engage the students and make maths more interesting. Just to make sure she had no time to herself Charlie was also delivering training sessions on behalf of a private training organisation to better teaching in maths. It was all non-stop and extremely fulfilling until a most bizarre incident happened at the college.

Charlie had a particularly difficult class of hair and beauty students. The college had no discipline policy and students could just sit through lessons, chatting, playing on their phones, or anything else they wanted to do if engaging with maths was not top of their priority list. Even though most of the class had settled down over the first few months of the academic year there was a small group of girls that were particularly distracted, and Charlie had tried everything in her teaching school kit to get them engaged.

On one particular afternoon lesson after demonstrating a particular topic, she tasked the students with completing some questions on their own. Again, most of the students complied and as a reward for completing the work independently and to a satisfactory standard, Charlie said she would let those who had completed go early, when they had finished. It was the last 20 minutes of the lesson and in view of the fact it was past 4pm, and Charlie could not start a new topic this late in the day at the same time as support those who were struggling, she decided this would enable her to spend more one-to-one time with the students who needed more support. Being nice and supportive backfired on Charlie vigorously. She was at the end of her desk, near the exit door, checking the students work as they brought it to her completed. Eventually there were just around ten girls left in the class who decided they wanted to leave also, despite not completing the work. Charlie reasoned with them that as soon as they finished the small plenary task, they could go, but they started behaving like a pack of wild animals. They surrounded Charlie by the door, shouting at her, threatening her, telling her to get out of the way so they could leave. She was not intentionally blocking the door it just happened to be where was standing. Charlie was quite terrified in the end and instead of breaking down into tears in front of them all she moved aside and told them all to go.

The minute the classroom was empty, Charlie broke down into uncontrollable, hysterical tears. One of the joinery lecturers was passing her classroom and came in to see what was going on. Charlie explained everything and he was really supportive. He suggested she report the incident to her line manager.

Charlie was still shaking but agreed that was best, that she would do it from home as the next day was not one of her days in the college, she was doing lesson observations for the university. Charlie kept bursting into tears on her way home and when she got back Brett and Jack wanted to know all the details of the incident. Jack was the same age as the girls and was really upset. He jokingly said that if it were allowed, he could sit at the back with his target rifle. He was in the cadets at school and was in the shooting team. Charlie thought it was just his way of being protective of his mum and clearly explained that his idea was not really the solution.

The next day Charlie tried to move on from the incident and continued with her lesson observations. This involved quite some travelling as she had three of her trainee teachers having an observation on the same day but it least it kept her occupied. On the Wednesday she was back in the college teaching classes. Whilst she was outside the front of the college chatting with some other lecturers, two of the girls from the Monday class came over to Charlie and apologised for their behaviour on that day. Charlie explained how upset she had been about the whole debacle, had gone home in tears that evening, and what her son and partner had said. The three of them had a giggle at his comments and they went their separate ways. She was not teaching that class until the following Monday, so it gave time for feelings to settle down. Thursday was another day doing work away from the college and as normal Charlie went into work on Friday, early as usual, to get ready for a day of teaching and department administration.

Charlie had not even settled at her desk when she was ambushed by her line manager and told she had to go to HR immediately. Bemused, she took the lift up to the top floor.

There she met with the head of HR and her line manager who informed her that she was suspended with immediate effect. When Charlie asked what this was about, she was told that it was a number of parents had called into the college to say she had threatened their daughters with a gun. Charlie could not believe this was happening, but it was clear that there was no room for discussion or further explanation, so she returned to her desk, collected her belongings, and walked out of the college. The rest of the day at home she kept racking her brain to find some reasoning for what had happened. She was sure it could not have been the conversation 2 days earlier with the girls as they had found it all amusing and they certainly were not girls that would go running home to their mothers, and Charlie very much doubted their mothers would be even concerned. Charlie had been told that she would receive a date for a disciplinary hearing in due course and more detail could be discussed at that point. In the meantime, she was to have no contact with any staff or students at the college.

Charlie immediately obtained advice on the contact issue as a few of the lecturers in her department were close friends, including Bella who was now renting her old house from her in the same village. Luckily, she was told by ACAS that the college could not impose this restriction. A day later she received a formal letter from the college detailing her suspension and informing her that an investigation meeting was to be held in January 2016. It was not going to be a good Christmas this year. It was not about the money, she was suspended on full pay, it was about the shame, the lack of understanding and ultimately the disappointment in herself. Charlie continued with her associate tutor role at the university and decided it was best not to tell them what was going on.

At the moment she was only suspended, and she was hoping after the investigation it would all be cleared up. For the time being she was also able to complete one of the training days she had committed to for maths teachers in colleges but as this was effectively organised through a colleague at the college, she knew this would not last. It was a horrible time for her – being in limbo – and not knowing by who, how, or when her fate would be determined. Her fellow lecturer from the college Bella, who was renting their old house and had become a good friend, supported Charlie as best as she could. It was really good for Charlie to know at least one person in her professional circle was on her side and Bella really kindly agreed to attend all the meetings at the college with her as there was a right in these circumstances to take a representative to the meetings.

The investigation meeting with an apparently impartial lecturer from the college, went reasonably smoothly. Bella recorded the whole meeting on her phone, and they had prepared and taken with them a detailed account of what had happened, including the events leading up to the 'incident' in December. It was at this meeting it became clear that there were never any phone calls from the girls' parents, and the whole complaint had arisen from one of the health and beauty lecturers who had overheard parts of the conversation in which Charlie had mentioned the gun and distorted the whole conversation. Charlie and Bella asked at the meeting for statements to be obtained from the girls as it was clear they had not raised a complaint. They also requested a copy of the CCTV which apparently failed to record voices, but at least would show the body language during the conversation Charlie had been with the girls outside the front entrance of the college. The college agreed both these requests would be provided.

To both Charlie and Bella's surprise a few days later Charlie received a letter from the college informing her of a formal disciplinary meeting in February. They were so taken aback as it appeared quite clear in the investigation meeting that a formal disciplinary would not be necessary, but it dawned on both Bella and Charlie that someone obviously had it in for Charlie and were prepared to have her sacked. Charlie knew, in hindsight, it was a stupid and possibly unprofessional comment to make regarding the gun, but there was no malice, no threat, and the girls themselves made a joke of it. Charlie had been pushing her line managers and the leadership to provide more support for the maths, and the English team, as the lecturers were either off sick frequently with stress or resigning. It was a toxic environment and certainly not one of consultation to find the best way forward. Any suggestions Charlie had made were ignored, so it was looking increasingly like the college were using Charlie's mistake as an opportunity to get rid of her.

The disciplinary hearing was a joke as far as Charlie and Bella were concerned. It was clear from the outset that the principal and her cronies had made up their mind before the meeting. The lecturer who had conducted the investigation did try and put Charlie's points across, but they were not interested. Bella recorded it all again on her phone, they did not know why they were recording it but somehow it felt like a wise thing to do. They went over the same things repeatedly. They had some statements from the girls that were noticeably short and almost identical making it clear they had been told what to write but even these did not express any more information than Charlie had said herself. The cronies refused to take any notice of events leading up to the incident and just dismissed them as irrelevant.

By the time the formal letter arrived a few days later informing Charlie that she had been dismissed due to Gross Misconduct, Charlie already knew what the outcome would be. The cronies had made it quite clear in the meeting that she was going.

Charlie and Bella carried on with their research to look at the next step. Charlie was still doing her university associate tutor role, but it was not going to keep the wolf from the door. The college had stopped her doing the training consultancy work as this was through the college who had submitted the bid for the funding. This hurt Charlie more than the dismissal as she had ploughed days and days into planning and developing the course and it had cost her significantly to create the resources. It was another big setback to Charlie although she was astute enough to recognise that she should not have had THAT discussion with the girls. Charlie decided to submit an appeal against the decision. She decided it was worth a try as an appeal board would include Governors of the college so they might take a more reasoned approach. It was not about having her job back in the college, never in a million years would she walk back into that place, it was more about clearing the gross misconduct from her name.

The appeal was another farce. Bella recorded it again, but it was clear once more from the outset that their minds were made up. There was only one Governor present who had obviously been handed the details on a plate, like a done deal. Not surprisingly the appeal hearing also found in the College's favour.

In the meantime, Charlie applied for other teaching roles, but it was obvious the jungle drums had been beating and her teaching career was over.

It was fortunate that an accountant she knew was advertising for someone to help out. Charlie knew him vaguely as Henry was a colleague of Gabriel whom she had sold her client base to some 9 years earlier and she had met him a couple of times. She walked into Henry's office on spec and spent a couple of hours with him and then left him to ponder over whether he was interested. Charlie had also been interviewed for and been offered a job some twenty miles away. This role involved looking after a case load of clients and accountancy training apprenticeships in the organisation. It really played to Charlie's strengths and varied skill set and would have been remarkably interesting and could have developed well with progression through the ranks. Before Charlie could accept the offer, she also received a phone call from Henry. He was prepared to offer her a good wage on a self-employed basis to start with as this fitted around Charlie's commitments to lesson observations and teaching sessions at the University. After some discussion with Brett, Charlie decided to accept the offer from Henry. It was not a career move, but it was doing what she had been trained for most of her working life and was only five miles down the road. Henry had clients that were similar in size and nature to her own when she had her accountancy practice, although he did have considerably more clients.

One of the trainee teachers that Charlie was mentoring for the University, Michael, was training to teach business and law in further Education, and was a retired Barrister, specialising in employment law. Charlie had told him all about the debacle at the college whilst they were chatting after his lesson observation feedback. He was very keen for Charlie to submit a claim for unfair dismissal and said he would represent her for free.

Charlie spent some time discussing this with Brett and Bella and decided to go for it. The cost to submit a claim was minimal and there was a hope that it might clear her name. Being an accountant again was a lot less stressful than all the roles she had in the college, but she still felt the whole suspension and dismissal was engineered. In a way she was hoping that the college would ultimately be told they could not treat people like they had done with her.

A tribunal date was set for February 2017. Michael and Charlie, and sometimes with Bella helping, had spent hours preparing all the documents for the judge at the tribunal. Michael had prepped both Charlie and Bella on what they were and were not to say and told them to follow his lead as the direction he would take could alter according to the way the judge was responding to the representations. Charlie had never been in a tribunal, and it was nerve wracking but knowing she had Michael and Bella to support her was easing her anxiety to some extent. She need not have worried though. Michael tore strips off both the head of HR and the principal from the college and made it obvious that the whole disciplinary was at least flawed, biased, and definitely unfair. When Charlie and Bella were questioned, they were calm and factual and repeated their side of the story with eloquence and consistency. The head of HR at the college tried to claim that the secret recording transcripts should not be allowed, but the judge made it clear that there is no reason why not as the college should not have anything to hide. The outcome of the hearing was a blessing. The judge had found in Charlie's favour and ordered the college to pay her one year's salary.

Under the rules of compensation, she would have been entitled to a lot more especially due to lost future pension, but there was a limit on the maximum award. The Judge also stated that the college had ruined a good teacher's career. Charlie could now put this whole episode in her life behind her and continue building her own self-esteem and confidence in her own ability again.

Chapter nineteen – building a new career.

In the summer of 2017, the role with the university finished. This time it would not restart in the autumn term as the whole further Education and training department was being disbanded. They were merging it into the PGCE secondary team and many of her full-time colleagues that she had worked with for a few years were being made redundant if they could not be redeployed in the new set up. As far as Charlie was concerned this meant that she could take the offer of full-time employment with Henry, rather than the self-employed basis she was currently on, and would still be able to find time for the marking commitments she had been building up. To enable to meet these commitments she arranged with Henry to reduce her salary pro-rata to enable her to have more days of holiday leave. This would give her the flexibility to be marking full time from home in the busy exam season, and it suited Henry as this tended to be the quieter months for Henry and would save him money on Charlie's salary.

Things were going well for Charlie and her family. They were financially sound; Jack had completed his A levels. He achieved reasonable grades but not enough to enable him to follow his preferred career as an officer in the forces. He had also failed the Medical as the misguided GP put his juvenile arthritis down on his medical form even though the consultant had stated he had been in remission for 3 years. Jack did not want to go to university despite Charlie's dad pushing him in that direction. In the end Charlie and Jack found a level 6 apprenticeship role as a project manager within the construction industry.

This meant that the company would fund a degree whilst he was earning a good wage.

It was quite a distance to travel every day, and Jack tried both driving and travelling by train but both journeys were taking a couple of hours each way. He was enjoying the work until the university decided his grades were not enough to be enrolled on the degree programme. Charlie searched long and hard for a solution and eventually decided with Jack that he should complete a level three diploma at the college near where his work was based so he could accumulate more UCAS points and start the degree a year later.

At the start of 2018 life took a turn for the worse. Charlie and Brett had been arguing just after new year and Brett had gone up to bed incredibly early, after a bellyful of booze. By the time it got to 9pm Charlie noticed she had not heard any noise or movement from upstairs for a long time. She was completing online marking at the dining room table and said to Jack that she would go and check on Brett. She would never know what compelled her to go up. They were not exactly on speaking terms right at that point and Charlie was really upset, but something made her go and check. It was a good idea she did as Brett was lying on the bed virtually lifeless, the bathroom was a mess, and he could hardly speak. She called 999 and tried over and over again to manoeuvre Brett to a sitting position following the instructions over the phone but nothing was helping, and the call handler called an ambulance to attend. It was not long before the ambulance arrived and with difficulty the paramedics carried Brett down the stairs to the ambulance. Every time they tilted him from a sitting position to get him out of the house, his blood pressure was dropping dangerously low.

Brett was taken off in the ambulance with the blue flashing lights and Charlie followed in the car, advising Jack to stay at home and promising to ring him as soon as she had some news.

When Charlie arrived at the hospital Brett had already been taken through to urgent care and trauma and Charlie was shown to where she could sit and wait. The nurse told Charlie that Brett was critical, really poorly, and they were doing all they could. Hours later the doctor came to speak to Charlie. She had kept Jack informed although there had not been much to tell him, and it was the middle of the night. She had messaged Henry to say she would not be in work and advised Jack to do the same. The doctor explained that Brett had been given six units of blood, they had to zap him to restart his heart and other organs were critical, but he was now stable but very weak. She was allowed to see him, but he really was not able to talk, or understand what was happening. The nurses advised Charlie to go home as Brett would soon be moved to a ward for some rest. They promised they would ring if there was any change. Charlie did as she was told and drove home and went to bed. Not surprisingly she could not sleep, and it was not many hours before she was on her way back to the hospital. She had called Brett's ex-wife who was a nurse herself and told her what had happened so that she could explain it to their two older children.

Shortly after Charlie arrived at Brett's bedside the doctor came on his rounds. He explained that Brett had been in heart failure, they suspected he had an ulcer that haemorrhaged, his liver and kidneys were under stress. Then the surgeon came to join them and explained he wanted to take Brett down to theatre to stop the bleeding and needed his consent.

He explained that it was a dangerous operation because of the anaesthetic and Brett's week state, but that it might save his life. Charlie tried to explain what was happening to Brett, but he really was on another planet although she managed to get him to agree to the procedure.

The wait whilst he was in theatre seemed never ending. Charlie was on her own and could not bear to tell Jack at this time the whole truth of how serious it all was. Eventually Brett was returned to the ward. The operation had gone well, and they had clipped the ulcer that was causing the issue. When he came round from the anaesthetic Brett still did not seem to understand the full picture and it emerged during the next hours that they had to treat him for hepatic encephalopathy. They were hopeful that there was no permanent damage and as he quietly went back to sleep Charlie made her way home. She had to give an update to Jack, Brett's ex and their close friends and family who were all worried but eventually after Jack had gone to bed Charlie collapsed in an exhausted heap on her bed.

Brett spent the next week in hospital recovering and improving. It had been a big wake-up call for him that he had to change his life. When he was eventually allowed home, he was medicated for all his conditions, but he decided he would no longer drink alcohol or smoke. The doctors had warned him that if he wanted to live, he needed to stop and he took it seriously. He spent some time recuperating at home before going back to work on the coaches.

By Easter of 2018 Jack was unhappy in his job as a trainee project manager. He said that he had been watching what the more experienced managers did and it was not what he wanted to be doing in 5 years' time.

Charlie explained to him that he was still so young and not to continue if it was not going to work. He had his whole life and career ahead of him and did not need to be stuck in a job he hated for the long-haul. She also told him a proviso that if he quit, he had to find something else to earn some money and be able to make the car payments for the new car he had bought.

With this in mind, Jack resigned from his job and was successful in securing a post at a local DIY chain whilst he looked at what else he wanted to do.

Life for the three of them continued fairly smoothly after that. They spent time with good friends, carried on being satisfied with their jobs, and enjoying holidays in Spain. Charlie's dad was doing really well, and it was great having him living next door. Jack had decided to apply for a new job, a career with a special police force, and had been successful in his application. It was definitely more along the lines of his career aspirations although it did involve a lengthy period of time staying away from home for training. Charlie missed him terribly but did not want to make a big deal of it for fear of upsetting the balance. It was during this training that Charlie realised her son suffered from exam anxiety. When he was home at weekends, he sometimes had to revise for modules of the training course and it had become apparent that even though he knew the subject matter really well, he could go to pieces when he was in the actual exams. After much research Charlie found him some herbal tablets to try to relieve the anxiety. To her surprise they worked like a dream, and he was coming out in the top section of the class in the frequent exams on the training course.

She only wished she had known about this a few years earlier. In hindsight it was apparent that the same pattern had been happening with his GCSE's and A levels. He clearly knew the topics, had good course and classwork and good predicted grades, but something went wrong when he sat the actual formal examinations. There was no point in dwelling on the past as Jack was now flourishing and his grades had been good enough to get him where he wanted. Once he finished his training Jack was posted permanently to Whitby, and Brett spent a lot of time with him helping him find suitable accommodation to rent.

Charlie would have loved to be more involved, but the timing was really bad. She was working full time and exam marking early mornings, evenings, and weekends.

Chapter twenty - Living the dream.

After years of being really good friends and working with Gretchen and spending lots of time together both at home and on holidays with the kids, talk had been ongoing both drunk and sober about the dream of a new life in Spain. It had never really been Charlie's dream retirement plan. She had constantly discussed moving to Anglesey or North Wales with Gretchen, Grunter, and Brett, but every time she brought it up, she was outvoted, and reasons galore were given for not staying in the UK. Charlie knew that if they could downsize and buy something much cheaper but with more land, be mortgage free, her and Brett could survive on her marking income and any other bits of part time work they wanted until they reached state pension age – which had unfortunately moved to 67 for both her and Brett now.

The others argued that the weather was better in Spain, the relaxed lifestyle, Brett said his arthritis would be better and so on and so on. In the end after countless efforts to show them all lovely suitable places in the areas Charlie wanted in North Wales or Anglesey, she gave up and went along with the idea of moving to Spain. They began looking into the details and finer points of relocating. There would be the issue that Brexit was looming – it was now mid-2020 and Brexit was due to kick in at the end of the year. There were plans to be made for removals, transporting the animals – Charlie and Brett had three cats and a Doberman, and Gretchen 2 dogs, making sure their son Jack was sorted and settled, selling the beautiful house they had built, and sorting Spanish residency before the Brexit deadline.

At this point in her career Charlie was working full time in an accountancy practice but Brett had recently finished working on the coaches. It was not that he could not work, but his boss had moved the coaches into Bridlington so the extra cost of fuel to get in and out to work four times a day for the school runs was not worth it for the wages he was getting. He was still available for any day trips that were needed but they had been lacking. In addition, Covid was at its height in the UK and across the country. That summer, Charlie, Brett, Grunter, and Gretchen, along with Gretchen's eldest daughter Chole and her family, had booked a villa in Mijas Costa already, and as long as all the Covid requirements were adhered to it was still to go ahead. Charlie and Gretchen were on furlough from work at this time, and the others were in essential industries which meant they would not have to isolate when they returned as long as they tested negative for Covid.

So, the holiday went ahead. Charlie' son Jack was not able to join them as his work would not allow him to travel with the covid restrictions, but Gretchen's younger daughter Scarlett and Brett's lad Noah were able to fly over for part of the 2-week holiday. The 2 weeks were lovely with lots of sun and swimming and delicious meals and days out. The 2 couples spent some days travelling around various areas getting a feel for them as had been suggested by Naomi, the lady who was helping them with their planned move. Naomi ran a business from Costa del Sol to help with all the administrative and practical sides of people from the UK moving to Spain. Charlie had taken to her when she had done zoom meetings from the UK, and they had decided to go with Naomi to help them with their move.

Naomi had agreed to do it all for them as the family package rather than 2 couples, so this saved some money on their fees, and most of Naomi's money was earned from the commission she earned from the estate agent when a house in Spain was purchased. They travelled round and looked at various towns around the Mijas area. Moving slightly East of Malaga was cheaper in places like Coin and Alhaurin, and even as far as Vinuela. It was difficult even at this early stage to find an area they could all agree on, but they kept on looking. Ideally, they all wanted to be near Mijas, but it might end up being too costly for what they needed. The most suitable layout would be a house split into two parts with 2 or 3 bedrooms in each part, a lounge and kitchen in each, and its own swimming pool and garage. This was looking like a pricey option.

After the holiday and they had all returned to the UK detailed plans were started. By this time Charlie had accepted that they were moving to Spain. The plans were in motion, and it was decided that Brett and Gretchen would travel to Spain in the October of 2020 and stay in a hotel. Whilst they were there they were to meet up with Naomi or Belinda her associate and visit potential places for them all to rent whilst they searched for a house to buy. The bookings were made for the trip and the plans carried on. The two houses – Charlie and Brett's, and Grunter and Gretchen's were to go on the market at the same time or just after they returned from the rental property trip. Grunter and Charlie had to continue working as they had no holiday left to take and could not afford the isolation time off on return from Spain either.

Before all of this started Charlie' father had decided to put his house on the market.

When Brett and Charlie built their beautiful house in her dad's garden, they had a semi-detached house right in the village. Bella and George, close friends of Charlie, had been renting the house for a few years but had decided to move to the neighbouring town to rent and were moving out. As it was smaller than dad's house and near to the train station and village amenities Dad thought it would be much better for him. So, it was decided, they agreed a price for the semi and dad's house went on the market.

The main problem with dad's house being on the market was the poor state of repair into which it had got. The house was built in art deco style, all white and with a flat roof that Charlie and her friends had spent years on when she was younger. It would be sad to see it go but it was riddled with damp as the flat roof had been leaking for years. This was despite her dad's attempts with his friend to solve some of the problems. It was a joke in the village that it was the house with the crane and the shed on the roof. It was clear that any buyer would have to be in for serious renovations or even the possibility of knocking it down and rebuilding. This would not be a problem but as it had a frontage of nearly three of the opposite houses on the street, the general feeling from the neighbours was that anything would be fine as long as it was not flats. This would have altered the feel of the street – it was not a snobbish thing, they just would not have fitted with the area at all, or the beautiful house that Charlie had built in the side garden area.

There were a number of viewers that thought the job was too big to take on, and surprisingly to them all, no builders viewing. Soon a couple in their thirty's viewed it.

The husband had grown up in the village and wanted to move back. He ran a roofing supplies company so knew his stuff regarding the work that was to be done. They made an offer which Charlie' dad accepted and the preparations for the move began.

These preparations were set to be a lot harder than Charlie could ever have envisioned. There was years and years of accumulated belongings in the large house and the garage. The problem was not getting rid of it but getting her dad to decide what he wanted to keep and wanted to take. In the garage there were large engineering machines and precision tools. Dad agreed to Charlie's son Jack trying to sell some of these on Facebook and some good success was made here. Brett and some others took some of the smaller items and in the end the scrap metal merchants that were in the village took a lot. Dad and Charlie had tried various colleges and workshop training centres to give the equipment to, but no-one was interested, and it was such a shame. At least some of the better equipment went to some good homes. The man who bought the milling machine was over the moon with his find.

Inside the house was no better. Charlie's friend Titiana photographed and advertised a lot of the ornaments that had been Charlie's mums, and some of the items of furniture that were not needed. It was not as though Charlie did not know how to do it, but Titiana had offered, and Charlie jumped at the chance. Titiana had sold lots of things online and was much better at it. Charlie went through each room in the house emptying cupboards and units and putting everything in the middle of the floor so Dad could sort it into a keep pile and a throw pile.

As the weeks went on and completion dates got nearer and nearer, there was extraordinarily little sorting being done and Charlie was getting increasingly frustrated. Then alongside this, her friends moved out of the house in the village and Charlie and Brett went round to check it was all ok for when dad moved in. Unfortunately, the smell of cat pee was overwhelming when they entered the house. Bella and George had three house cats and it seemed as though they had decided the carpet was a cat litter in some of the rooms. There was no option but to rip out the carpets throughout and replace with new ones.

Jack and Brett did the horrible job of ripping out the old smelly ones. They also had to put some special biological treatment on the floorboards in various places to get rid of the smell where it had soaked right through. Eventually it was all sorted. The house also needed a thorough clean and various other bits sorting and the new carpets were ordered after deciding on a colour with Dad. It was one thing ticked off the list and the house was ready to move in to.

In the meantime, the clearance of Dad's old house continued. Charlie rang her brother Stewart who lived in Scotland and said he was going to have to come down and help as she was getting nowhere with Dad, and they just kept falling out. The skip on the drive was only half full and the house had little less in it than when they started. Stewart could take a few days off work and came down to help. He was ruthless – if dad had not made a quick decision or wanted to keep something for no obvious reason it went in the skip. Beds and everything were going out of the windows upstairs and skips were taken away full and replaced a number of times.

It worked though; the house was finally down to the bare essentials that Dad needed to take with him. They decided he should move before completion date to make life easier, so a local firm was booked, and Dad was moved to Charlie's old house.

Completion eventually went through. The house that Charlie was selling to her dad was a long leasehold and his dozy solicitors made a meal out of the payment of £11 of ground rent which was owed. It was a strange arrangement for the ground rent – as it was a semi the lady in the other half had always paid the £1 a year for both properties, but since she had died the new owners had not paid any. Dad's solicitors would not accept, even from their client, her dad, that there was no issue and that the ground rent had now been paid by Charlie and just to continue. It was funny when Charlie thought about this whole episode in her life. They say moving house is one of the most stressful occasions – she thought moving your parent should be way above this in the list of stresses.

Once Dad was settled it was time to start back with the plans for Spain. The trip for Brett and Gretchen was booked for October, and the paperwork for Naomi and her team was being put together. There was a lot of information that was going to be needed for the Spanish residency. Charlie put her beautiful house on the market. They were hopeful of a decent price as the market was fairly buoyant, but a slight drawback was that a builder had created a small cul-de-sac of four houses near to the bridge over the railway in the village, and these were being marketed around a comparable price. Charlie did her research and planning with a view to having some ammunition if she received a low offer.

She worked out the square meterage of these new houses compared to her own, and even though they were new builds that apparently people liked more, her own house was more than double the area with a larger garden and more space and light everywhere. That was without including the loft that although they had created to be a fully functional room, had only ever been carpeted and a spare bed put up there as a den for Jack and his friends. Overall, Charlie was confident her house was well worth the value being asked.

Gretchen and Brett went on their trip to Spain. Over the few days they were there they looked at many houses, many of which were nowhere near suitable due to layout or more often location. One in particular was down a treacherous and bendy road around the mountain edge. Another one had a dead bird in one of the rooms, and another looked like it had not been cleaned in a century. In the end they went for one in a quaint Spanish town called Competa, up in the hills behind Torrox and Nerja. The viewings had been a revelation as they realised that because the location of properties is not revealed to potential buyers until they want to view, a lot of time is wasted travelling to areas that do not have suitable access. Also, because floor plans and measurements are rarely included on the selling details, the rooms can be small or poorly laid out when the viewing is eventually made.

When Gretchen and Brett returned, the 2 couples decided to go with the Competa house. It had four bedrooms and an enclosed paved and gravel garden and the whole of the underneath of the house was a large garage that could be used to store the furniture from the two houses. The plan was to rent for 6 months whilst they looked for something to buy.

In order to secure the house Charlie had to pay a deposit and they all had to sign the rental contract. The owners and/or agents insisted on a 3-month deposit as they said it was the norm with animals involved in case of damage, so Charlie sorted all of this for the group. Next was to get on with the house sales in the UK and start the marketing of them.

They had viewers fairly quickly, and the third one round, another couple in their thirties with young children, made a full price offer which she accepted. The market was having a boom despite Covid being at its peak. The house had gone on the market at the end of September 2020 and the offer was accepted mid-October. The planned completion date was 3 December 2020. It was all happening so quickly, and Charlie and Brett rarely had time to think. Charlie was still working full time at the accountants and was in a busy marking period so was really under pressure. In addition to all of this, she felt the need to make sure everything was in place and arranged for her son Jack as he was renting in Whitby at his new place of work.

The plans for Spain needed to be sorted. This included how to get the families, furniture, and animals all the way to Costa del Sol. Rather a lot to be sorted in a short space of time, but as usual Charlie took on the challenge with full gusto and enthusiasm. She had never been one to turn down a challenge.

Gretchen was in charge of finding transport for the animals, getting quotes and information from various pet transport organisations. Gretchen and Grunter had two small white fluffy dogs, tampons as Brett called them. Charlie and Brett had a Doberman and three cats, so it was a big challenge to arrange transport.

The initial plan was for Brett and maybe Grunter to drive over in the left-hand drive Ford F150 that Brett had bought, and Gretchen and Charlie were to fly over. Somehow, and she was not sure why, Charlie ended up speaking to the pet transport companies. The one that was favoured really worried her because it was an estimated time of 4 days to get the animals to Competa. As they had already been working on routes, distances, and timings for the boys' journey, this seemed like an extraordinary amount of time to Charlie for the animals. She managed to find out it was because they stopped on route both in the UK and across Europe to pick up other animals that were booked to be transported, and she was not happy with this.

Charlie took things in hand herself and started looking at the possibility of travelling via a motorhome. She knew this would mean her driving all the way, as Gretchen was very lacking in confidence with driving, but Charlie was prepared to rise to this challenge regardless. The first idea was to look at purchasing a second-hand motorhome, so Brett and Charlie began their search. They saw a lovely small motorhome in Bridlington but by the time they pondered over whether it was the right one at the right price, it had been sold to another buyer. With this one out of the picture, they continued looking for more options. They went to see a much larger one further afield. Brett test drove it but Charlie, and eventually Brett, had to rule it out on two main counts. Firstly, it was exceptionally large, more like a small coach, and Charlie did not think she would be able to drive it, especially on the wrong side of the road. The main reason was that the owner had made no attempt to clean it up and used it for fishing trips. It completely stank of dead fish throughout the whole motorhome.

Charlie hated the smell of fish anyway – even to the point of holding her nose through the fish market in Doncaster. Maybe it was something to do with the fact that her parents liked kippers at least once a week and they stunk the house out when she was younger.

Having ruled out this one, there was little on the market. Covid was raging and staycations were all the range, causing prices of motorhomes to rise and availability to reduce. Charlie had to think of another plan. She googled and researched the possibility of hiring a motorhome to drive over. Every single company she contacted did not do one way hire for motorhomes and she was hitting the same brick wall over and over again. Eventually, Charlie found a company in the Czech Republic that would do one way hire. She could not believe her luck as this company were prepared to drive the motorhome all the way over to Hull, and then collect it in Competa in Spain. They were amazing on the phone and Charlie discussed the time period with them, bearing in mind covid restrictions for travelling were in full force and the company's drivers had to get home from Hull and to Competa accordingly. After discussing this as an option with the intrepid travellers they decided this was the best course of action and the deposit was paid. Charlie found this scary as in the back of her mind she thought it could all be a scam.

In the meantime, Charlie was also had frequent video calls and email correspondence with Naomi in Spain. She was key to their move and as well as sorting the rental villa they had previously selected was going to help them gain the residency and eventually find somewhere to buy. They were all aware that the timescale was going to be tight as Brexit was looming. It was widely understood in the expat world that if you had your residency application in before Brexit at the end of December 2020, you would still be applying under the old and easier rules. Nevertheless, there was a need to gather extensive documentary evidence of ID, address, bank statements, rental agreements and so on, such that when they all arrived in Spain the residency paperwork could be processed as quickly as possible and submitted.

The removals company also had to be arranged. After speaking to a number of different companies Charlie decided to ask for a quote from a Doncaster firm. They also had a base near Malaga so made regular trips to the Costa Del Sol. The firm visited both Charlie's and Gretchen's house and gave a quote and availability. Luckily, the dates tied in with the ones that Charlie's buyer wanted to complete so the removals were booked, and the motorhome deposit paid, and dates confirmed. Suddenly Charlie realised that this was really going to happen. She explained to her boss at the accountants and agreed a finish date. The plan was that Brett would get on with the packing and sorting as a considerable amount of stuff to be moved was his in the garage, along with a motorbike that needed taking over to Spain. Charlie arranged to finish work the Friday before the completion date the following Thursday. She hoped that this would give her enough time to finish packing and get everything sorted for the massive move. Her boss still could not believe she was doing the move and expressed doubts, that Charlie was much, much later to realise she should have paid more attention to. But she was swept up in the excitement of it all and as usual loved the whole organisation thing and took the pressure she was under in her stride. It was what she had always thrived on and drove her to make achievements.

One thing that still had to be done was to get passports and rabies injections for the dog and three cats. When Charlie asked for a quote from their own vets it was astronomical – nearly £1000 in total. Gretchen had two small dogs that were also going with them, and she had found the animal sanctuary near where she lived would provide the relevant documents and vaccinate the dogs for a much cheaper price, so Charlie booked all her animals into the same place. Charlie's friend Abigail said she would help Charlie take them as it was twenty miles away. The two girl cats could share a cat box, with the larger tom in a box on his own, and the dog in the boot of her car. They had barely reached three miles from Charlie's house when Dexter the Doberman decided he did not like being in the boot on his own. Charlie had no dog guard in her car, and he crawled over the head rests onto the back seat. Charlie suspected it was because he was protective of his cats who were making a racket on the back seat in their cat boxes. It could have been an utter disaster as at the moment he decided to climb over and cause mayhem – there was no room for him on the seat with the boxes – Charlie was on a busy dual carriageway. Luckily, she found a place to pullover and Charlie and Abigail carefully extracted the cats in their boxes from the back seat of the car and relocated them to the boot. This meant Dexter could stay on the back seat, but Abigail had to keep her arm firmly positioned in the gap between the two front seats in case he mounted an attempt to get in the front. Eventually they arrived and had all the paperwork and injections completed. They did the same arrangement on the way home, but it was an extremely stressful experience and Charlie and Abigail just collapsed with relief when they finally had the animals all safely back home.

The days were whizzing past and before she knew it, it was time to complete the final arrangements. The motorhome was being delivered on the Sunday before the big move on the Thursday as it was in the middle of the Covid pandemic, and this fitted with the flights and arrangement the driver from Prague could make. This was great for Charlie, it gave time to get it all packed and loaded, and ready for the animals, and it also meant that she could have some practice driving in it. To this point, Charlie had not even considered what a big undertaking she was taking on. The drive was around 1600 miles and was going to take quite a few days plus sleeping time. It was already clear that Gretchen had no intention of doing any of the driving, Grunter was staying in Doncaster until they had a buyer for their house, and he could finish work, and Brett would be driving the F150 pickup over to Spain.

It was a relief that Charlie's son Jack arrived to help his dad sort out packing the garage. If he had not had, Charlie doubted it would ever have been done at the speed Brett was getting through it. Once she had finished work on the Friday, Charlie spent the weekend packing bits and pieces, putting together an emergency come overnight bag, and starting to put her clothes in boxes and the spare suitcase she had. Charlie had never been big on clothes and shoes, as her friends and Brett would laughingly agree to, so most of the space in the large packing boxes she had made up was taken up by bedding and towels. They were all not sure what would be provided in the rental house in Competa when they got there, it was like stepping into a complete unknown.

At the opposite end of the spectrum was the packing for Brett's clothes and belongings from upstairs.

There were already three large boxes that had been filled, plus a couple of large suitcases and more to do. It was complete role reversal from the stereotype woman and her clothes and Charlie found it amusing. Doing the upstairs packing and clothes was not too long a task, with the exception of trying to get Brett to decide what could go on the removal van, and what he needed to keep in the motorhome or pickup in case of any delays in the main delivery which was scheduled to arrive about a week after the friends arrived in Competa. In the meantime, Jack had to sort what he wanted to keep from his bedroom and 'his' dining room. He had moved out in the September that year to live in Whitby. Much of the year 2000 he had been on training and preparation courses over the country for his new job and had chosen Whitby as the place where he was going to be located. Jack and Brett had looked at quite a few rental properties and Jack finally settled on one he was happy with. It was fully furnished so he arranged with his good friend John that John would store the items Jack wanted to keep until such time as he could retrieve them. It was fortunate that John's parents had a furniture business which they ran from an old mill nearby, so there was plenty of room for storage. The young men arranged to take all of Jacks bedroom furniture, a few personal items, and the desk and computer setup he had in the dining room for his gaming. There were also some other odd bits of furniture he chose from around the house, and packed up spare pans and other kitchen items, as well as a fair number of tools and other stuff from the garage that were not going to Spain. There was also Jack's motorbike. Following in his dad's footsteps he was a petrolhead. The motorbike was not going to the mill but was to be kept in the garage at his Grandads house in the village, until such time as he had somewhere to put it himself.

After tackling the upstairs and helping as much as she could with Jack's stuff and him deciding what was going where, Charlie thought she had better start on the downstairs of the house. She was fully aware that apart from a couple of boxes with ornaments and other special bits, Brett had not got far at all with the packing, and it was a daunting task to complete. She had refused point blank to have anything to do with the garage or sheds. As far as she was concerned, they did not need any of that stuff taking all the way to Spain anyway.

The motorhome arrived on Sunday as planned and the excellent rental company driver went through everything from Ad-blue, to using the heating in detail with Brett. Charlie hoped that he was going to remember it all because her brain was boggled. Brett was deeply knowledgeable about all types of vehicles and caravans, having had many over his life, so she secretly knew there would be no problem. Then it was time to tackle the set-up for the animals in the caravan. A childhood friend of Charlie, Sophie, had recently sold her parents' house after they had both passed on. Sophie's mum had a massive blanket box and Brett and Charlie had been given free access to this to take what they needed. The motorhome had a U-shaped seating area at the end that would pull out into beds. They did not need this for the journey as there was also a drop-down bed behind the driver and passenger seats, and other smaller seating benches. This would give plenty of space for Charlie, Gretchen, and Brett when they needed to sleep on the journey.

The plan was to set up the three cat cages they had bought along the back seat of the U-shape, and Dexter the Dobermans cage on the seat on the left-hand side, and the other cages for Gretchen's 2 dogs on the right-hand side. She prayed they would all get on well enough for the journey, but at least this way, she knew they were all with their owners should they get into distress.

Jack took on the task of setting up the animal area. He made a fabulous job of it, not that Charlie thought he would not. After securing all the blankets and other bedding items from Sophie's all over the fabric surfaces of the fixed settees to prevent any animal damage, he used cable ties to wire the doors of the three cat cages open, and then wired all three of them together to form a long L shaped tunnel. This meant there was enough for one to have a cat litter in, and the other two to have room for the three cats and their food. Charlie knew they needed at least this much space as even though they were supposedly brother and two sisters, the cats did not always see eye to eye. Jack even put split bin bags underneath the blankets under the cages, just in case of any mishaps.

By the time he had finished all of this and over the next day or two, Charlie sorted the clothes and personal toiletries and belongings into three different piles. Firstly, were small bags for her and Brett for the journey. Things like toothbrushes, spare knickers and medicines and a change or two of clothes. The second pile was for travelling with them in the motorhome. Some of this was all the animal feed and paraphernalia for the journey. They decided that best place to put all the animal stuff was in the shower. The motorhome had a separate small shower cubicle and separate toilet, it was really well equipped.

They had specifically requested they did not want the push bikes as part of the deal as these were included. The motorhome also had an exceptionally large boot across the whole of the back end, which was accessed through a side door. The suitcases, cat boxes, and other items they would need for their first week or two in Spain were all to be stored in here. These were items that Charlie and Brett, and the animals, might need before the removals company arrived in Competa.

By now it was Tuesday, and Charlie had not made much progress on packing the downstairs of the house. The boys had not yet finished the garage either and the skip they had ordered was nearly full. As well as sorting out all the house move and everything else that went along with relocating to Spain, Charlie had been trying to sell surplus stuff on Facebook since the plans were finalised. Brett had kept the slate bed of a pool table they had outside in their last house in Auckley, the party house. The slate had moved house with them when the woodwork of the table had decayed past repair, and Brett always planned to make the slate into something. There was no way Charlie was going to let this go to Spain with them so that was sold on social media, along with the outside garden furniture, Brett's dad's record player, and various bits and pieces. The biggest sale Charlie had made over the few weeks of selling was to a second-hand record buyer. She had a hundred or so vinyl LP's and nearly as many singles. The collection was records Charlie had bought before the advent of the CD, with additions from her ex-husband as he never took them when they split up, and other records that Brett had kept from his divorce. Overall, after looking at each record carefully in Charlie's house, the record buyer offered her a couple of hundred for the whole collection.

Charlie was fully aware that some of the albums were worth something significant, but she did not have the time or willpower to check each record in detail, photograph, and list them all. She also knew that a lot of the favourites had been played frequently at parties after too many drinks had been consumed and suspected there may be a scratch or two on some of the vinyl.

It was too late to continue with the packing now. It was Tuesday, and they had arranged that today Charlie would drive the motorhome to Gretchen and Grunter's in Auckley so that Charlie could have a practice before they set off on the long journey. There was a second reason for the journey as well, to allow Gretchen to pack in the motorhome her doggy stuff and clothes and toiletries for the first 2 weeks. This all had to be sorted today, as the removals company was scheduled to pick up the next day in Auckley, all of Gretchen and Grunter's furniture and so on that they were taking and then go to Skipsea later on the Wednesday to load as much as they could from Charlie's house. They would return on the Thursday, completion day, to get the rest.

Chapter twenty-one – the move is really happening.

By midday, Charlie and Brett were ready to set off for Auckley. Brett explained all the controls in the motorhome to Charlie. She had driven automatics a number of times, but never anything quite so big and left-hand drive. After a few moments doubting herself, she pulled herself together, knowing she had an excellent instructor and mentor sat by her side. As she pulled off from the house; Brett had reversed it off the path for her; Charlie realised the enormity of the challenge she was about to take on. Her first mistake was not to use the exterior mirrors enough which was duly commented on. There was no back window in the motorhome, so the side view mirrors had to be relied on. Although Charlie considered herself a reasonably good driver and used her side mirrors in the car on motorways all the time, she was not lorry or coach trained like Brett and the new way of looking behind you all the time took some mastering. It also took her most of the journey to be able to feel confident in judging the width of the vehicle when driving through country lanes and overtaking on the motorway.

They managed to arrive at Auckley with no disasters and Charlie pulled up the 7.5 by 2.5 metre vehicle outside. Gretchen and Grunter and their daughters came out to see them straight away and everyone piled in and had a good look round. Charlie explained the animal set up that Jack had done for them all, and they all went inside the house to discuss the final plans and have a general chit chat.

Gretchen had all her belongings and dog stuff ready to be loaded, so after a while of chatting full of excitement they loaded and stored the remaining luggage and necessities and said their goodbyes. Charlie was very relieved that Brett said he would drive home.

That was it now, there was only one more day and the day after was completion day. They were leaving their beautiful home that they had lovingly self-built. They had both put everything they had into the house and had enjoyed it immensely for nearly 8 years. But the decision had been made. A lovely couple with a young daughter and a baby were moving in and would hopefully appreciate the care and detail that had gone into the house. It was not finished with stupidly expensive taps or kitchen and bathroom fittings. As with her own preference for clothes, the fittings and fixtures had been chosen for practicality, reasonableness of price, and pleasing appearance. The garden was the main area that they had not paid much attention to, hardly worth it with a large dog and the subsoil being pure sand despite the tonnes of good topsoil and turf on top, but the new people could make it something spectacular if they wanted. They had also never done much with the loft room. The intention had always been to put in a proper staircase, and Charlie and Brett knew exactly where it would go, but it had never been necessary. There was only the two of them now Jack had virtually moved out, and four bedrooms was more than enough. Even though all these thoughts passed through Charlie's mind she pushed them to one side and carried on with the agreed plan. There were, however, moments in the years to come, that she looked back on these times and wondered why she did not respond more forcibly to her doubts and stop the entire process dead in its tracks.

The day before completion arrived. Charlie's usual calm and collected self seemed to have left her to go on holiday or something. Gretchen rang first thing to say the removals company had arrived at her house to start. Charlie's childhood and lifelong friend Abigail was arriving to help with the enormity of packing the lounge and dining room and the immense amount of stuff in the kitchen and its cupboards. She was getting hysterical with Brett when she was looking in cupboards and on shelves as he had hardly packed anything except a few ornaments here and there. Charlie might have been over-reacting as by this time she was panicking. The removals company were due at their house in a few hours and even though they had the rest of the evening before the removals men came back on the next morning, completion day, she was cross with herself for not keeping a tighter check on things. But then Brett was supposed to be an adult, and it was his idea to move to Spain in the first place as far as Charlie was concerned.

When Abigail arrived, she got straight into the kitchen. There were loads of cupboards and equally enormous amounts of the usual kitchen pots, pans, gadgets and so on to pack, wrapping in the tissue paper and boxing up. Charlie and Brett's neighbours, actually across the road, and particularly good friends came over and ended up taking home boxes and boxes of tins, jars, and other food out of the cupboards, as well as the contents of the freezer and most of the fridge that did not warrant throwing away.

At one point during the packing process that day, the removals company had arrived, and as well as packing Charlie was directing them to what needed to be moved into the removals van.

Jack's friend arrived and the two young men loaded up his van with the belongings Jack was going to store at John's mill before he could buy his own place. It all suddenly got too much for Charlie and she broke down into a complete mess, crying her eyes out on the floor in the lounge. Jack and Abigail tried to console her as best as they could and after a while, she pulled herself together for the task in hand. The original plan was to get as much as possible shifted into the removal's lorry, with only the beds and essentials to be collected on completion day, the next morning. The plan was then to run round for a quick clean as much as possible before the keys were handed over. It was looking increasingly like a cleaning spree was not going to be possible. Later that afternoon Abigail left, promising to come back in the morning and continue helping. Once Charlie, Brett and Jack had stuffed a takeaway tea down them, Jack had walked Dexter on the sandhills, they all flopped into their beds exhausted.

They awoke early to their alarms. The removals lorry was due to arrive around ten to collect the last belongings for transport to Spain. Not long after they were up the optician rang to say Charlie's new varifocal glasses were ready to be collected. She had been nagging them for over a week as they were late. Her last eye test showed that her distance vision had deteriorated and although not essential it was advisable for her to wear the glasses for driving. She had used a separate pair of distance glasses to read things like the TV guide on the TV for a while and had reading glasses for years. With the long journey ahead in the monster vehicle, and on the wrong side of the road, Charlie knew she had to collect the new glasses. Luckily, Abigail had arrived early and said she would whizz Charlie to the opticians in the next town to collect them.

One of the things that had to be sorted before they left had been both her and Brett's cars. They were both on PCP, so a settlement arrangement and collection had to be arranged and now both cars were gone.

The glasses were duly collected and by the time the two friends got back to the house the removals men had cleared the upstairs and were working on the last few areas. Unfortunately, the buyers pulled up outside in the middle of this. There was nothing Charlie could do to speed things along. She checked her emails for news from her solicitor but there was none, so she got straight on the phone. The solicitor she used for this move, and the sale of the old house to her dad, was the best she had ever known. She was efficient and quick with communications, and it was in the middle of the worst of the pandemic. Her solicitor told her they had received the funds from the buyer and completion had taken place. She advised Charlie to check her bank account to see if they had arrived. Charlie did and was pleased to see that she was now cash rich, at least until they bought in Spain. She transferred a large amount to Jack straight away in order to help him get his foot on the property ladder, it was probably also a form of guilt payment Charlie thought as she sent the money; she could not help the feelings she had at the thought of leaving him.

Charlie had already typed and printed a letter for the new owners telling them where everything was and how everything worked. She had put the letter in a new home card and explained where there was a box with every single instruction, guarantee, and even the original plans for the house were left. Then she had to speak to the waiting buyers. It was not a difficult conversation, although they were getting a bit impatient, and understandably so.

Charlie pulled herself into a calm and collected state and went over to them in the car with all the spare keys apart from one set they might need in the next hour or so. She explained how sorry she was that they were so behind with everything and that they were expecting it would be completed later in the afternoon. She gave them the card with the letter in and explained that under the circumstances they were not able to do the cleaning they had hoped to do. Abigail had done as much as she could, so it was quite reasonable, but not the thorough deep clean they had planned. The lovely couple who was moving into Charlie's dream home seemed suitably placated for now.

In the next few hours things started to come together. The removals lorry was full and prepared to set off. The three cats, Oscar, Missy, and Cappy were transferred from the bedroom, where they had been shut in for the last half day, using the cat carriers into the cages in the motorhome. Dexter the Doberman was loaded into the motorhome after his business and Charlie, Brett and Jack put their remaining possessions into the cars and motorhome they were all leaving separately in. They said their sad byes to the house and wished the new owner's good luck and to call if they needed anything. They parked the motorhome, Brett's pickup, and Jack's golf at the end of the road. The last few bits were tidied away into storage or safely in the various vehicles and before they could have their emotional parting goodbyes, a couple from a house further down came running to the motorhome. They wanted to say goodbye to Oscar, the boy cat. Charlie and Brett had found out a few months earlier that Oscar had two homes. They had seen him wandering down a few houses to the end of the road and turning right but did not know where he went.

Sometimes he took a while to come back when he was shouted if Charlie was worried when had not seen him much that day. One particular day Brett was shouting Oscar outside the front of the house whilst walking down to the junction. Oscar appeared on the corner of the pavement followed by a man with a South African accent. It turned out that this man said he was their cat and was called Hunter. After a brief chat Brett made it clear he was his cat, called Oscar and was microchipped. The two men laughed about it and the man told Brett tales about Oscar in his house and summer house in the garden.

The man and his wife were distraught about Oscar moving away as they must have heard on the grapevine in the small village that Brett and Charlie were going to Spain.

Once the neighbour had said her goodbyes to Oscar, it was time for Charlie and Brett to head off to Auckley to collect Gretchen and her two little dogs and start their big adventure together. Charlie bawled her eyes out as she said goodbye to her son, Jack, and Brett struggled to control his tears. Jack was crying as they had last hugs, and all climbed into their respective vehicles. They followed in convoy until they recached the motorway junction where Jack headed off up the motorway to go north, and Charlie followed Brett down another motorway. By now it was late afternoon and quite a dark and rainy December day. It was not the best conditions for driving in a large left-hand vehicle you were not accustomed to, all the way to Southern Spain.

Chapter twenty-two – the mammoth journey

It was not long before they were pulling up outside Gretchen and Grunter's house in Auckley. There was little room for parking outside the house as there was a small communal grassed area. Brett pulled his pickup onto the grassed area whilst Charlie parked the motorhome behind. They had to get to Dover for the ferry in the early hours of Friday morning. They had booked a flexi-fare which meant they could get an earlier or later ferry but were aiming for the 3am ferry. Gretchen put her final belongings into the motorhome and loaded the two small dogs into the pre-prepared cages. All the dogs were to travel in the cages and just be let out for walks and food and so on. Charlie had no intention of letting the cats out in case they escaped, but they were fully set up in their cage tunnel with room for all three, the food and water, and cat litter tray. There was not too much distress from Gretchen and Grunter's dogs and the cats when they were all in the confinement of the motorhome together. Dexter the Doberman was allowed out to have a wee before they finalised the last bits of loading.

In the week before departure Jack had ordered some walkie talkies for them to use on the journey so Brett showed Gretchen how to use hers as she would be the passenger with Charlie. Brett had his set up in the pickup on the best hands-free arrangement they could do.

Gretchen's two girls and husband were there to see them off. Brett turned the motorhome round for Charlie in the small dead-end cul-de-sac, and after more goodbyes and tears, the three travellers, Charlie, Gretchen, and Brett, set off with the animals on board.

As Charlie pulled off down the street, she was looking in her side mirrors as instructed and bumped up the kerb, luckily not hitting anything in the process. Then she had to stop. She noticed that Brett was not following, and it transpired that the pick-up, despite its enormous wheels and tyres, had got stuck in the muddy grass outside the houses. It was soon behind her, with a lot of laughter all round, and Brett pulled in the lead, and they set off on their journey. Without any stops or hold-ups, the 300-mile journey to the Port was due to take over 5 hours. They had plenty of time according to the plans, and Charlie pressed the point with Brett that she wanted to tootle along down the motorway and keep well within the speed limit, as it was dark, raining, and all new to her driving the monstrous vehicle. She could not think about the possibility of the two vehicles getting separated as she had not even looked at the route they were taking. Charlie had full confidence that this side of things was all in hand by Brett, he was after all a coach and HGV driver, and would know the best routes to take.

Charlie and Gretchen chatted away as they made progress on the first motorway. They laughed at the state of the clothes they were wearing. Charlie was in comfortable leggings and layers of clothing she could take off if she were too hot. She also had her knee length boots on as it was winter and very cold along with the rain hammering down on them. They also did not know what weather to expect as they drove across the continent of Europe. Gretchen was wearing a purple velour tracksuit that Charlie had not seen before, but it did not matter what they were wearing as long as they were comfortable for the journey.

They travelled down the five different motorways in convoy and for the whole of the journey the rain battered down.

They used the new motorway toll road and stopped at the services to let the dogs out and to grab a hot drink takeaway.

As they were nearing Dover on the M20, the traffic was getting heavier and heavier with lorries and trucks everywhere. It was 29 days before Brexit, and the looming problems with travel to Europe were already rearing their ugly head. France had increased Covid checks at the border, and this was part of the problem. There were lots of reports on the local radio stations about the queues on the motorway and it seemed to be the lorries that were being held up mostly, Charlie hoped that their own journey to the Port would not be too delayed.

They travelled slowly down the motorway for the last leg of the journey. Lorries were stationary on the hard shoulder throughout this section, and it was clear that some of them had just given up for the night and got their heads down. Charlie looked forward to doing the same, even if it was only for a couple of hours. Concentrating on driving in the pouring rain and dark, after the week she had just been through with all the stress, was taking its toll on her. At least her new varifocals were doing the job. Eventually they arrived in Dover itself. Brett pulled over and said he needed to fill up with gas. Although this sounded like it was an American expression, the Ford F150 had a conversion with a big gas tank for LPG in the flat bed of the pick-up. It could run on LPG or petrol and the cost of LPG was much less than petrol, especially in the parts of Europe they would be travelling through. They found a petrol station that sold LPG, and after a few complications with the various adapters for filling the tank that the F150 had, both vehicles were fuelled up and ready to go.

Eventually they arrived at the Port and checked in at the drive through booths. They had to show their own passports and covid proof, and the passports of the six pets on board. Everything went through smoothly and they were directed to join a lined-up parking area to wait for the ferry to Calais. The ferry was not due for some-time, so Charlie and Gretchen decided to take the dogs over to a specially designated dog exercise area that was a bit away from the queuing vehicles. It was as much as a relief for Charlie to be able to get some fresh air and stretch her legs as it was for the three dogs. Her head was banging from driving in the appalling weather and from the concentration on the road. It was 1 o'clock in the morning and they were all very tired.

Surprisingly, it was not long before a ferry docked and was being unloaded. Charlie watched in amazement as the huge lorries and other vehicle poured off like a trail of ants. Very soon after this was completed the Port staff started loading the vehicles that were queuing with the threesome. It turned out they had been able to get on an earlier ferry than the one booked, as the earlier one was actually late. Charlie was scared as she drove the motorhome up the ramp to the ferry, although she knew it was safe in her heart, she was still suspicious that it might fail. Once on the deck of the ferry they were guided into a particular row to park. Brett was in the next row to the motorhome and came over to the Charlie once he had gathered up his belongings. The rules for animals, and humans, on the ferry were that the animals had to be left in the vehicles, and the humans had to leave the vehicles and go up to the passenger decks. They were all concerned about leaving the dogs in particular but had no choice.

Brett helped check that all the doors and boot to the motorhome were securely locked as there were a few dubious looking vehicle owners and passengers hanging around, for no particular reason.

Having checked it was all secure the three of them went up the stairs on the ferry to the passenger areas in the hope of finding a drink and somewhere to get their heads down for a while. The crossing itself was less than 2 hours so Charlie knew it would fly by, but she needed to get some sleep to carry on driving. There were very few open facilities on the ferry, but they managed to find somewhere to get a coffee and some sofas in a quiet enough area to close their eyes. Brett and Charlie were out like a light, and Charlie hoped that Gretchen would stay alert enough to ensure no-one tried to steal her handbag as she knew she would probably not notice.

It did not seem like long before the tannoy announced that all passengers with cars had to return to their vehicles. Charlie, Gretchen, and Brett dragged themselves out of their slumbers and went back down to the car deck. The dogs were so pleased to see them when they climbed into the motorhome and wagged their tales vigorously and delight. There was nothing they could do to let the dogs out until they had disembarked from the ferry in Calais and found somewhere suitable to stop.

As they waited to be unloaded from the ferry Charlie doubted her ability to complete the rest of the long journey. They had not planned any stops for rest, certainly not any overnight hotel stays, only naps in the motorhome as and when needed. Charlie followed Brett out of the port at Calais.

They were both using Waze as a satellite navigation method to get them to the rental house in Competa. As with the route to Dover, Charlie had only had a quick look at the way to Competa and was reliant on Brett in front, and her passenger Gretchen to get them there. This was a little worrying as Gretchen had never been known for her navigation skills, but they had technology to fall back on. As they made their way out of Calais they were on the right track. Brett and Gretchen stayed connected through the walkie talkie, and it was hysterical listening to the banter and the way Gretchen contacted Brett through it and called him Beefy. As soon as they could they pulled over in a suitable French service station area and let the dogs out to do their business and fed and watered all the animals. They tucked into more of the food Gretchen had brought and fetched themselves a drink from the shop.

Unfortunately for the travellers, they had mistakenly taken the road out of Calais that went through the centre of Paris and did not skirt around it. Distance wise it was not much different, but because of the early time in the morning they had left Calais this incorrect route meant they hit Paris at rush hour. It did occur to Charlie that it was always this busy in the capital of France, no matter what time of day or day of the week. They sat in queue after queue as they made their way around the endless roundabouts and busy traffic. Scooters were everywhere, whizzing past weaving their way around the cars and other traffic on the busy city roads. Charlie was scared that she would not see one of them or catch one of them with the back of the motorhome. It felt as if she was looking behind her in the side mirrors more than looking ahead. Her concentration was waning, and her eyes were tired, even though they had not been on the road for that long.

It was second nature to Brett, and he was not struggling in the least according to his regular communication with Gretchen.

Eventually they had made their way to the correct road to exit the city and make their way to Orleans, a city to the South of Paris, in Central France. Throughout their journey around the bustling city roads Charlie had been constantly aware of the number of makeshift tents she had been seeing. She felt sad and concerned for them as the weather was bitter and wet, and she wondered how they had come to end up in that position. On many of the embankments and under bridges and spare land there were tents made with items that could be little more than plain blankets. It reminded her of her first arrival in Delhi, many years ago, and how the typical tourist would not see what she was seeing now on their holiday trip to the Capital of France. She knew that it was similar in England, especially in the bigger cities, and wished she could find a way to help or support others.

Since they disembarked at Calais, they had now been travelling for 6 or 7 hours with little sleep and Charlie's eyes felt like they had a skip load of sand in them and needed to close. It was made worse by the fact that the rain was still hammering down and making the visibility extremely poor. The rain had not really stopped much for the whole journey and Charlie was finding the white lines on the French roads really hard to make out, even in the daylight. Brett came through on the walkie talkie as they approached Orleans. He suggested that they get past the city and then stop at the first available place for a rest. He was obviously beginning to suffer too. It was now getting towards teatime on the Friday and the threesome had not had a proper sleep since Wednesday night.

Even the Wednesday, the day before completion on her lovely home, Charlie had not slept much due to stressing and worrying about the whole move. The plan was to have something to eat and then rest properly as long as was needed, before starting off again most probably in the early hours. This way they hoped they would find the roads quieter and make the journey easier. Some miles out of Orleans Brett spotted a service station of sorts. Both vehicles needed refuelling and this one looked big enough to provide food and space to park up in a quiet area. As they drove in convoy into the service area, they spotted a parking area away from the hustle and bustle that was next to a large, grassed area where they could let the dogs stretch their legs. This time there was a break in the rain, so Charlie and Gretchen retrieved the dogs from their cages and put them on their leads. They all showed great relief at being able to go to the toilet and drank water with a passion. Charlie was adamant that Dexter needed some proper exercise, so despite her tiredness and hunger she set out across the grassy area and allowed him to jump and run and sort himself out. As they neared the back of the buildings Charlie had to keep him on a shorter lead as it was clear that it was not only dogs who had been going to the toilet and Dexter was finding the mess quite interesting. Charlie could not understand why even humans could not clear up after themselves but decided maybe it was a cultural thing after her experiences of being an au pair.

Back at the motorhome and pickup, Brett was now inside chatting to Gretchen. She had walked her dogs but as they were only small, did not need the same extent of exercise as Dexter. Brett and Gretchen had the butties and savouries out and were taking their pick.

Charlie fed Dexter and the cats and cleaned out the litter tray before heading over to the Café to get them all a drink. She really did not fancy anymore of the prepared butties, especially as they had been made a day or two by now, so she selected some baguettes to take back with the coffees. When she returned Brett announced that he was going to recline his car seat and sleep that way – he was after all used to it from his years of coach and lorry driving. Before he returned to the pickup, they discussed Dexter who had become increasingly restless and whiny over the last few hours. Between them they concocted a temporary barrier with suitcases and bags so that he could not break his way through to Charlie whilst she was driving but was still free to roam about the motorhome. Even though it was limited space, it was better than being in the cage. Putting him in the cage also meant muzzling him first as for him to jump up to the cage on the back seats Charlie had to half lift his back end, and she did not want to risk holding him in a place he might not like and getting a nip. The muzzle was always removed afterwards.

Once Brett had gone, Gretchen and Charlie started to try and get the overhead bed down. It was electric and came down from the ceiling behind the driver and passenger seats. They both decided as they were not exactly eight stone teenagers, they would only bring it down enough to get on top. It was a double bed size, and they were happy to head to tail with the sleeping bags they had at the ready. Gretchen took layers of clothing off and climbed up first. Charlie made sure all the doors to the motorhome were locked and secure before making the brave decision to let the cats out of the cages. The way she was going to be lying on the overhead bed meant she could keep an eye on them for a bit before she fell asleep.

She could also see that Brett was well away in the pickup. It never took him long to fall asleep when he was comfortable and closed his eyes, and Charlie wished she could do the same. She took off her long boots and jumper and climbed up to the bed, apologising profusely to Gretchen for the smell of her feet. They had been in the boots with the same socks for a few days now and none of them had been able to have a proper wash, just a quick teeth brush in the motorhome sink, and a wipe down with baby wipes. They had filled the onboard shower with all the animal paraphernalia. As she tried to doze off, Charlie watched her three cats slowly make their way out of the cages and explore the whole motorhome. Gretchen's dogs watched and snuffled a little at their presence near their cage, but Dexter just ignored them as usual. They had grown up from kittens with him. The cats went everywhere, and Missy eventually settled on the drop-down bed next to Charlie. After this, Charlie must have dropped into a deep sleep as the last thing she remembered was listening to Gretchen snoring gently, and then awoke with a start. She looked at her phone and the three travellers had been asleep for over 4 hours. This was the longest they had rested for, and Charlie felt thoroughly refreshed and ready to get going.

Gretchen stirred and woke as Charlie dropped herself off the bed. During her time asleep she had no way of knowing what the cats had been up to, but all three of them had made their way back inside the linked-up cage tunnel and settled down on the bedding and towels inside. She took the opportunity to lock the cage door whilst they were all safely inside, before any of the humans opened the motorhome door and one of the cats made a run for it. She thought to herself whether it was cruel to have brought them on this journey and felt for their bewilderment and confusion.

Apart from a couple of meowing sessions they had been very well behaved, and she convinced herself it was still better than sending them with a pet carrier company with strangers and a longer journey in time. She still could not get her head around that. Oscar had started pulling at one of the flimsy net curtains on the window behind one of the cages, but if that was the maximum extent of the damage, they had nothing to worry about. Once the cats were secure Charlie grabbed herself a bottle of water and settled down in the driver's seat. She could see Brett stirring in his vehicle and after a few moments he climbed out and headed to the motorhome just as Charlie jumped up to unlock the door. As he came in Gretchen pulled herself down from the bed. They took turns at using the bathroom and freshening up and then they headed across to the café to see if there was anything worth having. The rain had eased off a bit but was forecast to start again soon.

Plans and route decided Charlie and Brett got into their drivers' seats and prepared to head off. The next leg of the journey was to take them down to Bordeaux, and along the coast into the north of Spain before heading down towards Madrid. As this was another 12 hours of driving, they agreed to let each other know when they needed a stop. As they pulled away, it was still dark and despite having had some good sleeping time Charlie was really struggling with seeing the faded white lines on the French motorways. She was amazed at how backwards it all seemed compared to the UK, where the lines were always bright white and reflective, and had the added benefit of cats' eyes. It was like going back in time travelling on these roads. She vowed to get Brett to look at the lights on the motorhome at their next stop and see if either she had them on the wrong setting, or there were extra lights she could put on.

They drove solidly for 4 or 5 hours before needing a break. They pulled up in a large layby where there were some French public toilets of a sort. Brett nipped over to them whilst the girls let the dogs out for a break. Throughout this last part of the journey Dexter had spent most of it on the small bench seat behind Gretchen's chair with his head flopped over her shoulder. He had tried to do the same with Charlie but luckily the barriers they had put up and the suitcases stopped him getting too close so as not to disturb her driving. Once they were all back in the vehicles and settled, they reclined the seats a little and shut their eyes for another rest. Brett said he would set his alarm and come and wake them up after an hour or so; he was keen to make timely progress and the weather had improved.

For most of the route so far, Charlie had been in front with the motorhome as the pacesetter. It was still dark, and Brett had cleaned the motorhome headlights with a tissue and between them they had found the fog lights for the front to see if that helped Charlie. Charlie asked Brett to go in front for a while so that she could follow his taillights at least until it was proper daylight. This worked a little better for her as they started back down the motorways. Since they had been in France, they seemed to have to stop very regularly to pay out more money in tolls, and the motorhome was not cheap to get through the tolls. At this last stop Brett had also told Charlie that the tyre pressure in one of the rear tyres looked low so she constantly had this worry in her mind as they drove along. She had virtually convinced herself that the back end was going to blow and cause her to crash the large beast.

At the next fuel stop, both Brett and Charlie took turns in trying to pump up the tyre off the automatic air machines, but only succeeded in letting more air out. Brett was not sure whether it was a faulty valve or whether it was them being stupid and language barriers, but he assured Charlie that it was still safe to drive. She had her doubts though. She tried to take her mind off it by chatting with Gretchen and listening to Gretchen's descriptions of the scenery as they travelled along the coast and eventually crossed the border into Spain. There was no physical border as such, just a small sign and the obvious change of language for the road signs and other places they passed by. They continued driving through the day. At least the weather had improved, and they were scheduled to arrive near Madrid around teatime in the Saturday, three full days since departing their hometowns. On the ring road in Madrid, they needed a refuelling and refreshment stop. Once the necessary had been done at the petrol pumps, Charlie was watching two men in overalls that were with a breakdown truck, or grua as she was later to find out. She decided to bite the bullet and approach the two men as she had not stopped worrying about the tyre with the low pressure.

She explained as best as she could to the two Spanish men what her problem was – she had already told Brett to keep out of the way for this plea for help. They spoke reasonably good English and seemed to understand what she wanted. They suggested she moved the motorhome over to where they were pointing out the air dispensers but with another pleading look from Charlie one of the men agreed to move the motorhome over for her. The garage was remarkably busy, and it involved a lot of reversing and manoeuvring which terrified Charlie.

One of the kind Spanish recovery drivers jumped into the driver's seat, luckily with only a bark and sniff from Dexter who was still loose inside and proceeded to move it over to the air pump. Then he pumped up the tyre perfectly with no problem at all. Charlie offered him twenty euros as a thanks, but he refused to take it and wished them luck for the rest of their journey. Charlie and Gretchen drove to the car park next to the petrol station to where Brett was waiting. They all laughed their heads off at the thought of the poor stranger being accosted by two mad English women and a Doberman, in a Check Republic motorhome that must have stank to high heaven with their own sweat and that of six animals. There was enough space and rough ground in the car park to let the dogs have a stretch and play before feeding everyone ready for heading off.

As well as sorting all this out Charlie had found time during the driving stops to speak to the estate agents in Competa to inform them they would be arriving in the early hours of Sunday morning and how were they to gain access to their rental property. Charlie had paid the rent from October 2020 as that was necessary to secure the property and had committed to a minimum term of 6 months. This meant that they should have access as soon as they arrived as far as she was concerned. It had all been arranged successfully, hopefully. The property owner, Fernando, was going to leave the keys under a stone near the gate and send her a photo of where the stone was on her mobile phone.

The journey from Madrid to Competa was the last leg of the long weekend. It should take around 7 hours without any breaks, but as it was early evening now it was clear that they would be arriving at their destination in the incredibly early hours of Sunday morning.

As they pulled away from the garage where the tyre on the motorhome had been sorted, Brett took the lead again in the convoy. Gretchen was in contact with him through the walkie talkie's as they pulled onto the motorway. Both Charlie and Brett were following Waze, and as they came up to a split in the road Brett appeared to go off in the wrong direction to Charlie. Gretchen was desperately trying to get him on the walkie talkie to tell him he had gone the wrong way, but he was motoring and was soon out of reach of the wavelength. Gretchen tried to get him on his mobile but with no success so Charlie just carried on following the directions on the satnav, praying that he would realise and find them. As they were making good distance from the City Charlie kept checking her mirrors for sight of the pick-up truck. Eventually she recognised the familiar lights behind her, and Brett came past and retook the lead. He told them over the walkie talkies that as soon as he had gone past the fork in the road, he realised but had to travel quite far before he could find somewhere to pull off and turn back round.

The journey to Competa was to take them directly South via Granada and the Sierra Nevada down to the coast and then West towards Malaga along the coast. They planned to leave the coastal motorway to Malaga at Torrox to travel back North into the mountains and Competa. It was already dark but at least it was not raining as they made their way from the city. The roads were good and motorways clear as it was the middle of the night. After a long stretch of driving both Brett's and Charlie's eyes were starting to droop, and the travellers decided it was a suitable time to find somewhere to recharge their batteries.

There was a suitable motorway service area that had a café style bar and space to let the dogs have a leg stretch so they pulled in and found a suitable place to park away from the main carpark. Charlie put on her coat and headed across the car park to the bar to see what food there was available. She messaged Brett and Gretchen to let them know the choices and took their orders of burgers. She chose a hot cheese and ham baguette for herself and ordered the coffees. In the meantime, Gretchen and Brett let the dogs out and went about feeding and watering them. Once they were securely back in the motorhome, Brett walked over to the bar to help Charlie with carrying the orders. As he walked in, every eye, presumably Spanish, turned at gawped at him. It was cold, in the middle of the night, and he was wearing shorts, just proving the point about mad Englishmen Charlie thought as she heard chuckles and whispers all around. The bartender was putting the order together finally whilst Brett nipped to the loo, and then Charlie and Brett walked back over to the vehicles laughing about the reaction of the customers in the bar. Charlie had also managed to secure a litre of milk from the bartender so they could make more brews in the motorhome.

Once the humans had been fed and watered too, the food tasted really good and was 100% better than the stale butties and savouries they had transported from the UK and the bits and pieces they had grabbed on the journey, they took the dogs out for another walk around the area before settling down into their car seats as usual for a quick sleep. By now Charlie had got in the habit of shutting her eyes for an hour or so and feeling refreshed enough to drive on.

She had never been able to do it before in her life and struggled to see how it was so easy for Brett to do, wherever he was, but after the eye strain and concentration of continuous driving it was almost natural.

A few hours after parking they were on their way again. It was a shame it was still dark as they drove through some beautiful mountainous country on the way to and from Granada. They drove through ravines and tunnels and across lots of bridges, some scarier than others, but Charlie just kept concentrating on the road and keeping within the edges of it, rather than trying to look at the scenery. They drove through snow flurries and sleet and passed several snowploughs that were fully equipped to deal with any eventuality. Even when they got near Torrox it was still dark and they were not able to see the or appreciate the sights of the coastal route and the Mediterranean Sea. Before they made the last descent to the coast they decided to pull over in a bit of rough ground and have a half hour rest and stretch. There were hardly any vehicles on the road as it was now early on a Sunday morning and very few even drove past where they were parked. Brett had been travelling at the front of the convoy for most of the journey, and as he had a vague recollection of the route to the villa that they had rented in Competa, the threesome decided it was best if he stayed in the lead. If Charlie had known what was to come on the roads ahead, she would have stayed put where they were parked or gone on a driving strike.

As they made their way to Torrox, Brett took a right turn in the direction of the town and Charlie just followed. At the roundabout where they turned, there was a Spanish police car or Guardia parked up. Charlie noticed him look in bewilderment as a UK registered big black pickup drove by, followed by a Czech registered motorhome with two women in the front.

Unfortunately for him he was going to get the experience twice. Soon after turning Brett was on the walkie talkie saying, he had gone wrong, and they had to turn round. Charlie went into a panic at the thought of trying to turn the motorhome around in the narrow streets, but luckily Brett found a small roundabout for them to use. As they drove back out of the town, the lone police officer looked up at the convoy again. Charlie laughed with Gretchen that she wondered what he would tell his friends or family – she guessed he might say he had imagined the sight. She was only glad they were not pulled over as it must have looked very strange.

Eventually they were on the correct route that took them up the mountains. Competa itself was over six hundred metres high so there was quite a climb to go. Charlie thought that the journey had been hard and stressful, but it was nothing compared to this last 15km stretch. It was still dark, the headlights and extra lights that Brett had found on the motorhome were not brilliant, but Charlie could still see how close the raw rock edges of the mountains were and how steep the drops down the valleys were. She could see extraordinarily little evidence of barriers to stop any vehicle crashing down the mountain so put herself into full concentrate mode. Charlie and Gretchen followed Brett up the mountain road in silence and luckily, he was going at a steady, almost slow pace, for Charlie. Every now and then Gretchen would wave her arm to indicate Charlie was getting a bit close to the rock edges of the windy narrow road but somehow, they managed to make it to the outskirts of Competa. Brett pulled over in the forecourt of a petrol station that was still closed – it was about 4am – and the three of them had a quick chat.

Brett reckoned he remembered the way from here – Charlie found this amazing as he had only been there once, but she had full confidence in his navigation skills. They pulled off and went down narrower and steeper roads until eventually pausing at the top of a steep concrete road. Charlie dreaded the thought of driving down there but knew she had to, there was no choice and she had made it this far. Off they went again and in no time at all they were pulling up on the road outside a house that looked vaguely familiar.

Chapter twenty-three – start of their new life.

At last, it seemed as though they had arrived, and Charlie felt like twenty sacks of spuds had been lifted off her shoulders. She could not remember which one of them it was, but they found the photographed stone and the key under it. Luckily for the travellers the owner had left the outside lights on the villa for them as it was still pitch black. Brett looked round to check they were not blocking the side road for other people living on the same hill, and they decided to unload the vital bits and pieces and the animals and leave the vehicles where they were for now. They all grabbed their travelling bags and overnight essentials out of the motorhome and pick-up and let themselves into the villa. Brett and Gretchen had already seen the property on their search earlier in the year so knew what to expect. It was a first time for Charlie, apart from the photographs and brochure she had seen. It was not an unpleasant surprise she mused to herself as she looked around the property. It was very cold and felt and smelled damp but was cozy and at the same time big enough for the four adults and six animals. As the three of them looked around they decided on bedrooms. There was one with an ensuite that Brett was to have, and Charlie thought the one at the end of the corridor was the best for her as there was enough space by the built-in wardrobes for the cat paraphernalia and it would be more separate for them from the main living areas.

Gretchen was happy with the 2 double bedrooms opposite the main bathroom on the corridor for her and Grunter, when he arrived, so they all left their bags and other bits and pieces on the agreed beds and whilst Gretchen set about looking for a kettle and mugs, Brett and Charlie went back to the motorhome.

They carefully wrapped the two female cats, Missy, and Cappy, one by one, and put them in the travel crate together. Then they did the same with Oscar the boy cat into the other crate and made sure the doors were secure. There was no way Charlie was going to lose them now after the last few days of keeping them safe on the journey. She thought to herself how well they had travelled. Every now and then Oscar had meowed a bit but did not seem too distressed on the journey. They had all had their fair share of cuddles and strokes at every opportunity Charlie had been given, and they did after all have Dexter and Gretchen's 2 dogs to keep them company. Once or twice, including the big sleep night, Charlie had managed to let them out for a wander around the inside of the motorhome, but they had not spent long outside the cage tunnel and had soon sought the security of their temporary home.

Brett carried the two travel crates with the three cats in whilst Charlie took the cat litter and food and water bowls into the villa. They put them in the end bedroom and laid everything out before shutting the bedroom door and opening the crates doors to let them explore the room in their own time. Then they went back to the motorhome to get the three dogs. This time they were in the security of the 6-foot fencing around the property, so Dexter was able to run around freely, sniffing everywhere and doing his business.

Once the dogs seemed satisfied, they all headed back into the villa to settle down for the night. It was still dark, and Charlie felt she could sleep for a week or more. She did not know whether it was from the stress, the lack of sleep, or all of it, she just knew she was exhausted.

They had all kept in regular contact with family throughout the journey, and Charlie sent Jack a message to say that they had all arrived safely and would speak when they were up later. The villa was meant to have underfloor heating, so Charlie had a quick look at the control and thermostat. She tried to put the lounge one on a setting of around 20 degrees to see if anything happened. After a quick mug of tea and chat with her fellow travellers, Charlie said her goodnights and crawled off to bed. There were some sheets and blankets on the bed so she climbed under them although if there had been a bed of nails on top she still would have laid down.

As she dozed off to sleep Charlie heard Gretchen and Brett saying goodnight and making their way to their own rooms and was conscious of the creeping around of her three cats. She watched with love and fascination as they explored every corner and the wardrobe, under and over the bed, until tiredness got the better of her and she went out like a light. The next thing she remembered was a big crash like bang. Charlie opened her eyes to see that Cappy had jumped off the top wardrobe shelf onto the bedside cabinet, using the door as a springboard. When she saw Charlie's eyes open, she came purring over and Oscar and Missy appeared from their hiding places to see what was going on. She laughed to herself that it was really quite eerie with these small furry animals with bright eyes appearing quietly and slowly from the depths and dark corners of the room.

She guessed they were hungry and as it was now a reasonable hour, nearly 8 am, she thought she might as well stay awake. The sun was coming through the window at the end of her bed, and she could hear movement at the other end of the corridor.

She grabbed a couple of packets of wet cat food and filled the three separate cat bowls. They still had plenty of water and had munched through some of the cat biscuits in the dry food bowl during the night whilst Charlie must have slept like a log. They had also been having a good go at the cat litter as the white stones were kicked out onto the cold stone floor.

Charlie dressed herself in some clean clothes from the travel bag, they had after all been dressed in the same clothes for a few days and needed a good freshen up. As she sauntered down the corridor to the open plan kitchen, diner, and lounge, she heard Brett putting the kettle on. They had tea bags, hot water and milk and it was music to her ears to hear the familiar sound of a cup of tea being made. Dexter bounded up to her as she approached. Either he had slept like a baby on one of the sofas all night or they were all too tired to hear him, as both Brett and Gretchen had not heard him at all. Gretchen's 2 dogs had slept on their beds in her room and had emerged when they thought they heard food. After all the three dogs were fed, they started the regime that was to rule their life for the next week or more. Charlie was adamant that the cats had to be stopped from getting out for as long as possible. All the theories said 2 weeks, but she planned to see how it went. Luckily all three of them were nestling down again in Charlie's bedroom. She suspected they had been exploring the small villa all night and now they were fed were due a rest.

Whilst Charlie and Gretchen wandered around with the dogs Brett fetched the keys for the motorhome to move it from where they had left it in the early hours and into the grounds of the villa. There was a 6-foot wire fence completely surrounding the plot, with double gates onto the road at the garage level.

The garage was the whole area of the house above and was surrounded by gravel parking so there was plenty of room. As Brett drove the motorhome through the gates to the compound, the vehicle went down a shallow dip in the gate area and they heard an awful crunching sound. Once parked they investigated further and found that the plastic skirting on one side had been cracked in the impact. Charlie assumed the company would knock the repair off the deposit she had paid and hoped it would not be too expensive. It was when they opened the inside of the motorhome that Charlie realised the full scale of the work to be done. The company were sending someone from the Czech Republic to collect it on the following day, so it needed emptying fully and cleaning.

Whilst the dogs enjoyed the freedom of wandering around Charlie, Brett and Gretchen started unpacking the motorhome. The whole of the visible floor was covered in green fluff. During the latter part of the journey Dexter had broken through the fabric on his dog bed and had started pulling the stuffing out of the bed. It was under everything, on top of everything and trapped in every crevice. The cat cage tunnel was untied and dismantled and with the dog cages, removed from the motorhome, along with the various blankets used to protect the fixed sofas and sleeping come animal area.

There was no more damage from the journey except a net curtain or two that Oscar had been trying to pick at through the cage and had made pull marks in. Charlie pulled them back into shape as much as possible and thought she would just tell the collection man as if they needed replacing it could not cost that much. Once all their belongings were removed and the pickup unpacked, they returned inside and had something to eat.

They had brought bits and pieces in the fridge and small freezer in the motorhome so there was enough to cobble something together. The plan was that Brett and Charlie would head out in the pickup to get supplies from the nearest supermarket, and Charlie would get on with cleaning and tidying the motorhome ready for collection. Before she could start on this task Charlie had to speak with the rental agents in Competa. As her work and only income consisted of online exam marking, internet connection was essential. She had handwritten on the signed copies of the rental agreement that the let was subject to internet access being active on arrival and it was not. The TV would only work on Spanish channels and there was no Wi-Fi. Luckily, after a bit of a battle, the rental agency admitted they had messed up and said they would sort it immediately. Charlie had a contract for marking starting the next day, so it was important.

Once Brett had left on his and Gretchen's shopping spree, Charlie made sure the cats could not get out and returned to the large garage to tackle the motorhome. She was sweeping up dog bed fluff and cat litter stones for ever. Once the sweeping was finished, she used a small cylinder hoover they had brought with them to get in all the crevices around the bed and sofa set up, crawling on her knees to get all the bits underneath.

Then with a bucket of hot soapy water she wiped and washed every bit of surface and floor in the motorhome. Once she was satisfied, she used the air and fabric fresheners they had brought with them to spray everything possible to try and remove the stale animal and sweat smells. During this time, she had also left the three dogs inside the villa as they kept trying to get back in the motorhome – she laughed to herself that they were telling her they wanted to go back home.

It was only a couple of hours later that the TV and internet man arrived. He set them up with everything they wanted including the TV and Charlie's laptop, and after Charlie signed even more contracts, he went on his way. Brett and Gretchen had returned with supplies and the villa owner called by to check everything was ok. He spoke little English, but they managed to communicate with him. Brett had also picked up a large bag of logs and some kindling and firelighters from the garage and they planned to get the fire lit to warm up the house. Fernando, the owner had quickly shown them the underfloor heating and indicated how to set it in each room. They left the dial on a medium temperature to see what happened as the stone and tile floors were extremely cold on their feet. Once everyone had left, they settled down to see what the TV had to offer in between making a snack for tea, feeding the animals, and feeling still very exhausted. Charlie still had to set up her printer – she had a colour multifunction laser printer and scanner that had come with them in the motorhome. It was the best purchase she had made for her work as all the other cheaper, or inkjet printers, had not survived long, especially when she was teaching and had to print a lot of materials herself. She managed to connect the printer to the Wi-Fi and successfully sent a couple of pages to it from her laptop.

That meant she could switch off for the night until the standardisation process for her next marking began the next day.

It was not too long before they were all tucked up safely in bed. The animals seemed to have settled a lot more during the day, although it was clear to Charlie that the cats were becoming increasingly inquisitive at anywhere there might be an escape route to the big outdoors and were looking longingly out of the windows.

The next morning the whole tribe were more rested and relaxed. Once Charlie, Brett and Gretchen were all washed and dressed they decided the plan for the day. There was some bedding on the beds when they arrived, but they decided to try and find some more sheets and covers and have a wander around Competa town and have a bite of lunch in one of the outside cafes. The weather was in their favour, as though it was cool out of the sun, due to the altitude of the area, when the sun came out it was glorious. The plan would get Charlie back in time to set herself up ready for the marking contract and give her and Gretchen enough time to get the final bits of paperwork ready for their residency application for Spain. Throughout their journey so far, Charlie had been in regular contact with Naomi and Leah, the lovely people who were helping them with the move and had helped Gretchen and Brett find the house they were now renting. It was now 8 December 2020 and Brexit was looming. It was accepted that applications for residency had to be registered by the Spanish authorities before the deadline of 31 December if they were to be granted on the existing, rather than the post-Brexit and stricter rules.

There was more paperwork that had to be arranged before the application could be submitted and this included registering to get a Padron with the town hall, the equivalent of the electoral roll in the UK, Charlie had assumed.

Once they had sorted the dogs, they all climbed into the pick-up and headed off for the town. After weaving around the tight roads and lanes on the way to and in the town, they eventually found somewhere suitable to park the noisy vehicle. It was clear that the pickup had already caused a few heads to turn due to its size and exhaust noise and that another more suitable vehicle was going to be needed for everyday use.

Charlie was not an exhibitionist and did not enjoy the attention it was receiving. They soon set about exploring the town. They managed to find what seemed like a smallish general store, although upon entering it was like a tardis. Because a lot of the buildings were built into the mountains, they were deceiving from the front and first impressions. This particular shop was like a small department store inside, with four floors that were quite large in themselves. They managed to find the bedding department and bought the assorted items they needed. This was after some googling of the Spanish terminology.

This was not going to be the first occasion that Charlie was going to wish she had made a proper attempt to learn Spanish before they had arrived. She had never had a natural ability to learn languages, even taking three attempts to pass her French O level and she admired the skill of people who were fluent in languages.

After they had paid for their selections, Charlie laughed to herself how Gretchen was full of 'Grunter will love this' and other such comments as she selected matching bedding for his room in the villa, the three of them wandered more around the town. They wanted to get their bearings and find out where the Town Hall was for future reference, and then they settled on a lovely looking bar amongst others in the Plaza Almijara, in the centre of the town. Whilst they sat and enjoyed a drink and something to eat for lunch, Charlie noticed that there were many English people around, as well as a big mix of nationalities. There were languages she did not recognise as French or German, although she was hardly an expert, and surprisingly few who were Spanish. She assumed that this could be because it would be a normal working day and people had long gone from lunchtime breaks. The temperature was well into double numbers and the sun was shining which made a pleasant change from the extreme conditions they had been driving through a few days earlier. It was not quite T shirt and shorts weather because of the nip in the air but was still lovely enough to enjoy relaxing in the outdoor eating and seating areas.

Once they were satiated and refreshed, they sauntered back to the pickup, this time it was all downhill which was good as the altitude of their chosen place to rent seemed to be affecting Brett's COPD. They climbed in for the journey back to the villa. It was only a few miles but involved navigating the twisty narrow roads in the town centre and then heading back across the narrow country lanes. Charlie was amazed at the lack of any sort of barriers stopping vehicles driving off the mountain cliffs and even more astonished that she had negotiated these roads in the dark and rain, in the middle of the night, in the enormous motorhome that was left-hand drive.

Once they were back at the villa they let the dogs out for a run around, whilst Charlie ensured the cats did not sneak through the gap in the door. They took their purchases in and got on with their plans. Brett was already missing his newspapers. He had accepted he was unlikely to get his Hull Echo in Spain but was hoping to find at least the Mirror. In their wanders around the town and questioning of various people who looked they might be in the know, it was clear that there was no longer a newspaper shop in Competa, and that the nearest place he could get one was in the town at the bottom of the mountain called Algarrobo-Costa where there were more tourist style shops along the seafront and apparently a newspaper shop. After a quick cup of tea, Brett headed off down the hill. Even though it was a short journey of 10 miles or so, it would take over an hour round trip due to the windy roads and slow speeds that would have to be used.

Gretchen busied herself preparing Grunter's room and sorting her own. Charlie was not sure how to interpret the Grunter-Gretchen situation. It was clear she was missing him as in everything, including buying the bedding, Gretchen made constant reference to him. Despite this she had clearly told Brett and Charlie that she did not want him to come and wanted the move as a start to her new life without him. Once Gretchen had finished with the rooms, she prepared some meat and vegetables ready for cooking later for tea. Charlie had never been a good cook. There were somethings that she made well, especially if it involved mince and some chicken dishes, but as she did not particularly like cooking, she had always been lucky enough to have men in her life who did. Her ex-husband enjoyed cooking, and Brett was an expert.

She mused that the men she had known in her life, including her brother and dad, had been much more inventive in their cooking. Even her mum had never shown much passion or patience for mealtimes which might have been why Charlie had followed her lead. It was not that she could not cook, she just would rather not. So instead, she got on with what she knew best – how to work. She completed the standardisation process for the exam she was due to mark and submitted it knowing she would not know if she was approved for marking until the next day.

The last job of the afternoon was to take Dexter out for good walk. Since they had arrived, he had run around the compound, the wire fenced plot of the villa, but not been out for a proper romp. Gretchen decided to take her two dogs with Charlie and Dexter, so they gathered up the leads and the dogs whilst Brett started enjoying catching up on the news at the dining table.

He had always been someone who liked to sit in the same seat, preferably with good views of the outside and the TV at the same time, and with all his personal bits and pieces within easy reach. Charlie and Jack had always teased him about this and used to sit in his seat for a laugh and wind him up light-heartedly. As they left the side-gate of the compound, the partially concreted road led to a more unadopted style of road that wound around the mountain to the villas higher up so Charlie let Dexter off the lead.

To all sides of this access road there were fields of olive trees which Dexter was loving running around. It was obvious that Dexter was hunting for a stick. It was his personal preference of toy unlike Charlie's previous dog Buddy that always wanted a ball.

It got to the point where because he could not find a suitable stick on the ground, Dexter jumped up to one of the lower branches of an olive tree and hung off it until it snapped. She secretly hoped that there would not be some sort of weird Spanish penalty for this but there was no one else around and it made a cracking sound like it was already rotten. The problem with Dexter and his sticks was that it was impossible to pick them up and throw them for him. He was always too quick to dive for it at the same time as Charlie reached out her hand for it and having been caught by his sharp teeth before by accident, they had all decided it was easier to kick the stick using a booted foot. In the meantime, Gretchen's dogs. Molly and Blue, trundled along the steep road behind her. They were small white fluffy dogs, and both overweight, especially Blue the male dog, and it was clear that this was too much for them. Charlie enjoyed the company with Gretchen as they chatted away but wished the two small dogs were not being pushed to make the climb.

They went up to a point that was the end of the road without having to go up what seemed like a private drive or road and then turned to make their descent back down the hill. By the time they got back to the villa it had been nearly an hour up and down the hill, plus the walk around the hilly town, and they were all ready for a well-earned rest. That was the girls and the animals. Brett was already flat out asleep on one of the sofas when they returned. Charlie messaged Jack about the best time to call him – at least they could do this through free internet chat now with a good signal. The actual mobile phone signal was really poor at the villa and when it would connect it was intermittent even though they were on the main networks that boast how they work all over Spain.

Chapter twenty-four – the house hunt and start of downwards spiral.

The next few weeks continued in the same routine. Charlie had her marking to keep her busy during the day, but as she had always managed this as well as working full time, it now did not seem as much of a commitment. It took her right through Christmas and into the New year every year and usual finished in the first week of the New Year, or sooner if all the scripts had gone. Covid restrictions were in full force throughout Andalucía, and masks had to be worn even when walking around outside. The police in the area took a much harder role in enforcing the restrictions and Charlie thought that cases in the UK would not be as bad if people did what they were told and suffered prosecution when they flouted the rules. They were obviously there for a reason and was she the only one who thought that. During this period, they also met a few of their neighbours. In particular, Emma, who lived in the house up the hill from them who was a keen runner and ran past their villa every day, and Madelyn and Ralph and their granddaughter Lily who were one hundred yards up the track. They had three dogs and regularly came for a chat through the wire fence when they were out. It turned out that Madelyn owned, and had done so since moving there, quite of a lot of the land around the villa, and her daughter who had sadly died young used to keep horses on the land. Charlie and Madelyn hit it off, somehow, they were on the same wavelength, and the group of new friends would meet up for a quick drink in the bar at the end of the road every now and then.

In the first week of their stay, after leaving various thermostats set, they realised that the underfloor heating did not work at all.

They had a leaking toilet and at one point the catch on the handle on Gretchen's door somehow broke and she ended up being stuck in her room. Brett managed to release her, and the rental agency sent someone to come and fix the handle. They also ordered a couple of tonnes of logs for the log burner in the lounge as along with electric fires, there seemed to be no other way of keeping the old villa warm. It had extremely thick stone walls and Charlie assumed that once they had warmed the place up it might retain some of the heat. It was also very smelly of damp. They had originally let this go as the agent said it was because it had been empty for a while, but as the days went on it was apparent that it was a real issue. Brett's bedroom, and in parts of Charlie's there was visible black and fluffy mould growing up the walls. The clothes in the wardrobes were smelling musty when they took them out even though the wardrobes were open or curtained and even washing did not get rid of the smell. The microwave also packed in after a week or so and the sewerage smell from the bathrooms was unbearably strong. Fernando the owner came round and fiddled with the underfloor heating controls and made noises to infer the floor was getting warmer although it clearly was not. He put sealant around the base of the toilet stand which obviously was not the root of the smell, and he brought a new microwave and washed the spores of damp off the wall. They all thought this was the best they were going to get and let him leave without any more complaints. Charlie was annoyed that they had contracted one thousand euros a month for a place that certainly would not be deemed fit for human habitation in the UK.

The best advice they received had turned out to be from Madelyn, their neighbour, who suggested making sure they did not let food waste and fats go down the kitchen drain and to pour a cheap bottle of red wine down the toilet to restore the balance in the septic tank. After a few days this worked and alleviated the smell issue.

Charlie had always hated shopping, even for food, so she was quite happy to carry on with her work when Brett and Gretchen went out to the local supermarkets to stock up. Brett continued his trek up and down the windy roads of the mountain every day to get his paper. Sometimes he would call into the supermarket near the paper shop to get supplies and other times Gretchen would go with them and would do a big food shop with him. Charlie had noticed that although they had agreed to split all the bills three ways, there were some comments being made by Gretchen about his choice of food and that cheaper alternatives could be used. By this time Gretchen and Brett were sharing the cooking say 60/40 with Charlie doing the odd meal such as lasagne or fajitas when the mood took her. The original and informal discussion they had before making the whole move was that Grunter and Gretchen would do all the cooking, shopping, cleaning, laundry and so on and Charlie would work. She certainly could not remember agreeing to paying all the rent and her and Brett paying all the running costs of the car, and what ended up as time went on doing her and Brett's own washing as the cold 30-minute wash Gretchen used was not getting things clean, especially grease and other food stains, and definitely not disguising the damp smell from their clothing.

There was also exceedingly rare evidence of any cleaning being done, and the accumulating grease in the kitchen was getting to Charlie. She kept quiet for the sake of peace, but cracks were already beginning to show with Brett moaning about Gretchen leaving food uncovered and similar bits and pieces of niggles.

Gretchen had worked in hospitality for a large part of her life, and Brett had run the shop, so both should be more aware than Charlie of food hygiene although she did know the basics herself. Another issue that niggled her was the fact that the tea towel was always filthy, including with grease and food stains. One day whilst working at the kitchen table she realised why when she saw Gretchen wiping down the surfaces and the greasy hob with it, after cooking.

As it neared Christmas, Gretchen and Grunter had agreed a sale on their house in the UK. They were using one of those all-in fixed fee agencies based only on the internet and had not received a good deal in Charlie's opinion, but it was none of her business she concluded. Anyway, this freed up Grunter to come over to Spain and their daughter to move to her boyfriend's house. Grunter arrived just before Christmas and even though Charlie thought that Gretchen was desperate for him to come over, Gretchen told Brett and Charlie on at least one occasion that she would be happy if he did not. They really did not know what to think, as one minute she was full of enthusiasm, and wanting to get his room exactly right, then the next she did not want him to come. Anyway, it was done now, and he needed to be there to be able to get his residency application registered before Brexit.

Up to this point the daily routine had been established. Brett getting his papers, or Gretchen and Brett doing some shopping, Charlie working online most of the day, food preparation and eating, dog walking and every other day or so they would go to a bar in the town for a drink or something to eat. After a week or so of living in the villa Charlie had taken the cats out on a harness and lead one by one so they could explore the outside.

She was amazed that they had not yet managed to escape or sneak out themselves. After doing this, they left the small window in the lounge open 4 or 5 inches so the cats could come and go as they pleased. It was not ideal as it could be quite bitter, especially at night, but the drop from Charlie's bedroom window was just that bit too far for them to be able to come and go easily, or certainly to get back in. To stop the draft from the lounge window being too much, Brett cut a bit of cardboard to fit in the rectangular window gap with a cat-flap style bit at the bottom and a small arched hole. Charlie glued some tassels off a blanket over the hole to stop the flies and other insects coming in. This seemed to work well and in no time all three of the cats were coming and going. Unfortunately, there was a big black and white stray around the area and there had been a couple of cat squabbles. Dexter the Doberman was very protective of his cats and became terribly angry and distressed when he heard cat fighting noises, even to the point of nearly knocking the TV off in an attempt to get to the window. Because of this, and for the safety of her three cats, Charlie made sure all three of them were inside safely before they locked up for the night. This was getting a bigger and bigger challenge as the three cats became wise to being grabbed and were becoming increasingly evasive, but she still managed it eventually each night.

Running alongside the daily routine were the applications for Spanish residency. Naomi had been sent all the relevant information of income, and after some delay they had all eventually obtained evidence of their Padron in Competa, and the appointments were made for the immigration office in Malaga.

Leah met them there for each appointment – it was a journey and separate appointment for each of them and she provided them with a pack of documents they had to take to the meeting with them. All of these went smoothly, and their applications were all logged in time for the deadline. The next stage of the process would be to return to have photos taken for the ID cards, which could be collected at a later date. In-between marking Charlie was also working on a spreadsheet that Naomi had set up for her, to list properties that they wanted to view. The plan was to find somewhere with at least four bedrooms, room for the 2 couples, and preferably enough room for some sort of separate living area each and for family visiting. There were quite a few houses and villas that on paper looked ideal and shortlists were made between the group of four friends although it was clear that nothing was going to happen until into the new year. There was still tension in the air. Grunter and Gretchen were in the habit of doing a video call with their daughters each evening, and as the area and villa did not have strong Wi-Fi or phone signals, this could boot Charlie off her online marking at times. When she broached the subject with them and asked if they could both use the same phone rather than being on their phones separately in their own rooms in the hope this may not use as much, Grunter reacted nastily, saying he would speak to his girls when HE wanted to.

She had also asked if they could tell her when they were doing their call so she could stop working for the duration rather than losing work she had already done but it was clear that no compromises were going to be agreed on.

Charlie and Brett had also hired a car from the car rental agency they had used for years. It was a long term, month by month hire, as Brett was concerned about both the fuel usage and the wear and tear on the pick-up, going up and down the mountain's windy roads to the coast every day. The car was also much more comfortable for Gretchen and Charlie in the back when they were going out, and most importantly was much quieter driving around the narrow streets of Competa and easier to park. Needless to say, no contribution towards this car was offered either and it was costing some 300 euros a month to hire, Gretchen seemed to think that paying a contribution towards fuel was enough, even though Brett also acted as taxi driver for them all as he did not drink alcohol and hence saved a fortune in taxi costs. As the months progressed Charlie was in full swing shortlisting properties to be viewed, but unfortunately because of outbreaks of covid in various towns in Andalucía they were being closed to visitors for all except essential purposes; and the closures included some of the less expensive areas such as Alhaurin and Coin that they had been looking at. This meant that viewings were not possible, and they had to play a waiting game. In the meantime, the weather was slowly getting a bit warmer during the day but still could get very cold as soon as the sun went down. They were getting through tonnes of logs in the log burner and had given up on the defunct underfloor heating.

They had also bought some portable gas bottle fires to move around the villa as needed. At one point, the log burner was belching out smoke from everywhere. It caused Grunter to have a collapse on the floor. Brett was down in the garage at this point and Charlie had no first aid training at all. Her and Gretchen managed to make him sit up against the wall and take some breaths, but he fell down on his back again. Charlie had to stop Gretchen from pouring water down his throat whilst he was lying there – she did not know what to do but knew it might drown him if it went straight into his lungs. In the meantime, Brett had heard the shouts and screams and came running in. He made Grunter have a go of his inhaler which alleviated the problem quite quickly and Grunter seemed to come back to normal. Then Charlie had to get on the phone to the rental agency to tell them of the problem. They did not seem to take it very seriously even though Grunter could have died. They said they would send someone out. In the meantime, Brett examined the log burner, and it was clear that the exhaust pipe at the back was dislodged and causing some of the problem, but there were clearly more issues going on.

Eventually someone arrived and went up on the roof to find the chimney was stuffed with bird's nests. These were cleared and an attempt made to reconnect the loose exhaust pipe, although it was obvious to all of them it was not a fix that would last. Anyway, for now it had worked, and the smoke had stopped belching into the room. As the weeks moved on, they were having to light it later and later and even some evenings did not bother at all. Some of the coastal towns at the bottom of the mountain had eased covid restrictions and travelling around was becoming easier.

Sometimes Brett would drive the four of them down to a restaurant in Nerja or nearby for a change of scenery and they would have something to eat and drink. There was one particular evening when the weather was fine, and they tried an American diner style restaurant in Velez Malaga. It was lovely walking around the streets seeing all the younger people out enjoying themselves again, meeting up in bars and cafes and chatting freely in groups.

Charlie was not averse to a tipple and preferred to have a few glasses of red wine or a couple of gin and lemonades although it had become obvious to her over the last month that she had to make sure she stayed sober as for some reason Grunter would start to dig at her when he was tanked up. Brett had noticed too so Charlie decided that the best thing to do was to drink soft drinks when there was a chance of a situation arising. She did not trust herself to not retaliate vigorously if he started on her when she had drunk a few herself and it would have not ended well for anyone. On this particular occasion, when they were paying the bill at the American diner, Gretchen and Grunter moaned about the cost of the fresh orange Charlie had chosen to drink instead of alcohol. The non-alcoholic beer that Brett had was usually dearer than normal beer as well. How she managed to keep her cool during this uncomfortable moment she would never know as all she could think of was the cheek of them as her and Brett had paid for the car to get them there and back and Brett had driven them all. As usual she let it go along with all the other bits and pieces that were beginning to grind.

As the year moved into March it was possible to start viewing some of the properties that they had selected off the internet brochures.

This was when the realisation that the Spanish estate agency system did not work the same as the UK occurred. The first issue peculiar to the Spanish system was that the exact location of properties was not revealed until you were on your way to view. From what they had been told this was to stop buyers turning up at the door of the house for sale and the estate agents being bypassed and losing out on their hefty commission. This meant that properties that were in really unsuitable locations for them could not be ruled out in advance.

Charlie and Brett preferred the areas around Mijas for their future home, but unfortunately the prices in this area were significantly higher. There was one particular property on their list for around here that they loved off the photos. It had its own mini golf course and was big enough for the two families, but because of its price it was on hold for now. In the meantime, they viewed other places that fitted the criteria. One they liked needed some work, or really complete refurbishment, but they were not afraid of this and had done it a number of times before. The road to this house became a narrow track very quickly and it was clear access would be a bit of an issue if there was significant rain. They were undeterred and met the agent at the property. It had obviously been vacant for some time and needed more than 'doing up.' As they wandered around, there was evidence of rat infestations everywhere including their scattered dead bodies. The pool was a mess and was located on a narrow terrace at the back of the house in full shade of the trees and the agent said it would probably not be possible to get permission to move it. Another property they viewed was more of an old farm on the outskirts of Alhaurin.

The main house itself was in reasonable repair but it was too near a busy road, which they ruled out because of the cats, near to the prison and the farm buildings which were being sold as additional space for bedrooms were completely decrepit. In addition, one of the existing owner's family members would be staying in the cottage part attached to the back of the building. Even though they liked the potential, the money that would need spending to get it how they would want, took it off the list.

There were a number of properties they viewed that claimed to have 5 or 6 bedrooms. One of these made them laugh for days.

It had a lovely location, much better than some of the others, and sounded ideal on paper. When they arrived, it was clear that the details had been somewhat exaggerated as bedrooms 3 and 4 were makeshift rooms in attic room up the ricketiest wooden staircase, with no bathroom or other facilities. What surprised them the most about this house was that bedrooms 5 and 6 were basically sheds in the garden area. They could not even be described as summer houses or chalets; they were just sheds. Inside the decor was equally bizarre with the main bathroom being so covered in shells stuck to every surface. Charlie mused it was certainly a house for someone of a particular taste. They went to see more comparable properties, including some decent ones set on hillside developments. These tended to have a better layout and be in a better state of repair, but the number of staircases from the top floor to the terrace and pool would have proved too difficult if their mobility deteriorated and would not help Brett with his COPD issues. There was one house Brett and Charlie liked. Charlie because it was in a small hamlet style area in the countryside, and Brett because it had views of the car scrap yard in the distance and had a good garage for his motorbikes.

They nicknamed this house 'dog poo' house. When they arrived for the viewing, the Spanish owner eventually came to the door, wearing a dressing gown and not much else, swigging a bottle of beer. His wife was blind, and they could see her in the kitchen behind the owner. As the agent and dressing gown clad man showed them round it was also clear that it needed lots of work. There was a bathroom upstairs that was half finished and there must have been an issue with the blown air heating as all the vents were taped up. The pool was nice and was approached across a large, grassed area and this was where the nickname came from. They literally had to pick their way across the grass to the pool whilst avoiding hundreds of dogs poos. They had a good discussion with the agent about this house as they could see potential, but it was eventually ruled out as the agent said the owners were unlikely to reduce their price and the asking price plus the improvements that were needed took it out of Charlie's desired maximum.

This same pattern continued over a few weeks. They had planned with Grunter and Gretchen that because it could take over 2 hours each way to get to the viewings plus the time of the viewings if more than one, and discussion and lunch time, Gretchen and Grunter would look after Dexter as they felt it was too long to leave him, sometimes in excess of 6 hours. This had tended to work quite well although there were two occasions that concerned Charlie. On one of them, the weather had begun to get quite hot during the day, and Grunter had walked Dexter in the heat all the way to their nearest bar, kept him them for some hours, and then presumably staggered back. There was another time when Gretchen and Grunter had gone into the town of Competa shortly after Brett and Charlie had left and had been out drinking in the bars.

They claimed they had only been out for an hour or two, but it was clear from their posts on social media that it had been most of the day, only getting back shortly before Charlie and Brett. Charlie felt this was really unfair. She was the one buying the house, sinking her lifelong savings into a place for them all. It was not easy doing all the viewings with the plan to narrow it down to a few for second viewings they could all go too, and it was only fair in her mind that Gretchen and Grunter could stick to their end of the bargain.

It was becoming increasingly obvious that despite the prices, the Mijas area was where they wanted to be.

With this in mind they asked Naomi to speak to the owners or agent of the mini-golf house to see if they would be open to offers. Naomi called it the 'pink house' and found out that the owner would consider offers so it was worthwhile them going to see it. That was the plan, see the house that looked so unusual in the photographs. It had two big bedrooms with ensuites upstairs, a large lounge diner with fantastic windows although this room did look a little pink for Charlie's taste. The wallpaper was pink and so was the big corner sofa. The kitchen looked a decent size with a downstairs toilet behind. Down on the lower floor was another bedroom and large bathroom, and a big living area that could be partitioned to make more bedrooms for Gretchen and Grunter. Outside, there was a pool table, a beautiful big pool, and terraces and gazebos. The terraces ended at the top of the scrub area of land that went all the way down to the farms on the road at the bottom of the hill.

Attached to the side of the house was a large garage with another large room behind which was being used a bar with its own beer pull and kitchen. This room led directly on to one of the terraces with the pool table and then back down some steps to the swimming pool.

There was also time to see a couple of other houses in the area whilst they were over in Mijas. The first house they saw was a bit of a mess. It needed tidying up and did not have a pool although the agent was adamant that one could be installed on the hilly terrace. Charlie could not see that this would be particularly practical and anticipated it would be an expensive job. What made them laugh was the so-called 5th and 6th bedrooms. It was suggested in the particulars that the basement could be used.

This basement was down the stairs from the kitchen and consisted of an area with a low ceiling and covered in rubble, with a little route through someone had cleared for the washing machine.

Charlie wondered what planet some of these agents were on with their suggestions for these extra bedrooms. It was clear that whatever planet it was, it was one that paid very well, as nearly all the agents they had met over the weeks drove expensive cars and obviously earned enough to support such a luxury. Then it was on to see the pink house. The agent was meeting Charlie, Brett and Naomi at the house and the owners were in situ as well. The first room that they entered from the front door was the pink lounge, and it was as pink as it looked on the pictures. Just a cosmetic change Charlie mused to herself. At the end of the lounge in the dining room bit were the large windows and the views were as fabulous as described in the brochure. You could see the coast and Fuengirola castle in one direction and the village of Mijas Pueblo in the other.

The side windows of the lounge area looked over the pool to the mountains and beyond. Both Charlie and Brett loved the house – they had a sort of feeling that it was the one for them. Charlie chuckled to herself that it even had carpet on the stairs which would save any human or animal slipping and getting bruised or worse on the marble or tiled edges.

After the visits of the day, Charlie and Brett went back to Competa to discuss the options, the houses they had viewed, and to plan going forward. They enthused about the house to Grunter and Gretchen, rang their son Jack to tell him all about it, and chatted with their neighbours about the house, showing them all the photos. By the next day it was decided.

The two couples would go back to the house for another viewing and if it was still as magnificent as they remembered an offer would be put forward.

It was important for Charlie and Brett to go back as because of the vast numbers of houses they had viewed the details like layouts and room sizes were hard to remember. They merged into one in their minds, and it did not help that Spanish estate agents did not think details like that were important to include in the brochures. Even rough room layouts would be helpful. A viewing was arranged, and the others tried to convince Charlie that Dexter would be all right for the duration of the journey and the viewing although she had another idea. She asked Madelyn, their neighbour, to pop in and check he did not need a wee or anything and gave her the spare key. Madelyn was quite happy, or seemed to be, to do this for her and a few days later the two couples headed off for the viewing.

The pink house was a lovely as Brett and Charlie remembered if not more so. As they all wandered around and discussed what they could do with the downstairs they talked about how their children would love visiting and enjoying all it had to offer. There was one tense moment when Grunter suggested locking the gate that separated the steps from the terrace near the front door and the downstairs steps and pool area to keep Dexter contained away from Grunter and Gretchen's 'area.' Brett and Charlie gave each other a knowing look at this point. They were buying and funding this house and their dog would go where he wanted. As usual the comment was parked in their minds and the viewing was completed.

When they got back, Madelyn was sat outside with Dexter enjoying the spring sunshine and they told her they had decided to make an offer on the house. Shortly after, and when Charlie had talked about the costs involved, they asked Naomi to put in an offer of around 10% below the asking price. This would leave enough money for the taxes and costs in Spain, which funnily totalled around 10% on buying a property, and leave them with some in the bank for repairs, emergencies and living off.

Chapter twenty-six – the dream house in Spain

They were over the moon when Naomi rang the next day to say the seller had accepted their offer. Charlie was keen to discuss and agree on dates as this was the way she worked. There was a solicitor in Mijas Costa to instruct and various checks to be conducted. Charlie had decided to get a small mortgage on the property over 10 years as it seemed widely accepted that if you used a bank for a mortgage in Spain even more thorough checks would be carried out on the legalities. Charlie used a broker in Spain to start arranging the mortgage and the six thousand euro holding deposit was paid to her solicitor. This deposit was to secure the property and to take it off the market whilst the legals were being completed. A further 10% would then be payable at the time a date was set and this 10% was not refundable, a point of no return. Once a date was set there would be more visits to sign paperwork and removal arrangements to be made along with a host of other bits and pieces to be sorted. It was a waiting game, and usually a much longer one than a house purchase took in the UK. Charlie was also watching the exchange rates between the euro and the pound as she had opened an account with a foreign currency broker and transferred the bulk of her savings into their account. The idea was to convert it to euros when the rate was good as the house purchase had to be done in euros. She did not find it amusing when Grunter kept teasing her about how the brokers would be enjoying spending her money jet skiing all day. It was one dreadful thought she did not need to have or worry about.

Whilst all this was going on in the background the tensions between the 2 couples were building.

Charlie was getting really fed up with Gretchen saying 'this is Grunter's favourite food' – usually chicken chow-mein or something similar. Gretchen's dog Blue was struggling with his weight and Charlie did think to herself that offering all the dogs a treat less than an hour after breakfast was really not helping. Then she found out that not only was Gretchen giving him ibuprofen to help with his obvious joint pain she would also give him tramadol or something similar. Charlie was horrified when she looked up the side effects. Firstly, she knew that human medication should not be given to animals, secondly Blue was a small, albeit fat, dog and the side effects and other implications such as organ failure were clearly not worth the risk. This conversation with Grunter and Gretchen did not go down well as with many others Charlie had with them. She knew she should keep out of it but was worried for the health of Blue, especially after Gretchen had said there had been blood in his pee.

As the house was being purchased with all the furniture and Madelyn was after a new sofa, Charlie offered Madelyn the sofas they had brought with them from the UK as they had no room for any more in the new house. It was now April and in the last few weeks Grunter and Gretchen had bought their own car. Brett had been to look at it with them and it was clear they were being ripped off by the garage for the money it cost, but Brett kept quiet again for the reason of not wanting to stir trouble. The hire car Charlie and Brett were using also had to be changed as the power went on it, due to the constant journeys up and down the mountain, but the hire company were exceptionally good and arranged to swap it.

On one occasion Charlie mentioned about Brett not driving when they went into the town for a drink and lunch and suggested Grunter drove them for a change.

Brett struggled walking up and down the steep hills in the town due to his COPD so made use of his disabled badge, which still was honoured in Spain, to park as near as possible to where they were going. Charlie could not believe her ears when Grunter responded to her comment. He said, that yes, he would drive, but would park far away so Brett had to walk. The problem was that he clearly meant it and his true personality was beginning to show. Charlie had known them both as close friends for many years and somehow at that point in time she resisted the urge to tell Brett what he had said, for fear of repercussions. She did not pursue the suggestion anymore.

In the week before Madelyn came round to look at the sofa that was stored with the rest of their belongings in the garage under the house, Grunter had been polishing his new car outside the garage. Brett was out on his paper and shopping trip down to the coast and Grunter wanted the keys to move Brett's motorbike so he could get the car inside the garage. Charlie had no idea where the key was for the motorbike and said as much and so Grunter had to put just half of his car in whilst he polished it. Charlie could not help thinking to herself that at no point in the 4 months or more that Grunter had been out there, had he offered to do any cleaning or polishing of either the pick-up truck or the hire car. When he had finished his polishing Grunter pulled the large sliding door of the garage back over and had stupidly left the key in the lock. The key caught on the brickwork by the door and snapped off into the lock.

Grunter was clearly not the most practical of men so when Brett returned home, he removed the key and putting the lock back on the door. They clearly needed to have more keys cut as they were one down now, so Gretchen and Grunter went to the DIY store to have some cut. They had extra ones cut of the side gate and front door to make life easier. Grunter insisted on parking his car in the fenced compound area, so it made sense to have another key for opening the gates to get into the compound. Once they were back with the keys Gretchen and Charlie discussed what to do with them. There was one main bunch that Brett tended to take with him when he went out. It was not that he needed them all but kept them all together in one place and it was a good job he had them so that the garage door key could be cut.

Charlie suggested that Grunter and Gretchen had a spare key for the compound gate and front door. They did not need the side gate most of the time because if they were going out on their own in the car, they would walk down the steps to the compound and go out that way. It would leave Charlie, or whoever else, with a front door key and side gate key in case she needed to get out for any other reason. The new and spare garage door key could stay with these in the villa for whenever needed. They used the garage key regularly because all their belongings were in there, including all the non-perishable food that Charlie and Brett had brought with them and was being worked through.

Unknown to Charlie, this key arrangement was going to lead to more disagreements. Shortly after, on a morning when Brett had gone down for his paper, and Gretchen and Grunter had gone out in their car, Madelyn said she was popping round to look at the sofa with Ralph.

Charlie let her in through the side gate and did not notice at that point that there was one key missing of the 'stay at home' bunch. They walked down the stairs to the garage, and it was as they approached the garage door that Charlie realised it was missing and it cannot have fallen off, it must have been taken off. It was a puzzle she could not work out. She rang Brett to see how long he would be, half an hour or so apparently, and then rang Gretchen to see if they would be back earlier and ask if they had taken the key. It appeared that it would be a short wait until whoever returned first. She suspected it would be Brett as Grunter and Gretchen had gone out for a 'quick drink' yet again. In the meantime, she made Madelyn a drink and sat down to have a good chat with her. It was not long before Brett returned, and they went down to the garage to look at the sofa with Madelyn confirming she would have it.

After some debate about the fact that Charlie did not want her to pay for the sofa, Madelyn went back to her own house. Charlie explained to Brett the weird key thing, and they both settled down for the rest of the day. Charlie actually had a week or so off her marking. She had some bits and pieces to do online for her old boss, but nothing that would not wait a day or two.

Once Gretchen and Grunter returned it was clear tensions were riding high, and the pair of them were tanked up. Charlie explained what the problem had been, that she could not get into the garage, and asked why they had taken the key. The response was that Grunter needed a garage key in case he wanted to polish the car some more.

Charlie could not believe what she was hearing, if that were the case surely, he could just get the key from the kitchen hook when he was there, it was not as if it went anywhere. The discussion became increasingly heated with eventually Gretchen and Charlie, more so the former, screeching at other. Gretchen for some reason said Madelyn and Ralph were wasters which was a comment Charlie could not understand for either its validity or its relevance. At some point Gretchen was on the verge of throwing her mobile phone at Charlie according to Brett, she had it in her hand and was motioning like she was going to throw it at the back of Charlie's head. It had all got out of control over a stupid key and slowly they retired to their bedrooms. Charlie could not sleep and in the early hours of the morning went into Gretchen's room to try and talk to her calmly and quietly. She was met with more hostility and said she did not think this was going to work. Gretchen readily agreed with her, and they talked about Gretchen and Grunter moving out.

Gretchen threw another gauntlet or threat into the ring by saying if they had to rent elsewhere, she would have to get rid of the dogs which Charlie thought was unnecessary as there were plenty of rental places that took animals and she wondered how someone who gave the impression that the dogs were so important to her could even contemplate getting rid of them.

Over the next few days tensions were high between the four of them as Gretchen looked for suitable accommodation for her and Grunter, and the dogs. She found a terraced house in the centre of Competa she liked and by this time the 2 couples were on a more civil footing.

Gretchen showed Brett and Charlie the brochure for the town house and went about planning for their furniture and other belongings to be moved. By this time, it was nearly the end of April, and the purchase of the pink house was proceeding well. After Gretchen and Grunter had moved out Brett and Charlie avoided areas where they may bump into Gretchen and Grunter, they really could not be doing with any aggravation, and despite a few attempts by Charlie to message Gretchen there had been little or no response. They had to admit though that they quite liked the villa with just the two of them in. They no longer had to listen to words like 'panademic,' or 'iburofen,' that really niggled. They also found out that despite the original agreement earlier in the year to not use the underfloor heating due to the expense and fact that it did not seem to work in most areas, Gretchen and Grunter had the thermostats turned up high in their bedrooms. Grunter's bedroom stunk of smoke as he had been smoking out of the window and hence the curtains both on the window and the wardrobe were smelly.

They also found out that the rechargeable hoover that Charlie had bought not long before they left the UK was damaged and overheating all the time. The only one who had ever really used it regularly was Grunter who was always doing his room and rarely the rest of the villa. The final straw was when it was getting near Brett and Charlie's time to move to their new pink house, they found out that the cheap kettle the landlord had provided had disappeared. They had been using their own kettle and toaster and so on since their belongings had arrived with the removals company and there was only one answer to where the kettle could have gone.

Charlie searched every single cupboard and drawer, but it was nowhere to be seen. She messaged Gretchen about it, but she just replied that it must be there somewhere. May and June were Charlie's busiest months as it was exam season, so she kept herself occupied marking and doing some work for her old boss. Brett did all the cooking and shopping and between them they took Dexter for nice walks when the heat of the day had gone off. They spent time with their neighbours, Madelyn, and Ralph, and would meet up with them for a drink or bite to eat, or pop round to each other's houses. It was during this time that Charlie found out more information about Gretchen. She had told Madelyn that the beautiful pink villa 'was not for them,' whatever that was supposed to mean; and at some point, before they moved out Gretchen had been up at Madelyn's house crying her eyes out after a particular nasty incident with Grunter. They were both drunk and at some point, Grunter had threatened to throw Gretchen off the cliff in front of Madelyn's granddaughter who lived with her. They also heard that he was picking fights and arguments with people in the town, but Charlie had got past caring. She still could not believe that someone who had been a close friend for so long and had even told Charlie that they would not have been able to move to Spain without her, could turn so nasty. Brett had told her that Gretchen had always been a hard bitch, not an easy walk over like Charlie. It was certainly one of those live and learn moments.

The date for moving had been set for the beginning of July and Charlie organised the removals company for a few days later as they had the rental place until the end of July. Her and Brett planned for the completion day.

Charlie had to be at the notary's office in the morning with her solicitor to do the final paperwork and ensure the funds were all handed over, so they planned to drive there and back in the morning. They had done lots of cleaning of the rental villa over the week before including gutting the empty bedrooms and the kitchen, inside and outside of cupboards, even to the point of pulling out the fridge and other appliances to clean behind. Once they returned on completion day Brett was to take the three cats and some essentials in the pickup to the new villa. Charlie would do the last bits of cleaning, with the help of Madelyn's granddaughter Lily, and then follow on after Brett in the hire car with the dog. This would give Brett time to unload the cats and get them settled before Dexter arrived. When moving day arrived, they set off for the meeting in the morning. Lily had arrived earlier than planned and said she would look after Dexter and start some of the last bits of cleaning whilst they were out, which was truly kind of her. They had already arranged with the villa's owner that they could drop a couple of suitcases off inside the gate at the villa before the meeting, to give them more room in the vehicles for the journey later.

At the Notary's office Charlie met her solicitor and they went through to the meeting room.

It was all so different to the procedure in the UK as present at the meeting were the notary, Charlie's solicitor, Charlie's mortgage company, the seller's solicitor, and mortgage company, and to round it off the estate agent was there too. They came to the meeting to make sure no one ran off with their cheques. Again, Charlie was amused when it turned out the entire process was done through a series of cheques that Charlie had to sign an authorisation list for from the mortgage company bank.

There was one for the seller, one for her mortgage company, one for the estate agent and one for Naomi as they were splitting the commission, there was one for her solicitor and one for the little mouse who lived under the floor. She felt it was like a mad hatters' tea party and unnecessary, Spain did actually do electronic banking, but it was more of a feeling that nobody trusted anyone else. Eventually the cheques were all handed out and the paperwork signed. At this point, the seller handed over all the keys to the villa to Charlie. They had a chat and wished each other well before Charlie went out to Brett who was parked up and waiting outside. Charlie and Brett were excited as they drove up to their new home and let themselves in through the locked gate. It would hopefully only be a few more hours before they were relaxing in their new environment and properly starting a new life in Spain.

Chapter twenty-seven – on the move again

When they returned to the Competa villa it was down to work straight away. Charlie stacked up outside everything that Brett had to load into the pickup and hire car. This included all the animal paraphernalia and a suitcase with clothes and so on for before the removals company arrived. She had already made sure the cats were locked in her bedroom so there would be no last-minute shenanigans trying to find and catch them. Once the vehicles were ready, using a hand towel, she slowly wrapped each cat and put them in the travel cages. They carried the cages out to the pickup and Brett and Charlie said goodbye as Brett headed off to the villa. Charlie hoped the satnav would do her proud and get her there safely later on. She was also conscious of driving there whilst it was still daylight as she did not know the route at all. Once Brett and the cats had left, Charlie and Lily got down to the rest of the cleaning. They hoovered and mopped up cat hair and dust from behind and under everything. They even cleaned windows and brushed up outside, taking care that anywhere Dexter had done his business was thoroughly clean. Brett had called to say he had arrived and unloaded the cats and Charlie reminded him to set up the cat litters right away and make sure they could not get out. Once they were done Charlie thanked Lily from the bottom of her heart for her help and put Dexter in the boot of the hire car. She set the satnav to find the villa in Mijas and set off on her way down the windy roads of the mountain. She had not driven since arriving there in the motorhome many months earlier.

At the bottom of the hill, she joined the motorway towards Malaga as it was starting to go dark and made steady but satisfactory progress in the traffic. She had driven past Malaga when the power was going in the hire car. Charlie carried on travelling along with the traffic and then realised that there was something seriously wrong. She was in no way a mechanic but knew enough to guess that it was an issue with the gearbox, or more likely the clutch. She coasted to the side of the motorway and eventually came to a stop. She tried to move the car off again, but it was going nowhere. The traffic was pretty heavy, rush hour she assumed, and there was no hard shoulder on the motorway but luckily, she was as far over as possible to the right-hand Short of the carriageway. Now she had to decide what to do. Her first instinct was to call the hire company as their mobile number was stored in her phone. Unfortunately, this call went to answerphone, so she called Brett to tell him what had happened. She was really worried about the traffic and especially the lorries that were continually approaching fast from behind and the fact that if one of them crashed into the back of her, the dog would be finished as he was still in the boot of the hatchback. There was nowhere in sight to take him out and get out of the way and it was going dark quickly. There were no grass verges like on UK motorways, and there was no junction to walk to in front of or behind her that she could see. She called Madelyn to see if she could help, mainly because Madelyn knew Spanish things and spoke fluent Spanish. Shortly afterwards Madelyn messaged her with a gruer, or recovery truck, phone number for her to try. When Charlie called this number, she was so grateful that the man at the end of the line could speak good English. He asked her where she was, and she tried to describe it as well as possible which was difficult as there were no obvious landmarks or road signs to go off so in the end, they decided Charlie should try and send him a pin of location point from her phone. She did this and waited patiently for him to arrive. He was not the first to reach her though as within minutes the Spanish police pulled up. They asked her for her driving licence and then walked off with it to their car so she could only assume they had some way of checking it was valid. She was terrified as to what was going to happen next as the police officers spoke little to no English, but at least they put some cones out to stop the traffic coming up too close. The next arrival was Brett. He had left to come and rescue her as soon as he put down the phone and had to go past where she was broken down up to the next junction to come back to where she was broken down. He parked behind the hire car, sticking out further into the carriageway with his hazard warning lights on, again to keep the traffic at distance.

It seemed like a long time although was probably only minutes before the recovery truck came. As it arrived, the car hire company called back, and Charlie explained what had happened. The recovery driver spoke to the hire company on the phone and when he had finished, he said they had a plan. In the meantime, the police were still there and still had Charlie's driving licence. The recovery driver went to speak to them for a while and then came back looking incredibly pleased with the licence for Charlie. He explained to Charlie and Brett that he was going to tow the hire car to a nearby garage in Mijas Costa and leave it there for repair. Charlie and Brett were to put Dexter the Doberman in the pick-up truck and Charlie and Brett were to follow him to the garage. They also had to pay two hundred euros and did not have enough cash on them, but the recovery man said there was a cash machine near to the garage.

They transferred the dog, and the recovery man connected the hire car to his truck. The police prepared to leave, and the convoy of recovery and pick-up trucks made their way off the motorway into a compound at the back of industrial units on the outskirts of Mijas Costa. Once the hire car had been released from the hoist Brett went off to find the cash machine whilst Charlie started piling up their belongings from the hire car. Both vehicles had been rammed to the limit with belongings they would need before the removals came, and Brett had not had time to unload the pickup other than the animal stuff, so it was going to be a squash for the rest of the journey.

Once Brett returned, they paid the recovery driver and after telling Charlie he had got her off any fine or penalty he headed off on his way. Charlie and Brett could not believe that the Spanish police actually fined you for breaking down, but it was Spain. The pair managed to cram all their belongings into the pickup and then went in search of where they were supposed to leave the keys to the hire car. The company had told them to push them under a door, but with the exception of the large industrial garage door there were no other gaps or letter boxes. They concluded that they would have to be under this garage door and Charlie messaged the hire company with a photograph to show where they had left them. Then all three of them, including Dexter, climbed into the pickup, and headed off for the villa. Luckily, it was not too far as it was located between Mijas Costa and Mijas Pueblo, just 5km or so. Charlie was so relieved to have arrived at the new pink house. They let Dexter out and went in through the gate. Charlie went straight through to the kitchen after doing a quick headcount of the cats and poured herself a glass of red wine.

After the ordeal she had just been through she could have drunk the whole bottle, but she was too tired to even contemplate that. They decided to leave the vehicle unloading until the next day and after relaxing for a little while, collapsed into their respective bedrooms upstairs. Dexter was even allowed to come up on the bed with Charlie. It must have been traumatic for him too, and it was not fair to leave him downstairs in a strange place. It was not long before Charlie and Dexter were joined by three inquisitive cats, and Charlie hoped as she nodded off to sleep that there were no secret places the cats could get out through.

Brett and Charlie spent the next few days getting to know their new villa and trying out the swimming pool. It turned out that the previous owners had left virtually everything – books, clothes, food, and personal items as well as the furniture that was part of the deal. There was crockery and utensils everywhere – in the kitchen, the bar area, and outside the downstairs rooms where someone had fitted a few cupboards. There was even a fridge down there which had some old food in. It was clearly going to be quite a big job to remove all the stuff they did not want to make room for their own possessions that were arriving on the Friday after the Tuesday they had moved in. It had to be started before Charlie started marking again so they got to work, piling up what they did not want and slowly loading the bed of the pick-up to go to the tip. All of this had to be done whilst making sure the cats did not escape, so it was quite a tricky task. Charlie had spoken with Madelyn about all the clothes the owner had left as they were too small for Charlie, and it was agreed that they would bag them all up and Brett would drop them off when he met the removals company in Competa on the Friday.

Over the week Charlie and Brett settled into their new surroundings and began to find out how everything worked in the villa, and the things that did not. Charlie also took the three cats out one by one on the harness to let them explore the surroundings a little more. She was scared about letting them out properly, but knew it had to be done, and at least there did not seem to be a nasty cat around like there had been in Competa.

Dave the builder, and friend of the previous owner also came round to discuss the alterations they wanted to make. The main plans involved putting partitions in the large underneath lounge to make two new bedrooms for visiting family and friends. They also decided they had no use for the bar room so the idea was to move the wall and door from the garage into this room further back towards the garage so that the toilet could be incorporated as an ensuite, and Jack could have his own room when he came over. The other three bedrooms that were going to be in the downstairs area could be claimed by Olivia and Noah, Brett's two children from his previous marriage, as they saw fit. Dave started work on the plans with some building mates as soon as possible. There was going to be electrical work to be done so Dave started searching for a trustworthy electrician. This proved as difficult as it was in the UK but eventually, they settled on a lovely young electrician and security specialist called Rupert. By this time, his services were much needed as the electric kept tripping in the house. It turned out this was to do with the contract for the electricity in the house.

Another peculiarity to Spain was that when you purchased a house the solicitor signed you up for the electric contract, presumably for some commission from whomever they chose, and if you used more than the contracted amount you did not get billed for the extra, they just stopped the supply. It was like going back into the dark ages. Charlie managed to find a cheaper company that was being recommended on social media and cancelled the solicitor's contract with the help of Rupert, who spoke fluent Spanish and English, and started a new contract. She also signed up for an internet and phone package.

When Brett went to meet the removals company back at the villa in Competa everything had been organised in an orderly fashion. Before they had left Competa, Charlie had made Brett help her use multi-coloured electrical tape to label every one of their possessions in the garage and the few boxes in the villa using colour codes to identify which part of the new villa it should be deposited in. When they arrived in Mijas and started unloading, the removal men actually told Charlie that it was a really useful idea, and she was pleased she had not wasted her and Brett's time. There were boxes and boxes of stuff stacked up in the dining room end of the lounge and it looked like a very daunting task to unpack everything. Charlie would not have brought even a quarter of the stuff, but Brett was adamant it was important, even though the boxes had not been touched for over 7 months by this point. One of the removals men was extremely helpful in suggesting a company that provided firesticks or something like that so they could watch UK TV in the various rooms. They were not short of TVs, as in addition to the ones they had brought from the UK, the previous owner had left all of her TVs.

Damian came out for the TVs, and they decided on four of the firesticks. One for the main lounge and one for the lounge downstairs. The other two were for the TVs in Brett and Charlie's bedrooms. All the sticks enabled you to watch UK TV and to pause and rewind a programme which was all they really needed, and the monthly cost was not too bad in addition to the purchase of the sticks. In the next few weeks Charlie and Brett slowly worked their way through unpacking the various boxes and finding homes for everything. The dining room unit that had come from home was filled up with the junk it had been filled with before and various pictures were put up on the walls. Charlie did not like any of the pictures the previous owner had put up, so they all been taken down and stored in the garage for now. Whilst they were doing this and removing the last remnants of the previous owner's belongings from various cupboards and drawers, Dave and his team were putting up the partitions downstairs and doing the finishing touches. Having had more issues with the electric going off, Rupert was replacing all the outside lighting around the minigolf course and the patio walls. Many of these old carriage style lights had deteriorated with age and the electrics were shorting out, so they were all being replaced with more modern stick like lights and new wiring throughout. It was whilst Rupert was working on the electrics in much more depth like this that he discovered there was no earth at all for the house. He proceeded to sort this out by putting a long metal pole out in the garden and connecting to it to provide an earth. As he worked through various areas more problems emerged, some minor and some more desperate.

Once Dave had finished on the partitions and left the electrical work for Rupert to complete, Dave moved onto altering the bar into a room for Jack. Brett and Charlie had decided they would have no use for the bar as it was. If they were to have more than one or two friends over to stay, there were plenty of entertaining areas both inside and outside the house, so the inside bar at the back of the kitchen was surplus to requirements. Charlie had ordered a cubicle shower, a bit like the ones they had in Skipsea. She had worked out this was the most cost-effective way to put a shower in for Jack rather than all the separate parts of a base, walls, mixers, tiling and so on. Dave set to work on moving the wall at the back of the garage further into the garage so that the toilet was now included in the new bedroom rather than the garage. There was plenty of room now in the new bedroom for the new shower cubicle and the super king bed and storage units.

Whilst all this was going on, Brett and Charlie had a few visitors. Firstly Titiana, Charlie's friend from teaching, came out to stay. It was so nice to see a familiar face and Titiana and Charlie spent quite some time catching up whilst assembling the Ikea beds and drawer units Charlie had ordered. They made a great assembly team, with both having tackled Ikea furniture many times before. When they were not assembling furniture, they enjoyed the pool and the sun and going out to lovely restaurants for tea. Once Titiana had returned home Jack came out to visit. It was the best thing that could ever had happened as Charlie was missing her only son so much it made her heart hurt. His room was not quite finished – the builders were still messing with the shower cubicle, but it was not a problem as he could use the showers in the main house.

As soon as Brett arrived back from the airport with Jack and his girlfriend Lizzie, Charlie was overjoyed and full of emotion. She could not hug him enough, even though he seemed keener on saying hello to Dexter. It was lovely to meet Lizzie for the first time and to see him so happy and settled in his life. At the same time as Charlie had been dealing with the purchase of the villa in Mijas and the removal arrangements, Jack had been deciding on a house to buy in Whitby. He chose a 3-bed semi on Whitby Island that was a new build and because he was eligible for the housing association deal, he only had to find 75% of the value through his deposit and mortgage. Charlie could not wait to hear all about the house he had bought. She had seen the photos he had sent through on WhatsApp and had even had to intervene quite a few times with the legal process of the purchase.

Conveyancing solicitors were often neglectful and occasionally incompetent as far as she was concerned. She had laughed a few years earlier when Jack was looking at the possibility of going to university as the A level requirements for a Law degree were very low, and they did not seem to have to complete years of professional exams to be qualified. One of her theories was that on the whole conveyancing was not really repeat business so the solicitors concerned did not care if clients did not come back, compared to other professions where the aim is to keep clients year on year and provide an excellent service, so they kept coming back and making recommendations to friends and colleagues. The exception to the rule was the brilliant solicitor Charlie had used for the sale of the house in Skipsea as throughout covid with all the delays and issues this caused, Jenny was prompt, efficient and excellent at staying connected.

Whilst Jack and Lizzie were staying with them, Charlie's brother and his family also came over to Mijas. They had chosen to stay nearby and not in Charlie and Brett's house, but it was lovely to see Stewart and his family again. They spent a lovely week indulging everyone and enjoying the company. In the meantime, Dave and Rupert finished the work in the house. Rupert was also working on the water pressure and supply to the house because it was intermittent at best and was installing some filters from the pump from the water tank. They had been informed by the local community to not drink or even brush their teeth in the water from the main community tank as it was polluted and not safe for humans or animals, so it was down to water bottles even for teeth brushing and face washing. Dave also arranged for some quotes for a staircase down from the lounge to the outside patio. Because the villa was on a hill, the swimming pool was on the lower story, and Charlie and Brett had decided the best idea was to make one of the large dining area windows into a door and have a staircase directly to the pool leading from this door. The quotes were extortionate, and, in the end, they settled on Dave building them a wooden staircase as he had done at his own house down the road. This also meant they could have a dog flap fitted and not have to keep letting the animals in and out when the doors were closed.

Even though everything was going to plan, and Charlie was getting plenty of online marking work to keep them financially comfortable, Charlie was not happy. Brett was picking on her about everything, from what she wore to whether she had shut the bathroom door.

It was all getting too much, and she felt like she was sinking into a depression. She picked up when they had a visit from all the kids together, Brett's two from his previous marriage and Jack as well. Charlie had paid for all their travel costs so they could all afford to come out and it was lovely having them altogether.

Chapter twenty-eight – a big mistake?

The problem was Charlie was still not happy. Sometime after they all returned home, she sat down with Brett and discussed what they were going to do. Brett's daughter was now pregnant which gave a greater draw to go back to the UK. They decided they were going to go back to the UK in November, look for a static caravan or similar to have as a base, and then return to Spain and put their lovely villa back on the market. Whilst they were due to be away for 2 weeks, Rupert very kindly agreed to stay for them and look after the villa and the animals, so Charlie booked the flights and a hotel near Driffield for some of the trip and one near Whitby for the remainder to include Jack's birthday at the start of December.

After this had been agreed Charlie's friends, Titiana, and Bella, came out to visit during the October school half term. Charlie knew she was not herself but between Titiana, Bella, and Brett, they decided they were worried about her and wanted her to go to hospital. Charlie just thought it was because she was unhappy, but they were all convinced it was more than that. She refused to go to a hospital in Spain as she knew if there was anything seriously wrong, she would be stuck in Spain. Even though they had health insurance, and she knew that the Spanish health system was excellent, it was of no comfort the thought of being in a hospital in a foreign country with no other family around. In the end, she agreed to go back to the UK earlier than they had planned. Bella booked Charlie and herself onto a flight back to Hull as that was the most her friends and Brett could get Charlie to agree to.

The idea was Bella would take Charlie straight to Beverley A & E in Hull and then Titiana would follow on her original flight a few days later. She did not know what had prompted her, but Charlie had already sorted a power of attorney with the Spanish solicitor who had dealt with the house purchase for them and had arranged for the animals to have all their booster injections. It must have been some sort of sixth sense.

On the day Charlie and Bella were flying home, on the morning of the actual flight Charlie was not getting on with things very fast and Titiana had to take over to pack a suitcase for her and motivate her to get on with it. Brett took Bella and Charlie to Malaga airport in the morning for their flight and then returned to the villa to look after everything at that end and stay with Titiana until her flight home. Bella had arranged for her husband, George, to pick them both up from Hull airport and take them to the hospital. They waited in A&E for what seemed like an age with waiting for triage, and then to see a doctor. The A&E doctor went through everything with Charlie. When Bella was telling him about the symptoms – sleeping a lot, face not right, dawdling and dragging her feet, Charlie was a bit surprised to say the least. She knew she had been sleeping a lot and lacking energy but had not heard the rest. The doctor decided to send her for a scan and found a bed on the department eventually for her to stay in. At this point, Charlie asked George and Bella to go as there was nothing they could do until they found out more, and she felt very guilty that her friends were wasting their life sat in hospital with her.

After some time, Charlie was sent for scans. One of the machines had broken and was waiting for the engineer to come and fix it, but now they were catching up with the backlog.

When she had been scanned Charlie was taken back to a main ward and after chatting with the nurses settled down to a long-awaited sleep.

It was not too long before the nurses were doing their rounds. They explained to Charlie that the doctors would be round to see her soon. Charlie forced some breakfast down although she was really not feeling like it and waited nervously for the doctors to come with the results of her scans. It seemed like forever but was probably not and then she was surrounded by 5 or 6 doctors and the curtains were pulled around her bed. She thought to herself that this did not look good and even though she needed to know, she was scared of whatever they were going to tell her.

It turned out she was right to be scared. They explained to her that she had an 18cm tumour on her kidney and a small tumour on her brain. This was not the news she had even considered and found it really hard to take in. She really needed to be with Brett, but he was still in Spain.

Charlie was about to embark on the biggest challenge she had ever experienced in her life, and she did not know if she had the strength either emotionally or mentally to deal with it all.

Epilogue

The next book will detail Charlie's life and all the turmoil and mishaps arising after her cancer diagnosis.

Printed in Great Britain
by Amazon